THE
SKINNY
SPELL

Wilbow, Sarah (author)
The Skinny Spell
ISBN 978-1-922890-95-5
Fiction

Typeset Minion Pro 11/16

Cover and book design by Green Hill Publishing

THE
SKINNY
SPELL

For my grandmother, Bonnie, who loved to read.

AUTHOR'S NOTE

Dear reader

This book might not be for you. It started in my mind as a lighthearted fantasy, a 'what-if', wish-fulfilment kind of tale. But the process of writing it made me realize some of the themes and ideas explored in the story are darker than I'd anticipated.

Please decide, before proceeding, if you're comfortable being exposed to details of various weight loss regimes, references to weight, BMI, calories, discussions of bingeing, and spending time with the inner thoughts of a character who thinks she's not good enough because of how she looks.

Please proceed carefully if you are suffering from, or recovering from, an eating disorder. This book is about a weight loss journey, and also a journey to self-acceptance. I would hate for my lead character's sometimes misguided path to influence a real-life reader to resort to or return to dangerous behavior.

The solution my protagonist finds for her obesity is science-based and (in my personal experience) very powerful for weight loss and improved health. But I am not a doctor. Please seek advice from a medical professional about your particular needs before adopting any of the practices described in this book.

This story is fiction. Real life is not this neatly resolved. But I hope if you do read this book, you get something positive from it. My hope is that, like me, you will find the information my main character discovers to be life changing in the best possible way.

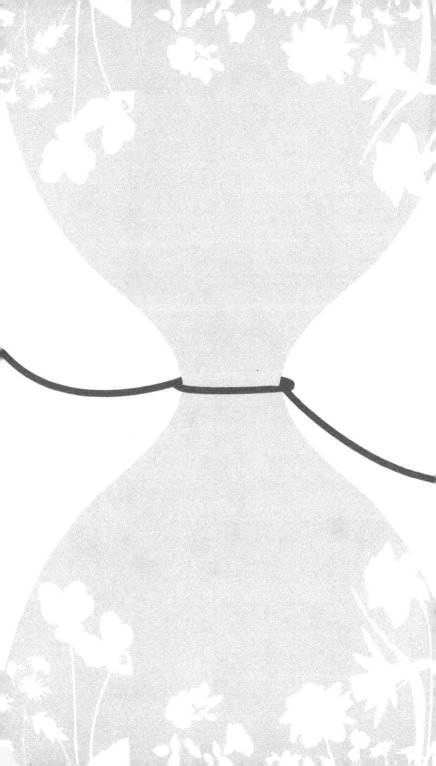

PART 1
BEFORE

CHAPTER 1

'You will always be fat.'

I choked on the coffee I'd just sipped and looked across to my sister Louise with wide eyes and, despite myself, a wide smile.

You could always count on Lou to tell you what she really thought. The morning sun bouncing off the marble and tile surfaces of the busy café temporarily blinded me as I shook my head in defiance. My stomach growled with a mix of annoyance and hunger.

'Gee, thanks very much!' I laughed. I'd just been telling her, with fervent optimism, about some organic weight-loss shakes I'd seen advertised and wanted to try. Lou had rolled her eyes as usual. Despite my laughter, my old frustration with her reared up.

'It's true,' Lou persisted. 'You will probably always be fat. Just accept it,' she shrugged. 'You'll be happier.'

Her certainty about my fate annoyed me. 'You can't predict the future, and I know that staying fat won't make me happy. So I'm trying the shakes. I'm really motivated to do this.'

But Louise pressed on. 'Countless studies have proven that 95 per cent of people who lose weight gain it all back. What makes you think science doesn't apply to you?'

'Why can't I be the five per cent that's successful?'

'Evie, chances are, the only way you're going to lose a significant amount of weight is if you get some hideous disease. Your body is biologically primed to keep you at your heaviest weight. I heard a podcast about it. Here, I'll send you the link.' She pulled out her phone and started tapping.

'Rubbish.' I shook my head, hearing my phone ping amongst the noisy chatter around us. 'It's simple math. Eat less, move more, I'll lose weight.'

Lou sighed. 'Yes, but it won't stay lost. Your body will do everything it can to get you eating again. If you do diet, even if you *can* stick with it, you'll just end up feeling miserable. You'll be cold and cranky all the time, and your mind will get obsessed with food until you can't take it any more. Then you'll eat, and regain what you lost, and then some.'

I sighed in frustration. 'Don't be melodramatic. It's just a matter of willpower. The reason I haven't properly lost weight since Vivi was born is because I haven't tried hard enough. I just haven't wanted it enough. I keep making excuses because I *really* like food.' I sat up straight and shook my head defiantly. 'My problem is that I haven't made a genuine commitment to a lifestyle change.'

Lou shrugged, as if to say, 'we'll see.' That irritated me more than any of her blunt words.

Well, I'd show her. I refused to accept what she was telling me. The consequences of that kind of thinking would be unbearable. Inevitable life-long obesity. A slow and steady heavying, year on year, for the rest of my life. It was too terrible to accept.

Lou must have noticed a hardness settle on me, because she tried to lighten the mood. 'Listen, I just want you to make a commitment to this delicious birthday cake.'

She pushed a slice of cinnamon apple teacake with butterscotch frosting across the table.

'No thank you,' I said, pushing it back. 'Look, I really appreciate the gesture, I do. But this is my year to do it. I want to be skinny before I turn 40. No, not skinny. I want to be *healthy*. I want to make this year count.'

'But it's your birthday.'

'I know. The perfect day to start. I know you don't get it, because you take after dad.'

Our father Brian was tall and lean. He could eat anything and not gain weight. Lou was naturally slender like him. But it wasn't just her body shape. I also envied her more mature approach to food. I still had the same food cravings I'd had as a teenager (pizza, burgers, chips, soda). Lou preferred healthy things like salad and seafood, and not just because they were good for her. She genuinely seemed to like them. It baffled me. I didn't understand how she got that way when we were raised the same.

I felt so guilty about how I ate. I knew all the theories of good nutrition but I always seemed to make bad choices anyway. And not just for myself. I wouldn't dare confess to Lou the amount of processed food I fed my daughter, Vivi. Instant noodles were her favorite. They were easy, they were quick, and they were eaten without complaint. I hated wasting food.

Lou rolled her eyes again. 'Yes, I have dad's body type. And you have mom's. And body type isn't something you can diet away. It's just how you are.'

She paused and looked directly at me. 'How long have you been trying to lose weight?'

I blushed. 'About 20 years.'

'And how much did you weigh 20 years ago, when you started trying to lose weight?'

'About 160 pounds.'

'And how much do you weigh now? After 20 years of trying to not weigh 160 pounds?'

'About 240. Thanks for pointing out what a failure I am.'

'No, I don't mean to. It's just... Have you ever wondered if you'd just accepted yourself at 160, that you might have stayed that way? Without that cycle of deprivation and bingeing, you wouldn't have been as tempted to go overboard in the first place.'

I scoffed. 'Of course not. I've always had a big appetite. Whether I accepted it or not, I would've always wanted to eat a lot. But you're right about one thing. In hindsight I was pretty thin back then.' I remembered a distant time when I felt awful about needing size 10 pants. What I wouldn't give to wear size 10 now.

'Well, here's another way to look at it,' said Lou, sounding as frustrated as I felt. 'Have you ever thought that you actually look pretty good just the way you are? You're lovely Evie. I wish you could see it.'

I shook my head. Deflecting compliments was a long-honed skill, and it's easy to reject what you don't believe. I jiggled my belly with my right hand, in imitation of a department store Santa Claus.

'Please. This? Don't give me that beauty at any size crap. What do they call it? Body positivity? Fat acceptance? I won't accept it. I can't accept it. It would be too, too...'

'Liberating?' suggested Lou. 'Think of all the time and energy you spend focusing on your weight that you'd be able to spend on other things, if you just accepted yourself as you are. You could put that energy into something productive. You could learn a musical instrument. Master a foreign language!'

We both laughed then, remembering my woeful attempt as translator on our trip to Paris years ago, after I'd bragged it would be *pas de problème*. The bubble of tension between us burst. 'Now you're just teasing.'

Lou took a bite of cake and exaggerated its deliciousness. 'Mm, this is really good!'

'Lou, I'm serious about this. I want to get healthy. I don't bounce back now when I get sick the way I used to. I get headaches and my legs hurt all the time. I'm always tired.

SARAH WILBOW

It's not just about how I look. I need to take better care of myself. It's no fun being this size. Not at my age. I need you to not sabotage me.'

Lou put down her fork and squeezed my hand. 'OK, I'll take your piece of cake home for the boys. Let's talk about something else. How's the building work going?'

I relaxed. Finally some safe ground. I gave Lou an update on the dramas with the home renovation Stu and I had just embarked upon. A bathtub for our new ensuite had been delivered but was too big for the space and needed to be sent back.

As I spoke, my eye kept darting to a glistening glob of butterscotch frosting on the edge of Louise's plate. I had an almost irresistible urge to reach over and scoop it up with my finger. I salivated and my tummy growled again. But I didn't eat it. I sipped my coffee and tried to put it out of my mind.

CHAPTER 2

I can't remember the first time I felt fat. It was somewhere between my carefree swimsuit-clad summers as a seven-year-old, and my self-conscious high school days when Linda Saville's brother, Darren, followed me home from the bus stop shouting that my legs were like an elephant's, that he just couldn't believe how big they were, and that that he felt the ground shake every time I took a step.

As small a kid, I never thought about my appearance. I was too busy having fun. But the older and bigger I grew, the harder it was to deny Being Fat. I remember the lady in the school uniform shop whipping back her tape measure, tsking under her breath and telling my mom in a doubtful voice she 'might have something in that size out the back, or we can order it in.'

My shadow, falling ahead of me as I walked next to ever-slender Jana toward school assembly each morning was, even in its stretched and elongated form, a wide puddle of shade next to Jana's slivered eclipse.

And the boys. Apart from Darren, they didn't tease or bully me. It was worse than that. They didn't see me at all. Their eyes and smiles and teasing were reserved for small-waisted Jana, or bony-kneed Seema. I was just an extra in the film reel of their imaginations.

I didn't understand why I was fat. No-one else in my family was. Mom complained about her weight but looked normal to me.

And there wasn't much I could do about it as a kid. I didn't get much choice about what I ate—that was mom's domain. I would snack when I was hungry. And OK, that might have been more often than some other kids, but I was growing. Listen to your body, mom would say. And my body was telling me to eat. I had to snack on boring 'healthy' things like peanut butter on a spoon, or a handful of sultanas, or a slice of brown bread, because Mom didn't approve of chips or cookies. But I seemed to always be hungry, so I was always snacking.

Of course, when I look back now, I wasn't fat then at all. I was just a bit on the heavy side. A solid, healthy girl.

Short-ish. Stocky. Squat.

But these are not descriptors a young girl desires. She wants to be described, like the celebrities profiled in teen magazines, as lithe or waif-like or slender. Or, of course, the most desired adjective of all—skinny. I was never skinny.

It wasn't until I was out of home and on my own, when I was able to choose what and when I ate, that my weight really started piling on. Without the maternal reins pulling against my choices, sugary morning coffees, burger lunches, takeaway noodle dinners, late-night TV snacks and alcohol quickly became a daily habit.

Jana, with whom I shared an apartment, seemed to eat the same things as me, yet remained her ever-slender self. Resentment and self-loathing grew. I was defective. Why was I the only fat friend in the group?

Over time, of course, my peers caught up. Each year, most found their weight creep up a few pounds, then more. The time and discipline required to maintain adolescent figures became harder and harder to find. Was it even physically possible?

Now I was middle aged, and I looked like most other pudgy people in the shopping mall. I blended into my surroundings perfectly. And in response to the growing plus-sized market, more and more clothing options had become available to me. Basic items that had previously been hard to find, like denim jeans over size 16, were easily attainable. And designers were starting to cater for bodies like mine. More stylish options were there to boost my self-esteem.

Fat social media influencers were legion, dancing joyfully in their reels. Celebrating their bodies at every size. I envied their self-acceptance and I tried to embody it.

I got angry at my internalized anti-fat bias. I challenged my own thinking. Who is the gatekeeper of what is beautiful? Why does beauty even matter? Is it because it's a currency to get things? A way of pleasing others? An obligation? And why do I care how I look anyway? I can't see myself. Is my appearance a gift to others that I am unreasonably withholding?

I almost convinced myself to get over myself.

I was almost able to pretend I didn't care about being fat. But.

Darren Saville's voice was still in my head. Your legs are like an elephant's.

Skinny bodies still proliferated as the default in all our visual cultural artefacts.

And now, on the cusp of 40, my palpitating heart charged me awake at 2am, racing in the effort to digest my dinner, triggering catastrophic thinking about anything and everything. I couldn't roll over without straining at the effort. Plantar fasciitis hobbled my first steps in the morning. A day without a headache or a tummy ache was unusual. If I got a cold, I'd be sick for three weeks.

I was tired. So very, very tired.

My buxom friend Renae, whom I met when we both worked the perfume counter at a fancy department store during our college years, regularly swapped diet tips with me. I remember one Sunday morning at work, back in our early twenties, when I complained to her with a deep sigh: 'I'd do anything to be thin.'

'Except eat less,' she joked.

I laughed. 'Well, that would be taking things too far.'

Renae and I had a long history of shared self-deprecation, so I wasn't offended, but her words stayed with me.

In my late 20s I got fed up with myself and decided to give this 'eating less' thing a red-hot go. By that time I had the help of the Internet. I learned about calories and macros. I carefully weighed and measured my food, ensuring I ate no more than 1200 calories each day, at six carefully planned intervals. I power-walked to work each day and did an hour of cardio at the gym each night.

I white-knuckled it through eight months. Beyond my wildest expectations, I lost 60 pounds. I bought lots of small pretty dresses.

But over those eight months it became harder and harder to sustain the weighing and measuring of food. Mustering motivation to exercise didn't get easier. I felt tired all the time, and cold. And I was always hungry. It was a deep hunger that never went away, even after a meal. It pulled at my belly and invaded my dreams.

Looking back, it was probably inevitable: the back-sliding into old eating habits. The just-this-one-won't-hurt thinking. Before I knew how to stop the train of compulsive over-eating, I was back where I'd started.

I sometimes wondered what would have happened if I hadn't said 'just this one won't hurt' all those years ago. Where would I have been now if I'd been able to maintain that weight loss? The thought tortured me, like a winning lottery ticket lost in the wash.

If I could've clicked my fingers and gone back to that skinnier version of myself, I'd have done it in a second.

CHAPTER 3

After the birthday coffee (and uneaten cake) with my sister, I went back to work. The café where we'd met was just across the road from my office. As I returned, with each step, my mind refocused on the problems I needed to solve that day. Birthday or not, the to-do list was long.

I worked at Blake & Timms Lawyers, which we called BTL for short. It was a boutique law firm and I was the practice manager. My job was really varied; I was like a fixer. I did pretty much anything that needed to be done to keep the business running smoothly, and to keep the fee earners earning.

BTL specialized in property conveyancing, family law, and wills and probate. The three big life events for which most people need legal help. Buying a home. Divorcing. Dying. We also drew up contracts for small businesses and did some workers' compensation matters.

The managing partners, Melissa Blake and Ryan Timms, were not interested in pursuing more lucrative commercial work. They'd started out doing that in a top-tier firm when they first graduated, where I'd been their legal secretary. Both found themselves burnt out by Senior Associate level, yearning for a slower pace. So they'd started their own suburban practice, and took me with them.

I was particularly friendly with Ryan. Of the two partners, he was the more laid back, the most fun. His charisma and sense of humor made the office a great place to be, despite the dry nature of our work.

Melissa, by contrast, was harried and serious. Even after walking away from corporate law, stress had clung to her like static on a balloon. The only things she focused on were her work and the frequent problems attached to single-parenting her two teenagers. She never socialized outside of work and walked around with a permanent frown. If you asked how she was, you'd get a very detailed and honest answer. I'd learned to just say hello.

Ryan was great at pulling clients in, and Melissa's strength was providing stunningly insightful advice. I tried to make their lives easier by ensuring the pesky details of keeping the business afloat were attended to, like making sure our clients paid their bills.

Work was my happy place. I know—that makes me weird. But it was a place where I felt in control and respected. The place where my brain was my currency, and my expertise was sought. I knew I was good at my job, and that brought me satisfaction.

The firm was big enough to bring in interesting work but didn't demand crazy hours or attract unchecked egos. Generally, the lawyers who stayed at BTL were committed

to helping people. We'd get a steady stream of recent grad-
uate solicitors rotate through, looking for some real-world
experience after the theory of law school. They usually
moved on after a few years, with an unrestricted prac-
ticing certificate under their belt, to something bigger and
better. I always looked forward to meeting the next influx
of recruits, watching them flail, then flourish and take off.

Our current junior solicitor, Jeremy, was delightful. He
was clever of course—not unusual for a young lawyer—
but also canny. He'd figured out pretty fast that I was the
glue holding the firm together. Seeing a strategic opportunity, he was soon offering to get my morning coffee and
inviting me to lunch. He kept me laughing with tales of
his weekend escapades, and volunteered to help when
our secretaries had large amounts of tedious copying and
flagging of documents to get through. He listened when I
spoke. Of course, he may have been using me to advance
his career, whether consciously or not, but I couldn't deny
I found his attention flattering.

I couldn't help imagining, sometimes, what it would be
like if my husband Stu paid me attention like that.

I wasn't remotely attracted to Jeremy, of course. He was
still a kid. He'd reach peak attractiveness deep in middle
age. By then he'd have made partner somewhere, or would
be at the Bar, or even a judge, and would have found an
attractive, intelligent, equally high-achieving wife. One
day he'd probably retire to a large house by the sea and
complain about conservative politics, despite being a
direct beneficiary of conservative policies. I tried not to

begrudge him the almost inevitably easy life he'd have. He was the kind of charmer for whom it was hard to begrudge anything.

The other youngster in our firm was Chelsea, our paralegal. She'd only started with us recently and was working part-time while doing her final year of law school. She was still finding her feet. I had high hopes for her, but she did have the slightly annoying habit of apologizing all the time. For everything. Sorry I'm late. Sorry I bumped into you. Sorry to interrupt. One of my goals was to train that out of her.

I couldn't imagine why Chelsea lacked self-confidence. She was very smart and well spoken (aside from the apologies). She was eager to learn and had a strong work ethic. She was also tall, thin, tanned, fit and seemingly at ease in her blooming youthful beauty. She radiated good health and natural glamour.

Each morning she strode into the office with an energetic bounce, seemingly unaware of her allure, easy in her movements, entrancing despite her simple clothes. 'Sorry I'm late,' she'd sing, as she arrived bang on time.

Oh, to look like that, I'd think, each time I saw her.

I knew very well that no-one would ever think the same about me.

CHAPTER 4

I was home by about 6pm on my birthday. While Stu was preparing dinner in the kitchen, I walked around our soon-to-be-finished main bedroom, to see what progress the builders had made.

The renovation was about half-way done, and it felt like the construction team had been part of our lives forever. I couldn't wait for them to finish. The novelty of camping in the living room had quickly worn off.

Our bedroom was fairly compact, but had a pleasant view to the rear garden, which was now accessible through newly installed French doors.

The French doors were great, but the thing I loved most about my room now, the thing that made my feet skip with excitement, was through a newly constructed doorway on the opposite wall.

We had claimed some space from an adjacent bedroom and, for the first time in my life, I was getting a walk-in-closet. I might even go so far as to describe it as a dressing room. I smiled as I opened the door to the large area into which cabinetry had not yet been installed.

Being plump, but not happily so, I had long ago resigned myself to never wearing what I really wanted to wear. I played it safe with clothes, steering clear of anything that drew attention to my belly, arms and legs. I wore the same uniform every day: black or dark blue trousers, paired with a loose-fitting top, always with sleeves. And flat, sensible shoes, usually black.

But despite my self-imposed uniform, and my preference to disappear into the background, I loved fashion. I pored through fashion magazines, and curated boards on Pinterest, and followed stylists on Instagram. Sometimes I would wander through the fashion halls of department stores, immersing myself in the always beautiful array of clothes sized for 'normal' bodies.

There were times I couldn't resist a beautiful print or a soft material. Knowing it was foolish, knowing it was futile, nevertheless I would buy a dress in the largest size available, swearing to myself that this was the one that would serve as sufficient motivation to Stick With The Diet.

Through these lapses of my usual good judgment, combined with the stash of smaller-sized frocks I'd bought in a frenzy during my brief weight loss success over a decade ago, I'd amassed a large collection of lovely dresses.

There were only a few that actually fit me. They were the ones that were Empire-lined and stretchy. But I hardly ever wore them. They were far more whimsical than my usual drab office attire. On the odd occasion when I was brave enough to wear them, the fact of their difference made me feel uncomfortable. Noticed.

So my dress-wearing days were infrequent. And yet I kept buying them, and couldn't bear to throw away the ones I'd outgrown. I just couldn't resist how pretty they were.

As I dressed each morning in my dull uniform, I would imagine myself in some alternate skinny realm where everything in my closet fit me and looked amazing.

It was a silly game, but it also felt like a kind of promise to my future self. One day I would wear these again. Somehow I knew it was true, despite knowing the odds. I'd read somewhere that an obese woman in her forties has a less than one per cent chance of achieving a healthy weight. Usually I trusted what scientists and doctors said. But this bit of science I would continue to ignore.

I'd lugged those unworn dresses through three different house moves. Stu suggested I cull the collection. And I tried to reason with myself to do so. If you lose weight again, you'll want to buy *new* clothes, I told myself.

But I couldn't do it. I couldn't let them, or the dream they signified, go.

And so, despite the fact that the clothes I actually wore each day would fit comfortably into a single chest of drawers, I was committing my family to the expense of a large walk-in-closet. All for a silly dream that would probably never come true.

I walked now through the empty space, mentally arranging where the shirts would go, and the skirts and the bags and the shoes when it was finished.

My reverie was broken by the sound of ten-year-old Vivi calling for help. I flicked off the light, closed the door and rejoined my family.

***

Stu and I generally shared the cooking chores, and it was just a coincidence that his turn to cook had fallen on my birthday. He wasn't the type to have spared me housework on my special day. He was far too unromantic for that. You had to eat, no matter what day it was. He wouldn't expect any different on his own birthday.

Over our coffee that morning, I'd suggested he do a veggie stir-fry for dinner. I hadn't told him I was dieting again. He'd seen me try and fail so many times that I was embarrassed for him to know. My plan had been to just quietly start cooking healthier meals when it was my turn, and eat smaller amounts of whatever he served to me. I'd drink those organic shakes for breakfast and lunch. I'd stop snacking and start exercising at lunch time. No need to make a big deal of it.

But Stu'd had other ideas. Instead of the healthy stir-fry I'd suggested, the hot oven was now browning three large, crumbed, garlic-butter-filled chicken breasts. Chicken Kiev. I was an equal mix of pleased and frustrated. One of my favorite meals. Was this his way of saying happy birthday?

I'd only had an apple for lunch and my tummy was twisting with hunger. I decided I'd try to eat just half the chicken.

'Yum, Kiev!' said Vivi, immediately piercing her chicken as she sat down to the table. A squirt of butter shot across her plate.

'Careful, it'll be hot.' said Stu. Vivi ignored him and tucked in. I looked from Vivi to Stu and smiled at our daughter's healthy appetite.

'So how was your day?' I asked my husband. He shrugged and nodded, as if that was all I needed to know, and started eating without looking at me.

I bit into the chicken, taking a moment to savor the crunchy buttery sensation in my mouth.

I waited for Stu to ask about my day, but he didn't. His dinner disappeared in a few bites. Then he carried his plate to the kitchen, rinsed it, and returned to his spot in front of the television.

Vivi and I continued eating together more slowly. She filled me in on her day, and while I listened, I ate every last crumb of that delicious garlic butter concoction.

CHAPTER 5

The builder's name was Dan. Tall, sandy-haired, with a patchwork of skin cancers over his forearms and face. He had a crew of three who worked on-site with him each day, including his sister, Angelica.

There was nothing delicate about Angelica. She had a rough gravelly voice, and a thickly lined face. No scars on her, though—she seemed to have been spared the basal cell carcinomas of her brother. She was tall like him, and strong, and she didn't mince her words.

If Stu and I were to ask if something could be added to the build, or changed from the original plans, Dan would scratch his head and stare into the middle distance, looking for the right words to explain why that thing would be hard, or wasn't a good idea. But if Angelica was in hearing distance, she'd jump in before Dan had a chance to talk. 'Ya must be jokin,' she'd cackle, 'nah, forget it.' She'd laugh to herself and shake her head at our extreme ignorance, until Dan could catch up with a politer, 'well, you *could* do that, but it'd be very expensive,' and then tell us why.

I was a bit scared of Angelica, but I envied her forthright manner. I fantasized about feeling confident enough in my opinion to talk to people that way. But I'd never dream of cutting people off or telling them their ideas were stupid. I wanted to be kind; to build people up, not tear them down.

I did wonder whether my preference for a gentle approach did me a disservice. I'd often find myself doing things for others I'd rather not, to avoid the risk of hurting their feelings. And I did get frustrated when people dissembled and wouldn't just get to the point.

Over the years I'd put up with some frustratingly ambitious junior solicitors who had no idea what they were talking about. I would smile and nod, and encouragingly propose other ways of thinking about an issue or tackling a problem. I imagined they probably laughed about me behind my back. My mumsy manner matching my mumsy clothes.

I wished I had more spunk. More energy. More presence. Angelica, the strong, forthright, green-eyed, long-lashed, silver braid snaking down her back no-fucks-to-give builder, was my secret hero.

Sometimes I felt as if Angelica was watching me when I walked past. Then I'd dismiss that as a nonsense thought. A weird paranoia. But whenever we spoke about the build, and Angelica looked at me, even though we may be talking about drainage pipes or the placement of power switches, or whatever, I felt unsettled, like she was looking straight into my soul, could read my thoughts, could divine exactly how small I felt inside.

***

The mirror in the walk-in closet had been Angelica's idea. I was huddled with Stu, Dan and Angelica in the empty room one morning to discuss the fit-out. I'd wanted cabinetry on all the available wall space. The more the better, I thought, for storing all those dresses. But as I was describing what I wanted to Dan, Angelica interrupted.

'Nah, that's dumb.'

'Oh?' I said, a bit offended. 'Why?'

'It'll feel too closed in,' she said. 'What you need is a mirror. A big one. Right here.' She tapped the far wall of the room with a partially extended measuring tape.

'A mirror? Well, I was thinking of having a full-length antique mirror in our bedroom—you know, one of those carved mahogany ones.'

'No. Dumb. Take up too much room. Remember that room's gotta fit a big bed in it yet. Won't feel so spacious once the bed's in. You won't be able to admire yourself properly in all them nice dresses of yours.'

As far as I was aware, Angelica had only ever seen me in jeans, or my work uniform of top and trousers. How did she know about the dresses, which were neatly packed in boxes in a corner of the living room?

'Oh, well…' I hesitated.

'A full-length mirror. Right here,' Angelica tapped at the wall again. 'Won't know yourself. Make the room look bigger too.'

'Will it cost much?'

'Not as much as your fancy-pants antique one. Couple hundred bucks.'

'I think she's right,' said Stu, who'd become quickly overwhelmed by the volume of decisions thrown at us each day by the builders. He'd realized that asking the builders 'what would you suggest?' was a good way to have matters resolved promptly.

I thought about the Edwardian repro mirror I'd seen online. Maybe it *would* be a bit heavy-looking in the bedroom.

'OK, you've convinced me. We'll put a mirror on the wall.'

Angelica's face usually betrayed little emotion, apart from annoyance, so I was surprised to see her smile and nod, and she tapped the wall once more. 'A mirror. Big one. I'll tell the glazier,' and walked away.

***

The mirror was installed two weeks later. As soon as I saw it, I knew we'd made the right decision. The walk-in closet, which now had the cabinetry installed too, looked so much roomier and brighter.

The mirror extended from floor to ceiling. For the first time in my life, I had a room in my house where I could see myself, completely, from top to bottom.

And while at the moment I didn't really like what I saw, I was sure this mirror would help motivate me to exercise and diet and get skinny again.

As I turned side on, to confirm that my stomach did indeed still stick out further than my breasts, Angelica appeared in the mirror, standing behind me.

'Oh, hello,' I blushed, turning around to face her. I always felt embarrassed when people saw me looking at my own reflection. I wondered if I could get away with pretending I'd been admiring the mirror and not appraising myself.

'Like it?' asked Angelica, nodding toward the mirror.

'It's brilliant. That was such a great idea of yours,' I said.

I winced. I could hear myself overdoing the praise. Stu and I felt vulnerable in our relationship with the builders. Neither of us knew anything about construction, so we had to trust they were only doing work that was necessary. I found myself unconsciously sucking up to Dan and his crew, to maintain friendly relations. But I had a feeling about Angelica. She was a straight shooter. No bullshit. She wouldn't rip us off.

I tried again, more honestly, 'I really like it. Thanks for the suggestion.'

'No worries,' said Angelica, and winked. I expected her to walk off then. But she lingered, looking at me with her head tilted to one side. 'Funny thing, mirrors.'

'Huh?'

'Well, how they show the world in reverse. Like, in your bedroom' (she pointed behind her), 'the window's on the left. But in the mirror here it's on the right. Things are opposite in there,' she nodded at the mirror.

I smiled politely and blinked. This reverse image thing was something only babies marveled at. Just how simple did Angelica think I was? But my conditioned response to be polite kicked in automatically.

'Yes, when I was a kid I used to imagine stepping into one and walking through a mirror image of my house.'

'It only looks reversed on this side. If you were in there looking out at us, we'd be the ones looking reversed,' said Angelica.

I laughed, 'Yes of course.' I wondered where this was going.

Angelica suddenly looked very serious. 'You know, when I was a kid I was really fat.'

'Really?' I was taken aback by the sudden personal turn in the conversation.

For a second I didn't say anything. I didn't know what to say. But Angelica seemed to want to talk about it.

'That surprises me,' I stammered. 'You're so strong and athletic looking.'

'Yeah, well, I got tall and stretched out. And my job's very physical, so I wasn't fat for long. But, see, when I was fat I was bullied. I was never that pretty, and there was this girl at school.' She paused and grimaced. 'Kerry Beaufort. Urgh. She made my life hell. Absolute hell. Didn't have no friends thanks to that one. Anyways, I used to look through the mirror to my backwards house and wish I could dive in and have a different life.' I smiled at Angelica but didn't say anything. She stared at me a bit longer. 'I even used to say a spell, to make it happen.' She closed her eyes and rasped, slowly, dramatically: 'Mirror, mirror, let me in. Let me in so I'll be thin.'

I laughed. I knew now that she was joking. 'Did it work?'

Angelica looked at me, unsmiling. 'What do *you* reckon?' I collected myself.

'Aw, I'm sorry for laughing,' I said. 'Kids can be so cruel.'

Angelica looked at me another second, then smiled and turned to go. 'Yeah, well, hope you enjoy it. See ya—got work to do.' She laughed then, wheezing and choking on her gravelly smoker's cough as she walked away.

I shook my head. That was weird. I turned back to look at myself in the mirror, and the reverse image of Angelica's retreating back.

CHAPTER 6

One month later, the renovation was finally finished, and I was nervous. I was going out to dinner with Renae, who was still my best friend all these years after our days working in the department store together. I hadn't seen her for weeks.

The organic diet shakes I'd started on my birthday had fizzled out after five days. I'd then tried a different approach that also hadn't worked out: an app that promised weight loss through behavioral change. It had promised to explain why my hunger was all in my head and could be cured with psychological strategies. But those strategies had failed to tame the very real grumbles in my belly.

After two failed diets in a month, I was back to eating normally, and looking forward to my dinner.

It was always fun to eat something delicious someone else had cooked. I felt a flutter of excitement, imagining what temptations may be on the menu.

But I was also worried because it meant dressing up. It meant trying to look nice. It meant self-scrutiny and, inevitably, disappointment.

'Mom, do you really need to go out?' Vivi broke into my reverie to demand my attention. She stood in the doorway to the new closet, as I stared at my clothes, working out what I should wear. Stu wasn't home from work yet, but he'd texted to say he was on the way.

Vivi was annoyed I was going out. I inwardly rolled my eyes. My daughter seemed to have a sixth sense for mommy guilt triggers. She would generally ignore me so long as I was in acceptable physical proximity to her. She could go hours at a stretch, when we were at home together, and not talk to me at all. She's so self-sufficient now, I would marvel with gratitude. But Vivi's independence annoyingly vanished at the slightest suggestion that I intended to do something interesting without her. Suddenly she was joined to my hip.

'Yes, I'm going as soon as dad's home. I'm supposed to meet Renae at seven-thirty.'

'I want to come too.'

'I already told you, you can't. This is a grown-up dinner. There won't be any other kids there, and we'll be talking about grown-up stuff.'

'It's not fair. I never get to go out.'

'You will when you're older. It's a school night, anyway. I want you asleep by nine, OK.'

'How can I fall asleep if you're not here to read me a story?'

'Dad can read to you. Or you can read to yourself. You're a good reader now.'

'It's boring reading to myself. I like hearing you read. You do the voices better. Please?'

Vivi looked at my reflection in the mirror. She clasped her hands together and pulled her sad puppy eyes look. It was a low blow. I felt the guilt she'd intended to cause, despite knowing I had absolutely nothing to feel bad about. I deserved a night out occasionally. But those eyes.

'Dad won't be home for 15 minutes. How about I read you a few pages before I go, then you read to yourself, OK? I don't have time to do a whole chapter.' Vivi frowned, unsatisfied. 'It's better than nothing,' I said in a take-it-or-leave-it tone. Vivi pouted and kept holding out for more.

'Ok then,' I said. 'Forget it. No story.' I turned back to looking at my clothes.

Vivi immediately capitulated when I called her bluff. 'No, no, no, I want it, I want it. A few pages is OK.'

I laughed. This kid was so easy to manipulate. I knew it wouldn't be long until the tables were turned and I'd be the one begging to spend time with her. I need to enjoy this while it lasts, I thought, smiling as Vivi pulled me by the hand to her bedroom.

'Where were we up to?' I asked Vivi, picking up the dog-eared book next to her bed. 'Ah, that's right, Isabeau had just asked the Beast if she could go home for a visit, and had discovered his mirror. Here we go.'

Vivi was far too old for fairy tales now, or so she insisted. The garishly illustrated compendium of abridged tales from her toddler years had been long abandoned. But I still loved the magic and fantasy of those stories. I'd worked out that I could now indulge my preference for these escapist tales by reading grown-up re-tellings to Vivi. This version of Beauty and the Beast was particularly delightful.

The cozy bedtime snuggle with Vivi took my mind off the night ahead. I was surprised to be feeling so anxious. When I was younger I went out all the time, with not a care in the world. But now I had the jitters.

I knew, objectively, there was nothing to fear. Renae was easy to talk to and the purpose of the outing was not in the slightest bit threatening. I could understand these butterflies in my tummy if, for example, I was going on a date. But my hook-up days were long behind me. I'd never so much as looked at another man since marrying Stu. Tonight was just a fun catch up with a friend. So why the nerves?

Because I need to dress up, I thought. Because I'm going to look and feel out of place.

Even though I tried to stop it, my internal loop of negative self-talk revved up. The neural pathways for that particular soundtrack were well established.

Look at her, people would think pityingly. Look at that fat frumpy mom who's usually in bed by 9pm. Who does she think she is, being out among us? She doesn't belong here. Look at those mom jeans, cunningly dressed up with a sparkly loose top. How sad. See the grey roots streaking through her DIY dye job, in that safe mom bun secured with the plastic clip? Oh God, there are cushion marks on the bridge of her nose where her glasses usually rest. She's made a special effort tonight and put her contacts in. See her wobble in those heels? She's out of practice. I bet she usually wears sneakers every day—even to work.

I sighed and tried to refocus on the book I was reading, and the uncomplicated love of my daughter.

***

Forty minutes later I took a deep breath and walked into the restaurant with my head defiantly high. Renee rushed over and squealed. 'Evie! Finally got you out!' She swept me up in a hug.

'You look great,' I said to Renae, meaning it, as we sat in our booth. Renae had a lovely, smiley face. She was an extrovert, and her body language matched. She was fun to be around. And she had the coolest collection of vintage clothes of anyone I knew.

'Oh shut up,' she shrieked, 'I look terrible!' Renee was about two inches taller than me and 40 pounds lighter, but despite her clear physical advantages, she couldn't help but moan all the time about how fat she was. 'Look at this,' she said, pinching some loose flesh on her upper arm. 'I'm such a fucking heffalump.' She looked around to make sure no one was listening, then leant across the table. 'These jeans are size 12!' she stage-whispered, with a look of horror on her face.

I ran my hands up and down the thighs of my size 18 jeans. 'Well, that's the same size as Marilyn Monroe, you know. You're in good company.'

'Aw, you're sweet,' said Renae. 'But look at you! Oh my God! You look AMAZING!' Her enthusiasm betrayed some insincerity, I thought.

For a second I wondered why I persisted with this friendship. Our interests had diverged so much since those department store days. But Renae was Renae. Once the obligatory exclamations of self-loathing were out of the way, she was a fun date. She always had good stories to share, and carried the conversation effortlessly, so there were never any lulls as we talked. Renae took me out of my own head. It was easy for an introvert like me to be around her. I didn't have to do much work at all, and usually enjoyed myself.

After the server had brought our food and we'd caught each other up on our respective work dramas, the wine had gone to my head. 'Have I told you about Skinny Annika?'

Renae's eyes gleamed with excitement—she could sense some fun gossip in the offing.

'No! Who, pray tell, is Skinny Annika?'

'Urgh,' I rolled my eyes, 'my neighbor. She moved in about a year ago. Of course, it isn't enough that she's gorgeous. It isn't enough that she's tall and thin. It isn't enough that she's a wildly successful businesswoman. Yesterday I read a profile of her in our neighborhood newspaper. She's gone and started a charity for homeless older women.'

'Bitch, how dare she!' laughed Renae.

'I know. How dare she be so perfect. It's just rude. It makes the rest of us look lazy. And then, on top of all that, she's taken to running laps up and down the park in front of my house. Every day.' I took another sip of wine. 'It feels like an accusation.' We both laughed.

'Is she good company?'

'I don't know,' I shrugged. 'She knocked on our door once to introduce herself, right after she moved in. She seemed nice, of course, but I kept forgetting to invite her back over, and now it feels like I've waited too long. It'd be weird to have a welcome to the street dinner more than a year after the fact. So I guess we're fated to not be friends.'

'Well that's her loss,' said Renae loyally.

I could tell from her body language that she wanted to change the subject, but I'd warmed to my theme and, in my drunken envy, I couldn't let it go. 'She's so god-damned virtuous. She has to rub it in my face with her perky pony-tail and her thigh gap and her long stride and her coordinating designer activewear. It's truly sickening.'

I felt a thrill verbalizing the jealous thoughts I sometimes entertained but never said. Seeing other people succeed where I had failed. Seeing other people enjoy exercise and live well. Seeing others lead the kind of life I felt I deserved, but for some reason couldn't achieve. It seemed easier in that moment to hate them rather than try to join them.

Renae held up a glass in a toast. 'Death to Skinny Annika!'

'Death to Skinny Annika!' I echoed, chinking her glass.

'So, I have a birthday surprise for you,' said Renae, jumping in to steer the conversation away from my maudlin and juvenile meanness.

'What? My birthday was last month.'

'I know, but you've been so busy and this is the first chance I've had to see you. I wanted to give this to you in person.'

'What is it?'

'Here.' She handed me an envelope. Inside was a folded piece of paper, with information about a place called Paradise Peninsula Resort, on the Gold Coast.

'What's this?' I looked up at Renae, confused.

'I was supposed to go there with Dean. For our anniversary. Before he dumped me, of course.'

'Oh Renae, I had no idea—I'm so sorry.'

She waved her hand. 'Good riddance to him. Cheated on me. Anyway, these are non-refundable tickets. So, I want you to come with me.'

'He did what? With whom?'

'Some skank at work. So are you coming?'

'Urgh what an asshole. I hate cheating.' I looked at the piece of paper again. 'Are you sure you want me to come?'

'Er, yeah!' said Renae, as if it was the most obvious answer in the world.

'When?'

'Look, it's not for three months, but I wanted to give you plenty of notice. Can you decide quickly, though, because if you can't come I have to find someone else. The plane tickets cost about $800 each, but if you give me $400 and buy me a cocktail, we'll call it even. Please come, Evie, I really want you to!' She looked at me pleadingly.

I thought about it for only a second. I thought about the pile of unsorted laundry on my dining room table as I looked at the photograph of a pristine beach on the paper in front of me. 'Yes,' I said.

'ARGGGGHHHHHH!!!!' shrieked Renae, 'Thank you, thank you, thank you!'

'No, thank *you*. I'm touched you chose me to invite. But I insist on paying my full share.'

'Well, I'm too broke to argue with that,' laughed Renae. We clinked glasses again.

'So tell me what happened with Dean,' I said, and Renae took gleeful center-stage, retelling the latest heartbreak in her drama-filled life.

CHAPTER 7

BTL was buzzing. It was the morning of the night of the annual Law Society Ball, and everyone was comparing notes about their outfits and hair styles.

The firm was paying for everyone to go. Chelsea was excitedly describing her frock to Melissa—a sequined number with a fishtail. I knew she'd look amazing. Claire, our receptionist, talked about her appointments for spray tans, gel nails and eyelash extensions. She was working a half-day, so she'd have time to get her hair and make-up done.

I didn't need such preparation time. I had a tried and tested formal gown, which I always pulled out for these occasions. It was plain black silk crepe. Full length, with an empire waist and three-quarter sleeves, its simplicity hid a multitude of sins. I changed the look each year by updating my jewelry, adding big colorful pieces to draw attention to my creamy decolletage and away from my stomach.

I did my own hair and makeup. Why bother wasting money on something like that, when you could easily do it yourself? It's not like I was looking to score, or that anyone would be focusing their attention on me.

That evening, at 7.30pm on the dot, my parents Helen and Brian rang the doorbell to commence babysitting duties. They were punctual as ever. 'You look beautiful,' gasped my mom, admiring me as I twirled before them. 'What's different?'

'I have contacts in.'

'Yes, that's it. And that dress is very elegant.'

'This old thing?' I downplayed. 'You've seen this one before.'

'Have I? Well, it's lovely. You look great.'

'It'll do. You're just used to seeing me in jeans and a t-shirt.'

'Just accept the compliment darling. A compliment is a gift. If you reject my compliment, you're rejecting my gift.'

I rolled my eyes. Thirty-nine years old and my mother was still trying to parent me. 'Yes mom. Thank you for your compliment,' I curtsied elaborately.

In truth, I did feel special. It was nice to dress up for once, and I was relieved the gown still fit. There had been a heart-stopping moment, as I stepped in and pulled it up, when it caught on my hips. For a second I feared I may have outgrown it. There was no Plan B for dresses tonight. I'd have had to wear one of the few other dresses that actually fit me, but they were all unmistakably day dresses, which I sometimes wore to the office. Or I'd have had to pull out my trusty black trousers, and team them with a plain black sweater. I would have gotten away with it, but would have felt uncomfortable all night.

With this gown on, there would be no discomfort about being inappropriately dressed. But there would undoubtedly be discomfort from sucking in my stomach for several hours, even with my industrial-strength shapewear on. The dress was fine when I was standing, but as soon as I sat down, the fabric around my bust, waist and hips pulled perilously tight.

Mom and Dad were in a playful mood. They immediately turned their attention to Vivi and commented on how grown up she looked.

'So when are *you* going to start babysitting *me*?' Brian asked Vivi. 'I'm going to be in old-person diapers soon.'

'Urgh, gross grandpa!' laughed Vivi.

'No, I'm serious, I'm going to need you to help look after me. I changed your diapers once, so it's only fair.'

'Mom, please tell me he's joking,' said Vivi, looking at me with a disgusted look on her face.

'Of course he is, dear,' laughed Helen. 'We have many, many years before we get that decrepit! We're way too busy having fun. What was that book you gave me, Evie, by that Australian lady? You know, the one who says 'adventure before dementia'?

'Oh, Kathy Lette! Yes, she's hilarious,' I laughed.

'Well, we're taking her advice. We're going ballooning over the pyramids next year. We saw the travel agent last week.'

'Gosh, that sounds exciting.'

'Yes,' Helen sighed. 'But it's so much work. It's just exhausting planning a holiday.'

'Well,' I said, feeling no sympathy whatsoever, 'I can understand why you may need a break from the unrelenting grind of retirement.'

'Hey now!' smirked my dad. 'I have a lot of responsibilities. Walking the dog every day is hard work.'

'And I appreciate you taking time from your hectic schedule to watch Vivi for us. Thank you again. Please don't forget to read her bedtime story. We're up to an exciting bit.'

'It would be a pleasure, darling,' said Helen, coming over to kiss me. 'Now go to that ball and enjoy yourself. You look like a princess!'

***

The Law Ball was in full swing when we arrived. Stu and I took our places at the BTL table with Ryan and Melissa, Ryan's wife Rebekah, as well as Chelsea, Jeremy, Claire and Claire's boyfriend, whose name remained a mystery the whole night. After a delicious meal (I had the chicken, Stu had the steak, but I stole some of his potatoes because they looked so good), there was a charity auction to benefit a local animal shelter. Then a DJ started taking requests for the dance floor.

I was content to watch the dancing. Stu hated to dance, and I wasn't drunk enough yet to lose my inhibitions.

Stu had become embroiled in an argument with Jeremy about some sports story that had been in the news, so I took that as my cue to escape to the ladies' room.

Naturally there was a queue for the stalls, and I found myself waiting behind Machiko Tanaka from Match Point Legal.

Match Point was the most notorious ambulance-chasing firm in the city, whose slick television commercials were always on high rotation. Machiko was the owner and the face of the business. And quite a face it was. A former fashion model, Machiko was six feet tall, with jet black hair long enough to sit on. Her dark eyes sparkled with merriment as if the daily opportunity to crush her opponents with her towering intellect and limitless confidence was an unending source of entertainment.

Machiko was always smiling, even in the most heated cross-examination. She had the best strike rate in court of any lawyer I knew. And she'd been trying to poach me from BTL to come and work for her for the past five years.

'Evelyn, how are you?' she leaned down to kiss me on both cheeks.

'Machiko. Hello. I thought I'd run into you here.'

'In the bathroom?'

'No, at the Ball.'

'Oh good. For a moment I wondered if I have a reputational problem.'

'You have many reputational problems, Machiko. But none of them involve restrooms, as far as I'm aware.'

'Well, let me know if that changes. I'd welcome the opportunity to sue someone for defamation; it would be a good chance to broaden my litigation experience. So Evelyn, when are you going to quit that third-rate BTL outfit and come join the grown-ups at Match Point? I need someone to lead our e-law transformation project, and you'd be perfect. You know I can make it worth your while.'

'Thanks for thinking of me, Machiko, but as I've said before, I'm not looking to move right now.'

'Not looking to move. You know what that sounds like? Stasis. Retardation. Stunted development. If you don't extend yourself soon, Evie, you'll be stuck at BTL forever.'

'It's a pretty good place to be stuck.'

Machiko shrugged. 'Well, the offer's still there.' A stall became vacant and she disappeared behind the door, calling over her shoulder, 'Call me if you ever change your mind.'

***

When I returned from the ladies' room, Jeremy had left the table to dance with Chelsea. Stu was sitting by himself, scrolling football scores on his phone. I sat next to him and poured myself champagne from an open bottle. Stu continued staring at his phone.

I turned to watch the dancing. Ryan was leading Rebekah across the room. That familiar pang of jealousy—which hit me whenever I saw a couple acting lovingly toward each other—hit me in the guts, but I pushed it away. It's not that bad, I told myself. Everything with Stu is fine. Generally, we're happy. Well, at least, we're not desperately *un*happy. Don't overthink it. Don't go looking for trouble.

Ryan spun around and noticed me watching him. He smiled. I looked away, embarrassed that he'd seen me. After a few more turns around the floor with Rebekah, she headed off to the bar and Ryan sashayed over, insisting I join him for at least one song. He was so charming about it that I couldn't say no.

I gulped the rest of the wine in my glass for Dutch courage and followed him to the dance floor. We laughed as we bopped awkwardly together, both agreeing I was a terrible dancer. Eventually we settled into the rhythm.

'How do you think Jeremy and Chelsea are performing at work?' he asked, shouting close to my ear.

'Yeah, they're doing well, I think. They both need to work on their confidence though. Chelsea needs to dial hers up a bit, and Jeremy needs to dial his down.'

Ryan chuckled. 'I remember being his age. I could never understand why other people didn't instantly agree with everything I said and thank me for sharing my opinion.' He laughed at himself.

'Speaking of egos, I was just talking to Machiko. She tried to poach me again.'

'Well, she wouldn't be where she is today without that legendary persistence. What did you tell her?'

'I told her no. For now.'

Ryan raised an eyebrow. 'For now? Do I need to offer you a pay rise?'

'Well, I hadn't been thinking of that, but now you mention it.'

Suddenly the music changed to a slow dance. We looked at each other awkwardly. 'Oh God,' I laughed, pulling a face.

'I'm game if you are!' said Ryan, offering me his hand.

I reached for him, and he led me around the dancefloor slowly. I tried to relax and was grateful for the champagne that was finally starting to mellow my self-consciousness. Ryan smelled nice. I felt gratitude for the millionth time that I'd landed a job where my boss was also my friend. We were so comfortable in each other's company and worked so well together.

I looked across at the tables. The elegant Rebekah had returned from the bar and was standing near our table laughing with a group of women I didn't know.

Rebekah was one of the reasons I harbored no romantic feelings for Ryan. I'd felt a flicker of something the first time I met him 15 years ago, but then I'd met Rebekah, and understood I had no chance with him. Rebekah was a perfect physical match for Ryan. Tall and gorgeous and self-assured. They were like a living version of Barbie and Ken.

While I was facing her, Rebekah looked across and met my eye. Was that a raised eyebrow I saw? I suddenly felt shy. I took a step back from Ryan. As I did, my heel caught in the hem of my dress. My foot fell out of my shoe and I stumbled.

'Ah!' I shrieked involuntarily and grabbed him for balance.

Ryan caught me by the elbow. 'I'll get that.' He picked up my shoe and followed me as I limped back to the table. 'Here you go,' he said, handing me the shoe. 'Are you OK?'

'Yeah,' I said, rubbing my ankle. 'I don't think it's twisted. Just my pride that's bruised. I'm such a klutz!' I laughed and held up my wine glass. 'I'm blaming the wine.'

'Yes, it was the wine. Undoubtedly,' he said chivalrously.

'No. She's a klutz,' said Stu. 'Take my word for it.' He put a possessive arm across my shoulder. Ryan smiled but said nothing and walked over to Rebekah.

My happiness soured. 'That was mean,' I whispered to Stu as we sat at our places.

'Why? You *are* a klutz. We joke about it.'

'Yeah, in private. When we're in public it would be nice if you had my back.'

Stu lifted his arms in defeat, as if I were a toddler he couldn't reason with. 'You expect me to be happy about you dancing with another guy?'

'What's it to you? You haven't asked me to dance at all.'

'You know I hate dancing.'

'So why did you come?'

'Because you made me. And also for the food.' Stu's irritation seemed to vanish as quickly as it had arrived. He smiled at me as he put a spoonful of dessert in his mouth. Then he grabbed a bottle from the table and refilled my glass. 'Come on Evie, let's not fight. Enjoy the free food and drink and dance with your friends if you want.'

After another glass I'd forgotten our tiff. It was a rare occasion for me to be out, and I was determined to have a good time.

The rest of the ball sped by in a blur of smiling shouted conversations, more food and wine, and thunderous laughter, courtesy of the MC. Stu and I continued drinking and circulated amongst the crowd with ease. One of the local magistrates flirted with me outrageously, having an in-depth conversation with my breasts.

Like many fat people, I was incredibly camera-shy. At first I tried to ignore all the phones in people's hands, flashing candid shots of everyone. But as the alcohol loosened me up, I was soon pulling colleagues and acquaintances in for hugs and demanding selfies.

Before I knew it, the night was over, and Stu and I were creeping quietly through our front door, trying not to wake Vivi. My feet and head were throbbing, evil silver heels clutched in my hand. My parents reported a quiet and uneventful night at home, and quickly left to get themselves to bed.

I went to my room and peeled off the dress, leaving it in a heap on the floor; I'd take it to the cleaners tomorrow. I rolled into bed and felt myself floating and spinning, with ringing ears, before I drunkenly passed out.

CHAPTER 8

Late the following morning, a Saturday, I was woken by the weight of Vivi lying on top of me. She was poking my nose flat, and then lifting each of my eyelids in turn. 'Wake up, mom.'

I groaned, pulled Vivi into a tight hug, and rolled her sideways so she was lying next to me on the bed. 'Good morning,' I mumbled. 'Mom has a headache.'

'Well I need breakfast. I'm hungry.'

'Why don't you get it yourself?'

'I can't open the milk. The lid's on too tight.'

'Where's dad?'

'I don't know.'

'Ask him to do it.'

'I can't find him.'

'Ok, just give me a minute,' I said. 'I'll get up soon.'

This seemed to satisfy Vivi, and she skipped off to play one of her games.

I sighed with relief, knowing I'd bought myself a bit more time in bed. Vivi would probably get distracted and forget she'd asked for breakfast for at least fifteen minutes.

But I was awake now. I knew I wouldn't get back to sleep. I rolled over and picked up my phone, which had been charging on the nightstand.

The first thing I did each morning, to help myself wake up, was to scroll through my social media accounts. My feed was usually full of boring advertisements, interspersed with carefully happy updates from extended family. Rarely anything interesting, and generally only one or two notifications. But today, my phone had forty-eight notifications.

I immediately sat up straight. What's happened, I wondered with alarm. I tapped on the alert icon and went to the first post.

I'd been tagged in several photos from the Ball. One of them, the most liked and commented upon, was a photograph of me hugging the magistrate. He had his arm tightly around my waist.

And gaping between his hand and my breast was a bubble of white flesh, bursting through the seam of my dress. The empire line had torn, but I had been too drunk to notice, and no one had told me.

I was unwittingly flashing half my torso—half my fat, dimpled torso—to the entire legal fraternity of the city. And my face in the picture was blissfully, drunkenly, heartbreakingly unaware.

I dropped the phone in horror. I lay back and put a pillow over my face. I was mortified. Not so much about being drunk, or about being too friendly with His Honor, but about being so unkempt, so slatternly, so enormous, that I was literally falling out of my dress.

The comments my colleagues had written were not malicious. I'm sure they were meant in jest, but people were clearly poking fun at me and enjoying the scandal of the drunken photos.

'I object!' someone had written.

'Judging from the evidence, Evie Swan had a fun time last night.'

'Things are getting a bit un-seam-ly!'

How would I face anyone at work again? How could I project any kind of authority or respect after this?

I blinked away tears. I punched myself in the belly and the thigh. You are so disgusting, I told myself. You are so fucking disgusting.

Stu came into the bedroom carrying a cup of coffee. He looked hungover too.

'Have you seen these?' I asked, holding up my phone.

He smiled. 'Yeah, the comments are gold!'

'You think this is funny? I'm so embarrassed!' I looked at him with a stricken expression.

'What do you mean?'

'My dress is torn! Everyone can see my stomach. I'm practically naked!'

'You're overreacting. It's not that bad,' he said. 'No-one will remember next week.'

Typical, I thought. He doesn't get worked up about anything. It's like he's moving through life anaesthetized. Never shows any feelings at all, except when he watches sport.

'Anyway, I just went out for coffee and croissants.' He handed me the cappuccino in his hand. 'Do you want yours with honey and butter, or with ham and cheese?'

I hesitated. My inclination a few moments ago when I saw that photo had been to never eat again. For the past few minutes I'd been vowing to myself that This Was It. This was my rock bottom. This was my turning point. This was the start of the end of me being fat. I would stop eating altogether. I would go on one of those extreme vegan raw food diets or something. Or at least go back on those stupid shakes. Goddammit I really meant it this time.

But then Stu mentioned croissants, and the memory of their warm flaky buttery taste overwhelmed me. As comforting as an embrace from Stu might have been, if he'd been inclined to offer one. More, even.

It's OK, I told myself, planning ahead, trying not to panic. You haven't got any diet shakes in the house today. You can buy them this afternoon and start the diet tomorrow. Or maybe start on Monday. This weekend can be your last hurrah. Your commiseration. You hereby have permission to eat all the feelings you want today and tomorrow. And then, that's it. You'll never be this fat again.

'I'll have jam and butter,' I said to Stu.

CHAPTER 9

On Monday morning I prepared the first diet shake for breakfast. I drank it down, holding my nose. It was disgusting. Chalky and lumpy. It made me gag. But I'd get used to it. I was going to do this. I slammed the cup down defiantly on the bench.

On the way to work I was filled with dread. What would they all say about the photos and the torn dress? But no one said anything. They were just getting on with their day, as if were a normal Monday.

In the cold light of day, and face to face, perhaps it was too embarrassing to mention. Maybe everyone had memories of the ball they were trying to forget. It was as if, by silent agreement, we were pretending it never happened. What happens at the ball stays at the ball.

Surprisingly, I didn't feel overly hungry that morning. My body was probably still digesting my final-hurrah gorge-fest from the weekend.

Plus, I was fueled by my new determination to Do Something.

At lunchtime I waited until no-one was in the tiny office kitchen, then went in to shake up my diet drink. I carried it discreetly back to my office, closed the door and scoffed it down as quickly as possible.

I wanted to keep this diet a secret. It was weird—everyone could see I was fat. Why didn't I want anyone to know I was trying not to be? Was it because it was so pathetic to even try? Was it a public acknowledgment of my past failures?

As long as I ate like everyone else in public, not too little, not too much, everyone could politely pretend I was normal like them, in the same way they were politely pretending to forget the photos from the Ball.

By early afternoon I was extremely hungry. Have a diet soda, I told myself. Drink lots of water. And then the receptionist Claire popped her head into my office. 'Melissa's meeting has just finished. There's leftover sandwiches in the conference room. I'm just letting everyone know they can help themselves. Chelsea said she's going to take some home, but there'll still be heaps more if you want some.'

'Thanks Claire,' I said, in as normal a voice as I could muster.

Our firm catered for client meetings from time to time. I personally thought it was a waste of money, because no-one ever seemed to eat much during the meetings—they were too busy talking. But it was an expected part of our corporate hospitality. There were always leftovers, which everyone at BTL shared between themselves later.

After Claire left my office, I banged my head on the desk in frustration.

I thought I'd planned this whole day so carefully. Day One of The Diet. I had assessed where and when my temptation points would be, and I had prepared myself for how I would manage them. I had rehearsed casual excuses to use if someone offered me a cookie or invited me to lunch. But I'd forgotten about Melissa's meeting today. It had caught me off guard. And now there was an almost-full platter of delicious deli sandwiches just sitting there. Just begging to be eaten.

I tried to get on with my work, but I was so hungry I couldn't focus. I had to sign a form for Claire at reception. Walking back from her desk, I passed the meeting room, and glanced at the platter. I could remember the taste of those sandwiches from previous meetings. I could almost feel the rush of pleasure it would give me to bite into one. I salivated.

At my desk I checked the work calendar. There were no more catered meetings booked for the next three weeks. No more unexpected bumps in the road after today. I bargained with myself. How about you have a couple of sandwiches today and start the shake thing tomorrow. Treat today as a trial run. A dress rehearsal. It's only a 24-hour delay. Besides, those sandwiches aren't unhealthy. They have veggies in them. Some of them are on whole-meal bread. Fiber is good for you.

Feeling relieved I'd made my decision, I walked casually back to the meeting room and put three sandwiches on a plate. I took them to my office, and almost swooned at the first bite. They were soft and cheesy and savory and chewy.

Almost as soon as the last mouthful was swallowed, I felt regret. Well, I've blown it now. Might as well write off the rest of today too. I went back and added four more sandwiches to my plate.

Driving home a few hours later, I passed a fast-food restaurant. I didn't eat fast food very often, but the awful taste of the diet shake that morning had made me crave a proper milkshake.

On a whim, I turned in and bought a chocolate thickshake for the rest of the journey home.

That was definitely your last treat, I told myself. You are definitely going back on the diet shakes tomorrow.

CHAPTER 10

Lying flat on my back in bed two days later, after two miserable days of diet shakes, I grabbed at my stomach fat with my hands.

I pulled at it like I was kneading dough, giving myself a pep talk.

I was very hungry again. I really wanted a fried egg on buttered toast for breakfast. I really did not want a diet shake.

C'mon Evie, you can do this, I thought. It's only food. Just choose not to eat it. It's all in your head. It's just a matter of willpower. No one is forcing you to eat crap. No one is holding a gun to your head and making you swallow. Just choose not to put it in your mouth. The answer is so simple. You know how to do it. Why don't you just do it? Do you want to wear all your nice clothes again or not?

To get extra motivation, I pulled out my phone and looked at some before and after photographs of strangers on the internet, proudly sharing their weight loss successes.

If they could do it, so could I. My resolve strengthened enough to get me out of bed. OK, let's go.

After my shower I was standing once again in my closet. This time, as further motivation, I didn't just grab the nearest work shirt and quickly get dressed. I decided to look at myself properly.

I closed the door and faced the mirror. I took off my bathrobe and stared at my body in my underwear.

It was rare for me to do this, and I wasn't used to the sight of myself almost naked. Sure, I was accustomed to seeing myself fat and dressed, but not fat and undressed.

My underpants were enormous. Granny pants. I didn't dare try skimpy bikini bottoms at my size. Narrow straps on anything, especially underwear, would get lost in the folds of my flesh. They would get damp with sweat, and chafe, and make every step painful. I needed full briefs and wide bra straps to hold myself together.

I look like an old lady, I thought sadly. I'm only 39. I shouldn't look like this.

All of a sudden, everything felt too hard. This mountain was too big to climb. The weight was literally and figuratively too much to bear. Lou's terrible words, 'you will always be fat,' filled my head.

I shook my head. Snap out of it. This kind of self-pity is futile. Drink the damn shake and stop wasting so much mental energy on this. I moved to put my bathrobe back on.

But then, for some reason, I thought of Angelica. I remembered her story about the mirror. What were the words she had used? Mirror, mirror something.

A little spark lit inside me. I walked up to the mirror and pressed my palms against it. I stared closely at my face. Despite my size and age, my face was nice. No wrinkles yet. Gentle eyes. A friendly smile. My cheeks were a bit round, and I had a double chin. But I liked my face.

I leant my forehead against the mirror, and suddenly Angelica's words came back to me.

I mumbled self-consciously. 'Mirror, mirror, let me in. Let me in so I'll be thin.'

Nothing happened.

I laughed at my own stupidity and went to lift my head off the glass. But it wouldn't move. I tried to lift my hands. But they wouldn't come off the mirror either. In trying to step back, my hands moved further forward into the wall. It felt like I was sticking them into a bowl of honey. A thick, oozy glob.

In a panic, I lifted a foot toward the mirror, to lever myself off. But my leg moved into the oozy silver too. Suddenly I felt as if I was being pulled forward. Like the mirror was quicksand, dragging me in. I took a deep breath before my face went in. It happened in seconds.

The next thing I knew, I was lying on the floor of my closet. I lay still for a moment, catching my breath. My heart was racing. What the fuck just happened? I looked up. Everything seemed as before. Maybe I fainted, I thought to myself. Maybe it wasn't a good idea to go on a very low-calorie diet without talking to my doctor first. Maybe I should quit the shakes.

I noticed my robe lying on the floor where I'd dropped it.

Still sitting down, I reached over to pick it up. And then I saw the label. XS. I blinked. The label still said XS. I held it up. The robe was tiny. Almost like a child's. I stared at it in wonder. I held the label close to my face. Yes, it definitely said XS.

Slowly, I turned around on my knees. There was the mirror. And in the mirror was someone I didn't know. A stranger was in my closet! I jumped in fright. The woman in the mirror gave a start too.

Wait, that woman was moving when I moved. Almost like my reflection.

I crawled to the mirror, unblinking, mouth agape. I put my hands against the glass. It was cold and hard and solid, as a mirror always is. I knocked on it. It echoed glassily.

I stood up with balletic ease, without any grunting.

I took a step back and looked at my reflection. Up and down. Head to toe. I could barely breathe.

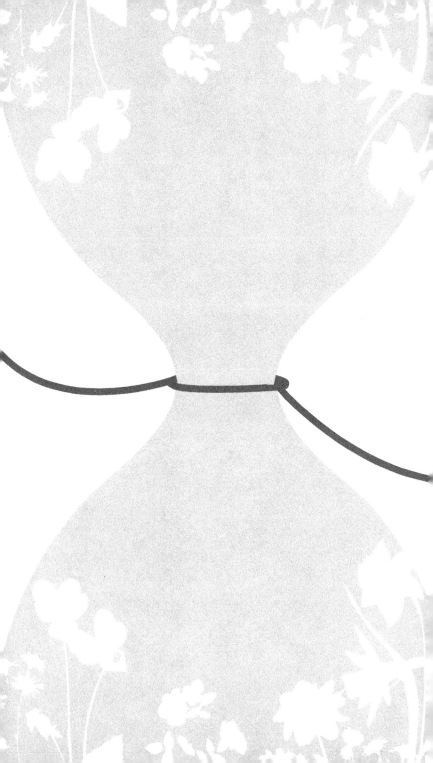

PART 2
THE
MIRROR

CHAPTER 11

I was gorgeous. I was perfect. I looked like a supermodel. OK, a short supermodel. But stunning.

Slowly, I turned around. Muscles rippled. Smooth skin stretched. I had a six-pack! My breasts were full but pert. My neck looked longer without a double chin and was emphasized by deep hollows behind my collar bones, stretching to bony shoulders.

My arms were toned. I held them out and flapped them. Nothing jiggled. No bat wings. No cafeteria lady arms.

I jumped up and down on the spot. Nothing wobbled.

I turned and looked at my bottom. No cellulite. Nothing. None. Just a perky curve down to my sleek thighs, my sculpted knees, my muscled calves and my slender ankles. Oh my God, even my feet look thinner.

Scales! Where were the scales? I needed to weigh myself. I dashed across my bedroom to the ensuite and pulled them out. Usually they were dusty, but not today. Usually I weighed myself only sporadically. Usually I didn't want to know my weight; couldn't face the truth. But now. Now I wanted to know.

I stood on the scales. After a second the number settled. 116. I blinked. 116. The scales were saying I weighed 116 pounds. I nearly screamed and put my hand to my mouth.

Suddenly I was fearful. What else had changed? Vivi! Stu! I pulled on my robe and ran out to the kitchen. They were both sitting there as normal, eating their cereal. 'Hi mom,' said Vivi, smiling at me.

'Hi,' I said.

I stood there, staring. Not saying anything. Stu looked up.

'Are you okay?' he asked.

'Why do you ask?'

'You're going to be late for work. You're usually dressed and leaving by now.'

'To go to BTL, you mean?'

'Yes,' he said, looking at me strangely. 'Unless you've secretly changed jobs and didn't tell me.'

'No. No. I'm still the practice manager at BTL. Aren't I?'

'Are you sure you're OK?' said Stu.

Vivi giggled. 'Mom, you're funny!'

'Viv, I need to take you to school soon. Finish your breakfast quickly,' said Stu, looking at his phone again.

Clearly neither of them were shocked by my appearance.

'I guess I'll go get dressed then.' They both ignored me as I walked away.

I went back to my bedroom, checking every room of the house as I went. Everything looked the same. Everything seemed the same. Everything *was* the same. Except me.

Back in the closet, I looked at my clothes. Some of the dresses were familiar, purchased when I lost weight many years ago, but there were other outfits too, which I hadn't seen before.

I pulled out my phone and rang the office.

'Oh, hi Claire,' I said, trying to sound casual when the receptionist answered. 'It's Evie here. I just wanted to let you know I'm going to be in late today. I probably won't be there until about eleven. There's a couple of personal errands I need to run. Can you let everyone know please? Great, thanks.'

I hung up the phone and looked at my clothes. With a gleeful squeal, I jumped up and down.

Then I started trying on my clothes. All of them.

Everything fit.

Everything looked amazing.

CHAPTER 12

Ninety minutes later, I was following my GPS through an unfamiliar suburb, looking for Builder Dan's new worksite. I had rung him after my clothesgasm that morning, to try to locate Angelica. Dan confirmed she was onsite at his new job, and he gave me the address.

Dan didn't seem surprised to be hearing from me. His sister seemed to make a lasting impression on lots of his clients—particularly the middle-aged female ones. He didn't care to think why and asked himself no further questions on the matter.

I pulled into the driveway of a half-demolished house and stood beside my car. I suddenly felt shy and ridiculous. What would I say? It was so absurd. Perhaps I was having some kind of psychotic event and this whole thing was literally all in my head. Some kind of strange hallucination.

Then I felt my belly. It was still flat and rock hard.

My hesitant thoughts were interrupted by a shrill wolf whistle. I turned my head, looking for both the source and the target. The source was quickly discovered—it was Will, the cheeky young apprentice on Dan's team, whom I'd often overheard making inappropriate jokes when he worked at my house. He hadn't spoken to me much then. But he was looking at me now, up and down, with an exaggerated movement of his head. He was positively leering.

'Looking mighty fine today, Mrs Swan!' he called through an empty window frame at the front of the house.

'Hello Will,' I said, and instinctively (where did this instinct come from?) gave him a coquettish smile. 'I'm looking for Angelica.'

Will nodded backwards into the house. 'She's in there—in the kitchen.'

'Can I go in?'

Will jumped down to the front of the house from the open window and ran to the end of the path whose steps were half-demolished. He extended his hand chivalrously to me as I came toward him. 'Allow me.'

He hoisted me up onto the path. 'Nice dress,' he said, as I walked ahead of him toward the house.

I couldn't help myself. I added a slight wiggle to my hips with each step. When I reached the door, I turned back and smiled radiantly.

'Thank you, Will.' I looked up from under my lashes. 'I really appreciate your help.'

He winked at me and went back to the front room where he'd been working.

Evie Swan, who are you? I thought to myself. Where did that confidence come from? And was that appropriate?

That is *not* how you respond to sexist attention. You should have called him out and reprimanded him for treating you like an object.

But I'd felt giddy, almost high, with this newfound physical power to attract. It was something I hadn't known before—ever.

Even as a young woman, at the height of my youth and beauty (such as it was), my pudgy bespectacled gaucherie had prevented me from developing any effective flirting skills. My boyfriends had all been friends first, who'd fallen for my mind and my conversation, not my body.

When I lost weight in my late 20s I suddenly unearthed a newfound confidence that gave me courage to try dating strangers. That was when I met Stu.

But by then I was already on an upwards trajectory back to fat. Our mutual love of wine and cheese, our cozy nights in together, and my sudden pregnancy, meant I'd returned to my usual, overweight size early in our relationship. After 12 years together, Stu had mostly only known me as fat, and didn't seem to care.

I heard Angelica berating a tiler about something in the kitchen. I took a deep breath and entered the room.

She stopped talking to the tiler immediately and looked at me. Again the penetrating stare. She didn't look at my willowy frame, but directly into my eyes. I shifted uncomfortably. All my newfound confidence dissolved.

Without saying a word, Angelica nodded her head toward the bi-fold doors behind her, leading to the backyard. I walked outside and Angelica followed.

We stood in the shade of a giant, autumn-tipped tree. 'Sorry to bother you at work. I, um, needed to talk to you.'

'Oh yeah? About what?' she half-smiled.

My eyes widened in disbelief. I spread my arms and gestured at my body. 'About this.'

'Your dress? It's very nice.'

'Not my dress. Me, my body. The mirror. The one you put in my closet. I did that thing, said those words you told me. And this…this happened!' Again, I gestured at myself.

'Yeah, I know,' said Angelica. She lit a cigarette and took a deep drag. 'You look great. But more importantly,' she leant toward me, 'how do you *feel*?'

'Confused!'

Angelica shrugged.

'Are you going to tell me what's going on?' I asked. 'Is this temporary? Is this forever? What else has changed that I don't know about?'

'OK, OK. Here's the deal,' she pulled up her sleeves. 'I meet a lot of women like you, and it's frustrating as hell. You spend all your time hating yourselves and your lives. You don't know how good you've got it. You live in beautiful houses. You have happy, healthy kids. You have good jobs and everything you need. Your biggest problem is whether to go with the dark tile or the light tile. You have god-damned options, lady. Choices. All that brain power you have, all that potential,' at this point she tapped my forehead, 'is stuck in an eternal loop about what's going on down here,' and she slapped the side of my thigh.

75

'Well that's a bit presumptuous.' I was suddenly indignant. 'How do you know I wasn't perfectly happy the way I was?'

'I didn't,' said Angelica, 'But the odds were good that you weren't. Every single time I've given a woman those words, she's used them. Whether she was fat or not. Every. Single. Time. So I guessed you were at least curious.'

'What are you? Some kind of fairy godmother?' My confusion and sense of powerlessness suddenly manifested as anger.

Angelica chuckled. 'If the shoe fits.'

'So, am I stuck like this? Is this my life now?'

'Well that depends,' said Angelica. 'As I said, you have choices. You have agency. You can make your life what you want it to be.'

'What else have you changed?'

'Nothing. Your life is still the same. I've just taken away this one problem. This one preoccupation. All the big things in your life, the people, the job—everything else is the same. Only your small, day-to-day decisions have changed.'

'Like what?'

'Like what to have for lunch.' Angelica wheezed at her own joke.

I blushed. 'So, everything's the same, except my body?'

'Yep.'

'Well, that doesn't sound so bad.'

'Maybe.'

'Wait, you said I have choices and agency. What do you mean?'

'I mean you can go back. At any time.'

'Go back?'

'Through the mirror. Back to how you were.'

I laughed. 'If nothing has changed except me being fat, why the hell would I want to go back?'

'Some people do.'

I stretched my skinny leg out in front of me and turned my slender ankle in its designer heel. 'I think I might like to stay on this side.'

'Well, you have a chance to think about it.' Angelica flicked her cigarette into a pile of building rubble and looked me straight in the eye again. 'This is the deal. You can try this life three times. You can go through that mirror, and back, three times. Over any period of time. Then it closes forever. No loopholes. Don't think you can keep going back to fill up on chocolate chip cookies on that side then come back here to swan around skinny. Three chances. And you'll still have to wear the consequences of your choices. On this side of the mirror, you didn't get that body for free. You had to work for it, and you'll have to keep working to keep it.'

I tried to ignore that last bit. 'Three times. So this counts as the first?'

'Gee, I wonder if you're as smart as I thought you were? Yes, dummy, this counts as the first.'

I felt wounded. 'I just wanted to check. I work with lawyers. I know how important it is to go over the fine print.'

'Fair enough. So, shall I tell you the words to go back to your old life?'

'I honestly don't think I'll need them,' I said, hugging myself. I felt colder in this skinny body and had started to shiver a bit. In doing so, I marveled at how much further around my body my arms could now reach.

'Well, if you want to go back, it's pretty simple. Same thing will happen in reverse. You just say: "Mirror, mirror, let me out. I don't care if I am stout".'

'Stout?' I laughed. 'Gee, what an attractive way to describe it. Why are all the words for being fat so ugly? Everything associated with fatness is portrayed so negatively.'

'I dunno that I agree with you. You ever look at Rubens? At Gaugin? Maybe the problem's with you and your attitude?'

'Wow, for a supposed fairy godmother you don't seem to like me very much.'

Angelica sighed. 'It's just frustrating, is all. Think of me as a coach. If you were a professional runner, would you want me to just tell you how great you already are at running? Or would you want me to tell you how to be better?'

'So you're a coach for fat, dissatisfied, peri-menopausal ladies?'

'Maybe.'

'OK, so do I need to check in with you or something? Let you know what I decide?'

'Nup. You never need to see me again. Just remember the rules. Three times in. Three times out. Then it's over. You either choose your fat body, or you choose your thin body.'

Dan's voice boomed out from the house. 'Angelica!'

'Break's over,' she said, patting me on the arm. 'I'm sure you'll make the right choice, honey. Just try to enjoy it.'

'Wait!' I called, as Angelica walked away. 'Why me?'

Angelica looked at me again with her incisive stare. 'You had sad eyes,' she said. 'Can't bear to see that.' And then she disappeared into the house.

CHAPTER 13

Stout. I sat in my car and made a note in my phone of the words Angelica had given me. Then I googled the meaning.

It was a word I knew, and sometimes read in books, but rarely heard. It was old-fashioned. It made me think of beer. Or of short, fat Englishmen with bowler hats.

The dictionary said 'rather fat or of heavy build.'

It wasn't a word that conjured glamour or sophistication. It was grandfatherly, not young-womanly. Not a way I wanted to be described.

I thought of the old A.A. Milne poem my father used to read me about a teddy bear who was 'proud of being short and stout'. Well, that's all very well for a toy bear, or an old Englishman. But not me. Never me.

I nearly deleted the note I'd just made in my phone, recording Angelica's spell to return to my old life. If I forgot the incantation, I'd be forced to stay here forever. I'd never have to think about being fat again.

My finger hovered over the delete button.

But something stopped me. What if? What if Angelica knows something I don't—a reason why I might need to go back.

I saved the note and put my phone back in my bag. I adjusted my sunglasses and looked at my watch. I'd better get to work.

***

I walked toward the front door of BTL feeling apprehensive. It was the same feeling as returning to the office after a radical haircut. I expected to be instantly surrounded by my female colleagues, who would cluck and fuss and heap me with compliments (some sincere and others polite). I would make a few self-deprecating jokes—why, yes, hadn't you noticed me trying to lose weight? I've been using those slimming shakes. They taste so bad, but it was easier to use them than count calories. Not at all complicated. I guess it worked.

Play it cool, Evie, play it cool. I took a deep breath and pushed the door open.

Claire looked up from the reception desk. 'Hi Evie. I took a few messages for you—just check your emails.'

I stood still. 'OK, thanks.' I kept looking at her.

She smiled at me. 'Was there something you needed?'

'Ah, no. Thanks for the messages.' I walked through to my office.

Those I passed on the way to my desk either nodded good morning or said hello. But nobody remarked on my appearance or seemed surprised when they saw me.

This is incredible, I thought. It's like nothing's changed.

I sat down and reveled in how much room I had, how comfortable it felt to cross my legs under the desk.

Before long the phone rang, and my focus shifted to work.

At lunch time I popped across the road to The Daily Grind, the café where Lou had met me for birthday cake only a few weeks (and what felt like a lifetime) ago. Bright sunshine poured in the large windows, and the clink of cutlery and smell of coffee made me feel warm and happy. Life is good, I thought.

'Hi Joe,' I smiled at the barista.

'You missed your coffee this morning,' he smiled back, sneaking a look at my breasts.

'Yeah, I had a meeting,' I said, casually stretching my shoulders, making my chest stick out slightly in his direction. 'I'll just get the usual for lunch, thanks,' I nodded toward the chicken glistening on a rotisserie behind him.

My 'usual,' which I purchased for lunch most days, was a sliced chicken kebab, with lettuce, tomato, red onion and a generous drizzle of garlic yoghurt. It sounded healthy, but deep down I knew it probably wasn't. In the past I'd tried not to think about its nutritional value too much. I suspected the oily chicken and full-fat yoghurt would disqualify it as a diet food.

Now, as the words came out of my mouth, looking at the fatty chicken turning behind Joe, I suddenly had a queasy feeling in my tummy—like a memory of food poisoning.

Joe looked at me quizzically. 'What usual would that be? We only ever see you in here for coffee. You want more coffee, you mean?'

'Ah, no, actually that's OK Joe. I'll um,' I scanned the glass cabinet in front of me, 'I'll take a small serve of that sushi.' Who am I, I thought? What am I doing? I hate sushi. But at the same time my mouth was watering.

'Anything else?' he asked, reaching for a small carton.

On top of the counter was an arrangement of donuts, pastries and gourmet cookies. I would often get one of these for a late-afternoon snack at my desk. In my mind I selected the caramel-frosted donut. But without another thought, out of my mouth came a confident 'No thanks!'

Back at my desk I bit into the sushi and was surprised to find myself enjoying it. It was firm and fresh and surprisingly tasty.

After three bites, Ryan walked passed my office. 'Evie!' he called, looking astonished. Finally, I thought, someone's noticed the dramatic change in my body. I prepared myself to explain the diet shakes.

But I was wrong 'What are you doing here?' he asked. I realized from his expression that he wasn't surprised by my sudden weight loss at all. He was just surprised to see me in the office.

'Having lunch,' I said, holding up my sushi. As I extended my chopsticks in the air, I couldn't help but admire the slender sweep of my wrist, on which a bracelet dangled delicately.

'No gym today?'

Oh shit, I thought. Maybe that's what I do now. I'd have to work out which gym I belonged to, and remember to bring workout clothes to the office.

'Ah, no, no gym today,' I said. 'I had some errands to run this morning, so I'm trying to catch up on a few things here.'

'Well, don't make a habit of skipping it,' said Ryan. 'We don't want you losing that delectable ass of yours.' He winked and laughed and walked on to his office.

I froze, the sushi-laden chopsticks suspended in mid-air. What did he just say? Did I hear right? That was way out of line.

I put the sushi down. I wasn't hungry anymore. The small rolls hadn't filled me up, but I now felt sick. It was only my fifteen-year friendship with Ryan that gave me courage to stand up and go to his office.

He was sitting at his desk, jacket off, sleeves rolled up, tie hanging loose, reading something on his screen. I knocked on the doorframe and stepped inside. He looked up, as if nothing had happened just now.

'Um, what's going on?' I said, my voice shaking. I cleared my throat and spoke a bit louder. 'It's not appropriate for you to say what you just said.'

Ryan looked at me silently. Then he stood up, walked over to me and closed his office door. 'Are we playing the Bosses game again?' he murmured close to my ear.

My heart hammered in my chest. My face flushed bright red. What?! Ryan? Oh my God!

Suddenly his hand was on my breast, squeezing and fondling me. I turned my head to look at him, outraged. He mistook this as a sign to kiss me, which he did.

I hadn't been kissed like that in a long time, maybe ever. Despite my shock I suddenly felt very turned on.

But it was so surreal. This was Ryan. Familiar, brother-like Ryan. Handsome, yes. But happily married to Rebekah. And my boss! And what about Stu?

I broke away, and pushed his hand off me. 'Wait. No! It's, um.' Now he was stroking my hair and smiling. He was completely at ease.

He looked through the blinds of his office window. 'Everyone's at lunch. We haven't done it here for a while. We could go to the stock room. How about it?' He put his hand around my waist and pulled me to him, grinding into me.

He thinks I'm worried someone will see us, rather than stopping because it's highly inappropriate. We must be lovers. How long have I been screwing the boss?

I looked at his full, wet lips, and his lustful eyes. I couldn't believe I was actually tempted to do this. Stop it, Evie!

'Uh, no, not now. I have to go. We'll talk later.'

I opened the door, walked quickly to my office, grabbed my purse and ran out of there as fast as I could.

Shit, shit, shit, shit, shit!

CHAPTER 14

I was home before Stu and Vivi, and had the house to myself. I went back to my closet and looked at myself in the mirror. I still looked incredible. But I saw my reflection in a new light. Clearly some things had stayed the same, but some things were very, very different.

How could I do that? How could I cheat on Stu? I mean, I know we have our problems, but really. And with a married man? Am I really capable of that? Am I that kind of person? I thought I was nice. I just couldn't believe it.

I felt twitchy and uneasy. My usual response to feeling this way was to eat something. But right now the thought of food made me feel sick.

I saw sneakers sitting on the shelf to my right. I grabbed them and changed into some leggings and a sports bra. I took my house key and phone, and before I knew what was happening, I was jogging away from my house.

I expected to tire out quickly, but I was able to keep going and going. The full length of our street, then into the reserve at the end of the block, across to the lake, then around the lake. It must have been at least 6 miles. And I was able to run the whole way. Up hills, down hills. Without my lungs or legs hurting enough to make me stop.

By the time I returned home, it was starting to get dark. I was sweaty and breathing a bit heavier than usual but I felt warm and tingly. In fact, I felt incredible.

The run had cleared my head and helped me sort out what I had to do. Shame caved in over me when I saw Stu's car in the driveway, but I set my shoulders straight. Somehow this situation wasn't my fault. I'd just stumbled into it. I had to find out what had been going on, and I had to put things right.

***

I crept into the house feeling like a criminal. I could hear Stu in the kitchen, cooking dinner, and felt heart-crushed with guilt.

'Hi,' I yelled out. 'Just been for a run. I'm gonna take a shower.'

'OK,' he called. 'Dinner will be ready in 10 minutes.'

I stood under the hot shower, watching the water stream down my body like I was a classical statue standing in a fountain.

I was still glowing from my long run, but also feeling agitated—nauseated but strangely excited from my encounter with Ryan. What other surprises was I going to discover?

I pulled on some yoga pants and a t-shirt and squeezed my hair dry. I wiped the steamed-up mirror with a towel and stared at my face. I still couldn't believe how beautiful I looked.

My face was much thinner now. My cheeks had hollowed out, making my cheekbones and eyes more prominent. My skin was clear and smooth, and currently slightly flushed, either from the run, the hot shower, or my embarrassment.

You can fix this, I thought. If Stu doesn't know yet, he doesn't need to know. Just end things with Ryan, then life with Stu can continue on as before.

But my heart sank a little at that thought. More of Stu's cold shouldering. More screen-staring silences. More emotional detachment.

'Mom, dinner's ready!' Vivi's voice echoed from the dining room.

'Coming!' I dropped my sweaty workout clothes into the laundry hamper.

I jogged to the table. Despite the emotional turmoil, I marveled how I could still have so much energy, even after a long run.

***

'Mmm, smells great,' I said as I approached the table. 'What's on the menu?'

Stu looked at me, a bit surprised. 'It's Tuesday.'

I looked at the meal. I couldn't quite work out what it was by sight. 'Tuesday. So that means…'

'Mom,' said Vivi, with exaggerated impatience. 'Tuesday's always cauliflower rice and chicken stir fry. D'uh!'

'Yeah, I know. Just testing you!' I joked.

As far as I could recall, I'd never eaten cauliflower rice in my life. And I'd never eaten to a roster.

I sniffed my spoon and took a bite. It actually tasted OK. Better than I was expecting, anyway. Maybe my tastebuds were different in this world, or had adapted after years of conditioning to eat this healthy shit.

We all chewed in silence for a few minutes.

'So, did everyone have a good day?' I finally asked, keeping my voice bright.

'Yeah, nothing special,' said Stu.

'And what about you, Vivi? What did you do at school?'

Vivi shrugged. 'I dunno. Nothing.' It was good to see some things hadn't changed. Vivi was as non-communicative about her school day here as she ever was.

'What about you?' asked Stu.

'Me? Um, yeah, just a normal Tuesday,' I lied.

'Vivi showed me the Law Ball photos today,' he said. I looked up, alarmed. I was sure I wouldn't have torn my dress in this body. Surely there would be no need for sniggering comments on Facebook on this side of the mirror. So I wondered why Stu was mentioning it. He was employed as a logistics executive, not a lawyer, so wouldn't be interested in anyone else there. Maybe

I'd disgraced myself in a different drunken way. Maybe with Ryan.

'Oh yeah?' I said, trying to keep my voice neutral. 'Were there any good ones? Any funny ones?'

'You haven't looked yet?'

'Haven't got around to it.'

'You should look,' he said.

'Why? Anything compromising?' I gave a light laugh. Ha ha ha.

'Well, I kind of regret not going,' he said. 'I would have had the most beautiful woman in the room as my date.' At this he smiled at me, sort of weirdly.

I should have been happy to hear this, but why didn't he go with me? And the way he talked about my appearance made me feel like Stu was congratulating himself, rather than complimenting me.

'Urgh, gross dad!' said Vivi.

Nevertheless, it didn't seem like he knew about Ryan. I'd try to find out later why he didn't go. Maybe I could discreetly check the calendar in his phone. Perhaps he had a conflicting engagement.

'So,' I changed the subject, 'what are we having for dessert tonight?'

They both looked at me blankly.

'Dessert? What's the occasion?' asked Stu.

'Um, Tuesday?'

'Oh can we? Can we?' asked Vivi, suddenly excited.

'No hon,' said Stu. 'You know the rules.' He looked at me with concern. 'Are you feeling OK, Evie?'

'Of course,' I said, far too quickly. 'I'm fine!' I looked across at Vivi. 'Sorry honey, Dad's right. We probably shouldn't have dessert tonight.'

'It's not fair!' she whined. 'Lily told me they have ice cream every night.'

Stu gave me a significant look. 'Well, that's up to Lily's mom and dad. In this house...'

'I know,' interrupted Vivi, 'party food is for birthdays and Christmas.'

'You can have an apple if you're still hungry,' I said, feeling like a complete hypocrite.

'OK,' said Vivi, 'but can you cut it up for me, and put cinnamon on it?' I couldn't believe how quickly she agreed to this. Gosh, we must be really strict parents here, I thought.

Across the table, Stu was close to finishing his meal. I looked at him properly for the first time since I'd come through the mirror.

He looked a little bit thinner than in my fat world, but not significantly so. He'd always been one of those long and lean men who could eat and eat and never gain weight. He also looked more tired than I remembered. There were dark shadows under his eyes, and was that grey hair at his temples? After the strange day I'd had, I didn't trust my memory.

Even though we lived together, we were usually so busy we hardly looked at each other from one day to the next, as we went through the motions of working and running a household. We might sit together in the living room after dinner, and sleep together, but we would invariably be staring at separate screens, driving in separate cars to separate workplaces, following separate schedules. Dinner was the main time we came together face to face each day, and then our attention was either on our food or on Vivi.

Maybe that's why we lost our connection, I thought, remembering Ryan's lustful gaze. Stu and I took each other for granted.

I stared down at my bowl of cauliflower rice. I was only two-thirds of the way through but felt full. Another meal I couldn't finish. Maybe I'm sick? Or maybe this is what happens when you're used to eating small portions.

'I'm done,' I said, standing to take my bowl to the kitchen. 'Thanks. That was nice,' I smiled at Stu.

'No worries,' he said.

CHAPTER 15

I tried to watch some TV after dinner but couldn't focus on the story. I was exhausted. The day had caught up with me. 'I'm going to turn in early, catch up on my book,' I told Stu.

'OK, I'll put Vivi to bed.'

'Thanks.'

I fell into bed, and doing so felt just as good in this world as it did at home.

At home? Isn't *this* my home, I wondered? Everything is the same here, except for how I look. Why does it feel different? Ryan intruded into my thoughts. OK, things aren't *exactly* the same.

I could see a half-read novel sitting on the nightstand. Interestingly, it was the same book I'd been reading in my fat world. But as I went to pick it up, I remembered Stu talking about the Law Ball photos. I decided to look at those before reading.

Cringing at the memory of my busted dress, I scrolled through my phone. As before, I'd been tagged in photos from the dance in this skinny world. In composition, they were identical. There I was being hugged by the leering magistrate, and there I was laughing in a candid shot with Ryan.

But now, in all of them, I looked like a movie star. I wore a strapless, beaded gold sheath that skimmed the floor. My shoulders were sparkling, as if I'd applied some kind of glittery bronzer. My hair, which was a few shades lighter in this world than my usual brown, had been professionally styled in an elegant updo. My jewelry was discrete, so as not to detract attention from the incredible dress. 'Wow,' I thought, jealously wishing I could have experienced that moment.

I scrolled backwards through my feed, seeing older posts that I remembered making (sharing silly memes, liking certain news articles, sending birthday wishes to family and friends) but there were other posts I hadn't seen before. These were generally photos (either selfies or shots taken by others) where I was doing things I wouldn't normally do—going on hikes, triumphantly punching the air at the finish line of a half-marathon, standing in a bikini on the beach, doing the warrior pose at a yoga retreat. Hashtag blessed.

In one snap, I was doing a star jump in my sunny back-yard, with the caption 'FINALLY warm enough for shorts!' In the photo I was wearing very small red shorts with a navy singlet and white tennis shoes. In my fat world, not only did I never celebrate the arrival of shorts weather (I hated summer), I didn't actually own a pair of shorts.

I wore the same full-length clothes year-round. In summer I just resigned myself to feeling hot and sticky and chafed and uncomfortable. And tried to stay in air conditioning as much as possible.

The next post on my phone was a link to an Instagram account called *Shrinking_Violet_1983*. 'Some useful tips from my friend Violet,' I'd written in the post, linking to the page. I clicked on the link. The Insta feed loaded. The bio described the page being about 'my journey from fat to fit. How I got it off. How I keep it off. And how you can too. Follow me for tips on how I conquered the demon of compulsive over-eating and found my path to health, happiness and inner harmony.'

Despite the attribution to 'Violet', I could tell from certain details that this was my own work. And what kind of New Age nonsense was it? 'Inner harmony'? I hoped I wasn't spruiking magic water or anything dodgy. I was glad Skinny Me had the sense to use a pseudonym. There might be personal stuff here I wouldn't want my colleagues to read.

I'd always been guarded about my privacy. I'd once read that we lead three lives—a public life, a private life and a secret life. Clearly my fatness was part of my public identity. I couldn't hide it. This was a source of discomfort, not only because I absorbed and must have subconsciously believed some the terrible false messages society projects about being fat (lacking in moral virtue, unclean, smelly and lazy), but also because my fatness displayed publicly an aspect of my private life I would prefer to keep hidden—my dysfunctional relationship with food.

My efforts to diet, I also tried to keep private. Hiding it was hard because so much eating happens publicly. Indeed, food is a primary way for public lives to connect. I could try to make excuses ('no thanks, I just ate'), but I never felt these were terribly convincing.

As for my secret life—not even accessible to my most beloved family members—I would include my self-loathing, my stash of unworn dresses and the occasional binges that thrilled and disgusted me.

While no one knew these aspects of my life, they ate away at me—literally—limiting the person I was able to be, in public and in private. And today I'd discovered that my secret life was even more complicated than I knew.

There were numerous lengthy posts on the *Shrinking Violet* account. I was too tired to read them all now, so I bookmarked the page to read later. Hopefully these would help me understand and navigate this skinny world better.

I put my phone down and picked up my book, but I couldn't focus on the words. Lying back in bed, I felt sylph-like. When rolling onto my side, I didn't need to carefully lever my body in a clumsy three-point turn. I could just roll over. Flat on my back now, I lay my palms on my tummy. No more handfuls of fat to knead. I was able to pinch up a little bit of flesh in my fingers, but that was it. I stroked my smooth stomach, and all the unpleasant aspects of the day were forgotten. It felt so amazingly good to be this thin.

I thought about my past. Why had I let myself gain weight after I lost it that first time in my twenties? Why had I allowed myself to miss out on this exquisite feeling for so many years? What food could possibly taste better than this feeling of taut, athletic sexiness? One thing was sure—I was never going back to fatness again.

I thought of Lou's words on my birthday—you will always be fat. Ha! Just wait until she sees me. Although she'll probably be used to Thin Me in this world, so I won't be able to tell her 'I told you so.' Damn!

I grabbed my phone to arrange a coffee catch up with her the next day. But for some reason Lou's phone number wasn't in my contacts. I searched for her name but couldn't see it. That's strange. I'd call mom tomorrow to get her number. Maybe she lost her phone or something.

I picked up my book and was finally able to get absorbed in the story. After a while, Stu stood in the doorway, and cleared his throat. His brow was wrinkled. 'Is it OK if I come in?' he asked.

That was weird; it was his bedroom too. 'Um, of course,' I said. He sat on the edge of the bed, looking awkward. 'What's up?' I asked him, slipping my bookmark into the page I was up to.

'Nothing. It's just, I've been thinking. Are you OK? It was really weird for you to be talking about dessert.'

I blushed. 'Yeah, I don't know. I feel fine. I just had a craving for it.'

'Well, that's what I was thinking,' said Stu. 'The last time you asked for dessert you were pregnant.' He winced, as if he'd just said something dangerous, and was bracing for my reaction.

I felt a pang. I didn't know what the story was with Skinny Me, but in my fat world Stu and I had tried unsuccessfully to get pregnant for five years after Vivi was born. No doctors could explain our lack of success. 'Secondary infertility,' they had said. 'Just don't overthink it and keep trying. And lose some weight.' So we'd kept trying, both for a baby and for weight loss. There'd been six miscarriages but no more babies. And no weight loss. In the end, we decided Vivi was more than enough to make our family complete. We let go the idea of more children and moved on. At least, I thought we'd moved on.

But was that a glimmer of hope in Stu's eyes now? Had my uncharacteristic request for ice cream dislodged a carefully placed emotional plug holding down a buried dream, allowing the idea of more babies to float to the surface? I felt terrible. It was hard to navigate tender feelings when you didn't have all the information. I took his hand and said, as gently as I could, 'I'm not pregnant. I just had a really strange day.'

Stu flinched when I touched him. He lifted my hand off his. 'Well I know *I* don't need to worry about you being pregnant, Evie. That would require sex.'

Wait, what? No sex? Coming into possession of this skinny body had created many uncertainties, but I'd had no doubt about my ability to attract and seduce men. Didn't today's kiss with Ryan prove it? Wasn't I now the walking embodiment of sexy? Objectively sexy. Exactly the kind of sexy you'd see in any movie, commercial, fashion magazine or music video. Of all the things I imagined learning about my skinny life today, marital celibacy was not on the list. I'd assumed that, in this body, all my inhibitions would be gone and my sex life with Stu would be amazing. Better than ever.

Since that kiss with Ryan I'd been all churned up, yearning to connect. I had been looking forward to Stu coming to bed. Maybe we'd had a fight that had led to a dry spell. But that could be easily fixed. A night of passion would be a re-set. Would bring us back to each other. He was a man, after all.

I tilted one shoulder toward him, and stretched one leg along the bed, trying to look seductive. 'Well, we could remedy that,' I said in my best husky voice.

'Evie, stop playing games.' He stood up. 'Well, as long as you're OK, I'm going to turn in.'

I shimmied back to my side of the bed to make room for him. But he didn't get into bed with me.

He turned and walked out of the door, and down the hall to the guest room.

CHAPTER 16

I sat frozen on the bed. What just happened?

I jumped up and went to the closet, not interested for once in my reflection. It was the clothes I was examining. Women's dresses, skirts and blouses. Folded sweaters, T-shirts, leggings.

No suits. No business shirts. No ties. No menswear at all.

Was it possible Stu and I had split up, but were still living under the same roof? And still sharing household duties like cooking? Pretending to be a family? I couldn't imagine ever agreeing to something like that. Whatever could have possessed me?

Vivi.

I crept quietly past the closed door of the guest room and on to Vivi's bedroom. Her door was open, and although the ceiling light was off, I could see from the soft glow of her nightlight that her eyes were open.

'Hey honey,' I whispered. 'Can I have a hug?'

I slid under the covers and spooned against her back. She was growing fast but still fit snugly within the contours of my body. I breathed in her smell, grateful it was the same in this other world. The potency of her infant scent was diluting with each year, but notes of it were still there. I greedily inhaled, storing up memories, knowing she wouldn't let me do this for much longer.

Vivi pulled my arm tight across her chest. I could tell she enjoyed the snuggle as much as I did.

After a few minutes I asked the question I'd been rehearsing in my head. After Stu's rebuff I needed information, but I didn't want to alarm or upset her.

'So, how are you feeling about dad sleeping in the spare room?'

Vivi shrugged, but stayed silent.

'I mean, we're still your mom and dad and we still live in the same house…'

'Yeah, yeah, yeah, I know the drill,' she said impatiently. 'Sometimes mommies and daddies stop being in love with each other but they'll always love their kids and we'll always be a family even if things look a bit different, blah, blah, blah.'

My heart was hammering. So Stu and I *were* separated. Were we divorced? I'd just assumed I wasn't wearing my rings in this world because they'd become too loose on my skinny fingers.

'That's right,' I said, trying to keep my voice neutral. 'I know you know that. But it's important we keep talking about our feelings. To keep processing how things have changed.'

'Geez mom,' Vivi said, 'I've had nearly a year to get used to the idea.'

I swallowed. Nearly a year?

'And, um, how do you feel about dad still living here when he and I aren't together anymore? Is that weird for you?'

Vivi rolled over and looked at me, suddenly wide awake. 'Do you want him to move out?'

'No, no, I'm not saying that,' I said.

She relaxed. 'Good. You told me you were going to keep sharing the house to save money, and so that I…'

She stopped.

'So that you what, honey?'

She was quiet for a long time. Her eyes watered. 'So that I wouldn't have to choose who to live with. Her voice was small and she suddenly looked much younger.

My heart broke. 'Oh baby, you don't have to choose. I'd never ask you to choose. Oh, I'm sorry. I shouldn't have brought this up when you were trying to go to sleep.'

I embraced her again. Vivi wiped her eyes and looked embarrassed about crying. She turned back to face the wall and didn't say anything more.

I lay next to her and stroked her hair until she fell asleep.

***

That night I dreamt I was at a cocktail party, wearing a little black dress and looking amazing. The room was noisy and crowded. Waiters were circulating with trays of delicious smelling hors d'oeuvres. I kept trying to make eye contact with one of the waiters, to get him to come my way. My mouth was watering. But he wouldn't look at me. He kept moving around the room. Whenever he came near me, a group of people materialized out of nowhere, moving between me and the food. I finally caught up with the waiter and took the last fried dim sim from his tray. Just as I was about to bite into it, an alarm sounded.

After a few groggy moments I realized it was the alarm clock next to my bed. I looked over and saw it was 5am. I groaned. Why so early? I turned off the buzzer and rolled back over. A minute later the alarm on my phone buzzed.

'No, it's too early,' I groaned to nobody.

I rubbed my eyes, propped up on one elbow and grabbed the phone. A calendar alert was displayed on the screen. I read the details. A recurring appointment: running club, five-thirty, Lakeside Park.

I flopped back on the pillow. No way, no how. I'd always hated exercising first thing in the morning, when I was sleepy to the bone. I needed a few hours upright, and a few coffees inside me, before I could even think about facing exercise.

Then I remembered Angelica's words: 'you're going to have to work to keep thin.'

Maybe this was what she'd meant. I'd have to stick to Skinny Evie's schedule, including her exercise routine, if I wanted to stay this way.

I took a deep breath and sat up. OK, I'll give it a try. And later today, I'll find this infamous schedule, if it's written down somewhere, and I'm going to rearrange things so that no exercise occurs before 10am. Ever.

***

There was a huddle of cars and bicycles near the café at the park, with some athletic-looking men and women hovering around, doing stretches, yawning and greeting each other with smiles and hugs. It was chilly, and their breath made little clouds as they talked.

They looked like a tight-knit group. Urgh, I thought. I definitely won't fit in. They look so professional and intimidating. And I don't know any of their names. How am I going to pull this off?

'Hi Evie,' called a couple in unison, who looked to be about my age.

'Hi,' I mumbled.

'How was the Ball?' the woman asked. 'I saw your photos on Facebook.'

'Oh, it was great, thanks!' I smiled. 'I, uh, I've just gotta get something from the car.' Facebook! Good idea! I gave silent thanks to the social media gods.

I lifted the trunk of my car and, hiding behind it, opened my phone and scrolled through. There it was: the Roosters

Running Club. Probably roosters because they got up so early. It was a private group.

I scrolled through the members and found thumbnails of the couple who'd greeted me. Bianca and Adam. I looked up. They were talking to someone else. I searched back through my phone. That looks like Sally. OK, you can do this. Sally, Adam, Bianca. It'll be fine. How much talking are they going to do anyway? Everyone will be busy running. Just make sure you go at a separate pace to avoid any conversation.

A whistle blasted. 'OK, folks, off we go!' yelled a man with a stopwatch. The group set off and I joined them, running slightly behind the pack.

I was wrong about the not-much-talking thing. This group chatted non-stop for the whole three miles of our run. There was friendly banter about training schedules, disagreements about politics, chit-chat about kids, talk of work. I stayed quiet and relied on the fact that, because I wasn't a morning person in my fat world, I was unlikely to be a morning person in this skinny world either. I hoped I had a reputation for being one of the quieter ones in the group.

About three-quarters of the way through the run we passed a woman who was out on her own, walking in the opposite direction. The woman was walking slowly, red-faced and sweaty, and very fat. The group split and jogged past either side of her. A few feet on, Sally turned back to look at the woman, and made eye contact with me in the process. She slowed her steps a bit so we were running together.

'Imagine being that size,' she said. 'I mean, good on her for getting out there and trying to improve herself. But I just don't understand how anyone can let themselves get that big in the first place.'

I said nothing. Sally continued. 'It doesn't just happen overnight, you know. You have to really *commit* to eating enough to get that fat.' She laughed.

I felt a hot anger and quickened my pace. Sally sped up too, matching me stride for stride. Was this how skinny people talked to each other, when they were safely out of earshot from the fatties?

'I dunno,' I said. 'It's not really our business what she looks like, is it?'

'It is when it offends our eyes!' laughed Sally. 'And our taxes have to pay for their hospital care when the inevitable heart attack strikes.'

'Hmm,' I said vaguely, uneasy about burning any bridges before I knew who was who in this new life of mine. I couldn't believe I'd be friends with a person like this, but decided to play it safe for now. 'I don't think it's that simple. Every body is different.'

'Baloney. It *is* that simple. Calories in, calories out. There's no excuse for people not knowing that in this day and age. It's pure laziness.'

I said nothing, realizing that what Sally said was almost exactly what I myself had said to Lou on my birthday. Why hadn't I felt the same empathy for myself then that I felt for the fat woman behind us now?

We were interrupted by the man carrying the stop-watch, who'd suddenly stopped, blown his whistle, and demanded everyone drop and do twenty push-ups. From the complaints of others, I found out his name was Derek.

I ran to the other side of the group away from Sally and, to my amazement, completed a quick set of twenty with barely any effort at all. With each movement to push my body up, I imagined my hands grinding Sally's face into the dirt.

CHAPTER 17

Walking into the office an hour later, I felt jittery, steeling myself to see Ryan. Then I remembered it was Wednesday, a day he typically worked from home. I sighed with relief.

After logging on, I checked my daily calendar. I had a lunch date scheduled with Renae. Seeing this gave me a rush of warm feeling. I always came away feeling better after spending time with her. It would be comforting to see her again, even though it had only been a short time since our dinner date. After everything that had happened, I felt like I hadn't seen my friend for years.

Next, I sent a meeting invitation to Ryan, for Friday afternoon. I needed to have it out with him. I wanted to find out what I could about how we got together. And then I needed to end it.

I hoped, by having the talk right before the weekend, we'd both have a bit of time to process things before work resumed the following week.

How could I be so dumb starting something with someone at work, I berated myself. And my boss, no less. Stupid, stupid, stupid.

***

At lunchtime I met Renae at our usual corner. She worked a few blocks from me, and we'd generally meet halfway, then decide where we felt like eating. But today Renae was holding a brown paper bag with a sandwich in it. After kissing hello, she asked me where my lunch was. 'Oh, I thought we'd go to a café,' I responded.

'Oh, OK,' she said, looking pleased and surprised. She held up her brown bag. 'I'll have this for afternoon tea then! Why the change of heart? You're usually so militant about bringing your own lunch.'

I made a mental note to start bringing my own lunch. I'd already guessed I didn't go to the gym at lunchtime on Wednesdays, because of the morning run, but this was another thing I'd have to check.

I shrugged. 'I've had a strange couple of days. I forgot to bring it.'

'Well, what about Akira?' asked Renae hopefully.

'Sure,' I said, and we set off in the direction of a popular Asian eatery. It felt weird that Renae hadn't commented on my figure. But I reminded myself that this Renae was used to seeing me thin.

On the walk to the restaurant, Renae caught me up on her dramas at work, and the latest fight she'd had with her mother. She was her usual bubbly self, and I was pleased this one thing from my old life seemed to be the same.

But I couldn't help thinking about how the tables had turned. Usually when we were together, I was self-conscious about being the fat friend, and would be jealous of whichever stylish outfit Renae was wearing next to my drab trousers and top. But today, I could feel passersby staring at me, in my figure-hugging wool crepe dress.

Renae was far from fat. She was a voluptuous hourglass woman, and I didn't know anyone with better style. She usually dressed like a fifties starlet, with her hair dyed pink or blue or purple, or all three, and rolled into flattering waves. She had immaculate makeup, with cat's-eye eyeliner expertly drawn above her beautiful eyes. She always looked amazing.

And for all Renae's diet talk (which she was refreshingly open about, compared to my secret hang-ups and furtive schemes), she didn't actually have anything to worry about. I envied her slender arms and legs, and wondered why she couldn't see what a great figure she had. It was interesting she hadn't said a word about how fat she felt, or what diet she was trying. This was out of character. She usually made some self-deprecating remark as soon as we met. Almost like she was subconsciously apologizing for looking better than me. Wanting to equalize us for the sake of our friendship.

Once we were settled at a table in the restaurant and had ordered our lunch (beef satay sticks for Renae, miso soup for me), I smiled across the table and said 'I'm so excited about the Gold Coast. Thanks again for asking me. I can't wait for us to be taking off.'

Renae stopped smiling and stared at me. Her face went pale.

'Er, what?'

'The Gold Coast,' I said. 'You invited me to go with you.'

'No I didn't,' said Renae, looking alarmed.

Uh-oh, I thought to myself. Tread carefully here. 'Oh, I'm sorry. I...'

'I'm going to the Gold Coast with Lucy.' Lucy was Renae's sister. 'I don't remember telling you about it.'

My mind raced. Should I tell her the truth about the mirror? She's one of my oldest friends. I can trust her. But how could she believe it when I could barely believe it myself, despite the evidence of my own eyes. She might think I'm crazy.

I decided to bluff.

'Well, I know we drank a bit at dinner the other night, but you must have had more than I realized. You definitely mentioned the Gold Coast, and you definitely asked me to come.' Was this a lie? Why did I feel so terrible saying it?

'I must be getting early onset dementia,' she said, looking worried, 'because I have no recollection of that at all.'

'Well how else would I know about it if you hadn't told me?' I asked, feeling rotten for gaslighting my friend.

Renae looked perplexed and shook her head. 'Wow, I need to be more careful when I drink. I've never blacked out like that before. At least, I don't think I have.'

I didn't know what to say, so I stared into my soup.

'I'll need to change the booking if you come,' said Renae. 'Unless I tell Lucy not to go. The booking's for a twin room.'

'Oh no! Don't do that!' I said. 'It's fine. I don't need to go. I didn't realize you were, um, confused when you asked me. Please forget it.'

Renae looked relieved. 'Well, if you're sure?'

'Absolutely,' I said. 'It's fine. Forget I even said anything.'

***

Later that day, I texted Stu. 'Sorry, just checking—are you getting Vivi from school today?'

'Nice try,' he wrote back. 'It's Wed. U bin rly spacey lately.' I vowed to sort out my schedule that night. I'd tell Stu I wanted to renegotiate it or something, as a ruse for working out what my usual routine was.

I drove to Vivi's school and found her waiting for me at the after-school care service. Once back behind the wheel, I waited for her to speak, but she stared out of the window in silence.

'Nice day?' I looked in the rear-view mirror. She scowled and shrugged.

'How's Lily?' Vivi and her best friend had a complex relationship. Sometimes they loved each other, sometimes they were at war. I could never keep up.

'Fine,' said Vivi. Uh-oh, I thought, it must be war.

'Did she say something mean to you?'

'No.' She didn't elaborate.

I decided to broach the subject later, maybe on the weekend, when Vivi had a bit of distance from her school day.

At home, she dropped her bag at the front door, as usual. 'Bag!' I yelled at her retreating back. She huffed and stomped back, picked it up and put it in the front entry closet. She closed the door perhaps slightly harder than she needed to, giving me a significant look when she turned back toward her room, as if to say 'satisfied?'

I smiled ruefully to myself. Yes, Vivi was just the same here. Wonderful, but also sometimes moody and melodramatic.

I walked through to the kitchen to start dinner. I planned to make lasagna. This was Stu's favorite, and I had a feeling I wouldn't have made it often in this skinny world.

Lasagna was my way of apologizing to him for the whole Ryan thing, even though Stu wouldn't know that. And perhaps I could entice him back. Even though we had been going through a rough patch in my fat life, I wasn't anywhere near ready for separation or divorce. Perhaps the situation in this thin world was redeemable.

It was the first time I'd cooked since I came through the mirror. In fact, I'd barely been in the kitchen this whole time. Since I'd arrived I'd only had coffee and fruit salad for breakfast, purchased at the café near work, as I'd been too busy each morning (either exercising or trying on clothes) to make something at home. Each lunchtime, I'd eaten out. And Stu had cooked dinner up until now.

I was looking forward to this hearty meal. I hadn't been hungry on my first day here. The shock of falling through the mirror had been all-consuming. But now that shock was starting to recede, and a hunger the likes of which I'd never known before had roared to life. It was an incessant, almost painful ache. I'd tried to make a game of it; I'd even given that constant gnawing feeling a name—Norman—because I figured we'd need to make friends with each other.

'Hello Norman,' I would inwardly sing. 'You back again already?'

I also dealt with the hunger by rubbing my hard, flat belly, to remind myself what I'd gained. I told myself the presence of Norman was a small price to pay for looking this good.

I'd stopped at the store on my way home with Vivi to buy some groceries, having no idea what was in the fridge. When I opened it now, I could see my hunch had been right. It was half empty. The pantry, while it had plenty of cooking staples, had no pasta and no snack foods.

The freezer, however, was stuffed chock-a-block. There were rows and rows of small plastic containers, with seemingly identical portions of food in them. I took one out and inspected it. Some broccoli florets, a few slices of white chicken breast and a small amount of brown rice.

I turned up my nose. It looked so bland. There were enough portions in there for two weeks. I guess this is my lunch, I thought to myself. No wonder Renae had looked excited about going to Akira today. She must feel bored by association, watching me eat this stuff.

I shut the freezer door and saw, amongst the familiar confetti of magnets pinning down photos and school certificates on the fridge, a new piece of paper. A-ha! That's what I've been looking for. I pulled it down to have a read.

It was titled 'Mom's schedule' and was a two-week planner, with our lives described with military precision.

Each weekday lunchtime, except Wednesday, involved a visit to the gym. Wednesday was my morning running group and lunch with Renae. Thursday evening was swimming with Vivi. ('Well,' I thought to myself, 'at least one thing in this schedule is the same as my normal life.') Friday night was grocery shopping. Saturday morning was laundry, including remaking all the beds. While the washing machine was running, on alternate Saturdays, I had 'meal prep' penciled in. That must be when I made up my weekday lunches. Saturday afternoon was 'go for run'. Sunday morning was house cleaning. Sunday afternoon was 'Pilates with Annika'. Annika? Skinny Annika? Well that's interesting, I thought, feeling guilty for the bitchy jokes I'd shared with Renae about my innocently healthy neighbor. Every Sunday night was 'work on Insta posts'.

Each day had my planned meals written against them. Stu's breakfasts and lunches were not accounted for. Given we'd separated, it made sense he made his own arrangements. Even if we weren't separated, he probably wasn't as rigid as I was. My breakfasts were listed as skim-milk coffee, with oatmeal and low-fat yoghurt. Lunch was one of the frozen chicken, broccoli and rice things. On the weekends I splashed out with an egg white omelet and veggies, or a salad and hummus wrap. Dinners each night were all variations on a theme—a salad and a protein in some combination. No dessert. Ever.

God that sounds boring, I thought. How can I live like this? Where is the spontaneity? Where is the joy?

I picked up my phone and searched my contacts for 'Annika'. Yes, there she was. I looked at our previous text messages. They were all logistical—arrangements for getting to Pilates and the like. We must do most of our talking face to face. But several weeks back, there'd been a text from her accompanied by exclamation marks: 'Got a promotion!' And I'd responded with 'You deserve it, Einstein' and love heart emojis. We seemed to be close friends.

I felt ashamed, again, that I hadn't made an effort to get to know her before. An interesting person living right next door, and I'd been too shy to say hello, all because of how intimidatingly fabulous she looked.

I made a mug of warm chocolate milk for Vivi before I started cooking. It was her favorite afternoon snack. I called her to come and get it, but there was no response, so I took it to her room. The door was slightly open, and I walked in without knocking.

Vivi was lying on her bed with headphones on, watching a YouTube video on her iPad. She hadn't heard me come in. I looked down at what she was watching. It was a frail-looking teenage girl, sitting on her bed talking about something. But before I could make out the title, Vivi noticed me standing there. She whipped around and put the iPad face down on her pillow. 'Haven't you heard of knocking?' she asked, crossly.

I ignored her tone. 'I made you a hot chocolate,' I said, holding the glass out.

'See? You NEVER listen to me. I TOLD you months ago that I don't want that anymore. I'm not a baby!'

'Hey, hey, hey,' I scolded. 'That's no way for you to talk to me, especially when I've just done something nice for you.'

Vivi stared at me for a second, then seemed to relent. 'Sorry,' she mumbled. She looked at the drink. 'I'm not in the mood for it.'

'OK,' I said. 'I'll have it.'

'Mom! Are you crazy? That's like 400 calories or something.'

'Since when do you know about calories?' I asked, shocked.

'Um, since forever? Every meal we have is 400 calories.'

I held my breath. What had I done here? A kid her age shouldn't be worrying about calories. This was the brief window of time in her life when her body was young and strong and healthy and beautiful. She should be taking it completely for granted. There was plenty of time—the rest of her life—to worry about food and healthy choices and how she looked.

She's obviously picked this up from me. From my rigid approach to food and exercise. As a fat mom I used to worry about setting a bad example for Vivi, giving her too much unhealthy food and hardly ever exercising with her. Maybe on this side of the mirror I'd gone too far in the opposite direction.

I walked back to the kitchen with the chocolate milk and held the mug to my lips. But I stopped before I drank any of it, catching my reflection in the glass of the oven door. I looked at the milk again, then tipped it down the sink.

CHAPTER 18

While the lasagna was cooking, I went to my bedroom and looked at myself in the mirror, turning from side to side and sucking in my tummy. I undoubtedly looked great. I'd started forgetting sometimes, when I was focusing on work, or talking to Vivi, that I was so much smaller now. But then I'd remember and feel a thrill of excitement at the novelty of my new normal. I'd discretely admire myself and hope no-one noticed.

Now, in the privacy of my own room, I could admire myself with abandon. On my left, peeking out among the many dresses, I spied my red silk tea dress. It was made from chiffon and embellished with sequins. It was one of my favorite things, but I'd never worn it. I'd bought it 12 years ago, in that magical season when I was thin. It was a small-fitting size four, a kaleidoscope of red and other colors swirling in a delicate floral pattern. Perfect to wear to a wedding.

It had been half-price when I'd bought it, and it had only just fit me when I tried it on. The fact that it fit had been one of the highlights of my weight loss journey back then. But it was a summer dress that'd I'd found on the discount rack in winter. It was probably left over as a sale item because so few people could squeeze into it. That was always the case—the nicest items on the sale rack were usually impossibly small sizes. All the sale items in larger sizes were the ugly things no one else wanted.

By the time summer had rolled around again, in those slimmer days, with warmer weather bringing opportunities to wear the dress, I'd met Stu and started nesting with him. And this beautiful frock no longer fit. So I'd never actually worn it. But now. Maybe now.

I quickly stripped off my work clothes and pulled the chiffon over my head. It settled delicately on my hips. I zipped it up. It fit me. In fact, it was maybe even a little loose.

Out of nowhere, my eyes filled with tears. This is why, I thought. This is why the stupid schedule and the stupid running club. This is why the boring frozen lunches and the repetitive weekday gym visits. It's so shallow, I know, but this feels so unbelievably good.

It was like a drug I wasn't sure I could give up now. But a shadow crested my happiness. Polluting Vivi's mind with diet culture was a steep price to pay for my own vanity. It had become clear to me that this body was only achievable due to a complete commitment, an unyielding, rigid adherence to rules and timetables.

Despite my misgivings, I justified the lifestyle to myself. There were undoubted benefits to having a strict routine.

It would lessen my emotional labor by reducing the number of decisions I needed to make each day. It was simpler to eat and exercise to a plan. And the number of temptation points in my day would be significantly reduced, having everything pre-prepared like that.

Maybe it wasn't as bad an approach to living as my initial reaction had thought. Maybe the warning voice in my head was just Fat Evie missing chocolate and trying to tempt Skinny Evie back to the fat side.

I was filled with a new resolve to protect this amazing body. Surely I could teach Vivi some healthy balance without jeopardizing my own wellness. Surely I was modelling good habits now. Better Vivi have a fit mom than a fat mom.

I changed into some leggings and a sweater and pulled open my laptop. I found a folder where my draft Instagram posts were saved. I knew I wasn't 'scheduled' to work on this until Sunday afternoon, but what the hell. Breaking this rule wouldn't hurt.

I started pouring my heart out about my experiences over the past few days. I can never post this, I thought, as I wrote about magic mirrors and fairy godmothers. People will think I'm loony.

But as I read back what I'd written, I was able to massage it into something more believable. I wrote about how I'd been thinking lately about that time, long ago, when I'd been fat, and what a negative mindset I'd had back then. But how, just now, I'd been able to pour a mug of chocolate milk down the drain with no regret at all. And how it's so true that it just takes the right attitude to not over-eat, and that exercise actually feels pretty good.

By the time I'd finished writing the post, I felt positively smug. This is easy. Maybe Sally at the running club was right after all. It is simple math.

I ignored the voice in my head reminding me that my smugness was not earned.

***

The timer on the oven buzzed. The lasagna was ready. I paired the heavy pasta dish with some steamed green beans, and glasses of red wine for Stu and me.

Cheese oozed voluptuously from the edges of each slice as I lifted the lasagna from the baking pan to the three dishes I'd lined up on the kitchen counter. But now, after trying on the chiffon dress, the prospect of this meal no longer delighted me. Instead I felt anxious about eating it. Foregoing food like this was the reason the chiffon dress fit.

I cut through the slice of lasagna on my plate and returned one of the halves to the baking dish. Stu could have the leftovers for lunch. The serving on my plate was now about one-third the size of my usual helping on the other side of the mirror.

I called Stu and Vivi to the table. They both stared at their meals as they sat down. Stu smiled at me disbelievingly. 'Is that lasagna?' he asked. 'You haven't cooked this in years!'

'Where's our salad?' Vivi asked.

'We had that yesterday.'

'We have salad every day,' said Vivi, picking up her fork. She inspected the meal suspiciously, lifting layers of pasta with her knife to peer at what lay underneath.

Why do kids do that, I wondered. Ask them to find a lost shoe and they prove themselves completely incompetent at discovering anything. But serve them unfamiliar food and they're suddenly the world's greatest detective, carefully dissecting each morsel to find hidden vegetables.

But Vivi wasn't looking for hidden veggies—this version of Vivi had been conditioned from birth to eat veggies. She was cautiously exploring this strange new cheesy meal because it was possible, I realized, she'd never eaten it before.

'I just thought it would be nice to try something different. Have a taste,' I encouraged. Stu was heartily digging in. He looked up with grease running down his chin.

'It's really good,' he said. 'Your mom used to make this for me a lot,' he told Vivi. He smiled at me, seemingly remembering the good old days.

Vivi took a cautious bite but said nothing. After three mouthfuls, she said she'd had enough. 'It looks fattening.'

'You shouldn't worry if something is fattening,' I said, moving the food around my plate with my fork, but not eating either. 'It's our job as parents to decide what food to give you. But you can choose how much of it you eat.'

'So I've chosen. Can I go now?' she asked, slightly impatient.

'Yes honey,' I sighed.

'Good on you for trying something new,' Stu called after her, as she left the table. He leaned over and grabbed Vivi's plate, scraping her leftovers onto his dish.

I forced myself to eat all of my dinner. It tasted good— just the way I expected it would. But I didn't enjoy it. The guilt of what my diet lifestyle was doing to Vivi made me feel sick.

That dinner stagnated in my belly, heavy, rich and oily.

***

Later, watching TV, I was enveloped by nausea. I ran to the powder room and threw up in the toilet. Stu heard me and came over to the open door. I turned to look at him, wiping my mouth with toilet paper. I was sweaty, and my heart was racing. He looked angry.

'You're not doing that again are you?'

'What do you mean?' I asked defensively. It felt like he was blaming me for being sick.

'You know what I mean. The vomiting.'

I covered my face with my hands, not sure what to think. Maybe this was another way I'd been keeping the pounds off. But I hadn't seen 'purging' on the schedule, taped to the fridge.

'We talked about you not doing that anymore. For Vivi's sake, if not your own.' He didn't say it in a caring way. He sounded exasperated, as if this had been a sore spot, a cause of arguments in the past.

'I promise, that wasn't deliberate,' I said, looking at the toilet. 'Dinner was just a bit richer than I'm used to. It just didn't agree with me.'

Stu shook his head and walked away.

CHAPTER 19

The next morning, Thursday, I was working from home at my dining room table (pretending to need 'focus time,' but actually trying to avoid Ryan) when my phone rang. It was Annika.

After discovering yesterday that we were friends, I'd found her Facebook page and tried to work out who she was. It seemed she'd trained as a clinical psychologist, but was about to start working for a tech start-up, doing something complicated involving computers and behavioral economics.

I picked up the phone tentatively. 'Hello?'

'Hi Evie, it's Annika.'

'Hey, how are you?'

'I'm doing great. A bit nervous about the promotion, but excited.'

'You'll be amazing. When do you start?' I was grateful our past text messages enabled me to participate credibly in the conversation.

'So that's why I'm calling,' said Annika. 'First day is in two weeks, and before then I want to buy a power suit. I'll be going to some pretty high-level meetings with Very Important People. I need your help choosing what to wear. I thought maybe we could go shopping together.' She must have known I can't resist a good frock shop.

'I'd love to. When were you thinking?'

'Maybe after work this evening? Shops are open late tonight.'

'OK,' I said, surprisingly relieved this wouldn't interfere with my gym workout at lunchtime. *Who am I?* I marveled for the millionth time.

'I'll meet you in the driveway at six?' suggested Annika.

'Sounds like a plan.'

***

The department store opened before us like a shining, treasure-filled cavern. Piped music, crystal light fixtures, warm air and clinking bottles of French perfume seduced us into its high-end embrace.

We walked past the make-up counters to an escalator, riding to the top floor. This was home to ladies designer fashion.

Racks of velvet, silk and linen in every color stretched as far as we could see. Skinny mannequins were artfully posed in beautifully stitched, carefully constructed gowns, smiling serenely, unpinched by the stilettos in which their plastic feet swam.

When I was fat, I would buy most of my clothes online. But from time to time I'd wander into a place like this, like a tourist, weaving between the racks, discreetly feeling the fabrics between my fingers. Sneak a peak at the prices.

If I saw something I thought I might be able to wear, I'd thrust my hand straight through to the back of the rack, where the largest sizes were always hung. Only sizes two or four, or an XS or S, would be allowed to face the front.

On pushing aside the smaller sizes, I usually found a 12 lurking at the back, occasionally a 14, and sometimes an XL. But I knew from long experience that XL in these designer brands tended to be not very extra, nor very large.

Garments sized in the 20s would generally be found one floor below, in the plus-sized fashion department, with brand names euphemistically connoting maturity and volume. Words like 'Curve', 'Shape', 'Full' or—worst of all—'Real', would swing on the tags attached to the garments, leaving no doubt about the intended demographic. I grumbled to myself, remembering how annoyed I used to be at being relegated to that department. 'Fat', 'Ordinary' and 'Crone' would have been more honest. But perhaps less lucrative. I wondered for the millionth time why 'normal'-sized brands didn't just came in larger sizes.

I sometimes wandered through the ladies' designer fashion floor in the early days of a diet, to shore up my stores of mental resolve. To flex that willpower muscle. Look at what you could be wearing in only six months, if you just put in the hard work now, I'd try to motivate myself. You are the only person preventing yourself from wearing this loveliness.

Sometimes, if I'd already lost, say, 10 pounds, and was certain I was now on an unstoppable trajectory to skinniness, I would buy a dress that was too small for me as a goal to work toward. No-one ever disturbed me as I wandered, fat and invisible, amongst the racks.

Now, as I strolled into the department with Annika, we were approached several times by elegant sales clerks, offering their help.

'Yes please,' said Annika comfortably. She belonged here. These were her people. This was her place. 'I'm looking for some suits for work. Nothing too fussy.'

One of the women led us to the business wear section, and hovered around, carrying Annika's selections to a commodious fitting room for her to try on. I'd never known such attentive service at the Real Woman counter.

It seemed, too, that the smaller you were, the larger your fitting room was. Up here there was a chaise where I could recline and give Annika my opinions on the various outfits she tried.

Eventually she narrowed her choices down to a navy sheath dress with matching jacket, and a gray coordinating jacket and trousers. She twirled before me in both, asking which was my favorite.

'They look equally good. You should get them both,' I said.

Annika laughed. 'Some help you are!' She held the jackets up in front of her again before the three-way mirror, switching each over her chest in turn. She sighed, with a smile. 'Oh dear. I can't decide either.'

After Annika had paid for both suits, she suggested we get a drink before heading home.

'Yes, that would be great,' I said, pretending to be relaxed but feeling slightly worried. Although we'd spent the last hour together, we hadn't talked about much at all, apart from clothes. The prospect of sitting face to face made me nervous. Would it be obvious to Annika that I was a total stranger?

In the tea shop Annika ordered a spiced apple blend. I liked the sound of that and ordered the same. Our taste in clothes had proved to be similar, and now our taste in drinks was too. Maybe we were well suited as friends. I regretted, again, my previous dismissal of Annika, out of envy, when I'd seen her jogging on the hill. Who else, I wondered, have I missed out on getting to know because of my stupid prejudices and insecurities?

Annika talked about a TV show she and I both enjoyed, and after we laughed together over the latest plot twist, she stirred her tea, and looked at me with a more serious face.

'So, I have to confess, I had an ulterior motive for asking you to come shopping,' she said.

My heart started pounding.

'Oh really?' My voice squeaked in a slightly higher register.

'Stu texted me last night. He said you were vomiting again. He's worried you're regressing. He's worried about Vivi.'

'Oh!' I laughed, relieved. 'Is that all?'

Annika didn't say anything but kept looking at me seriously. We must be really close, I thought, if I've talked to her about disordered eating. If *Stu* has talked to her about *my* disordered eating.

'No really, I'm fine. It's silly, really. For some reason I had a craving for lasagna. I just ate too much of it and it made me queasy. I didn't make myself vomit on purpose.'

'You weren't purging then?' asked Annika.

'No.'

'Because I know you have a bit of stress going on in your life at the moment.'

'What do you mean?'

Annika looked from side to side then leaned forward. 'I mean Ryan,' she whispered. 'Have you made a decision about that yet?'

Oh wow, I thought. We really are close friends if I've told her about the affair with Ryan. I hoped Annika hadn't discussed *that* with Stu.

'Yes, that is definitely finished,' I responded firmly. 'In fact, I've set up a meeting with him tomorrow, to make it clear it's over. It's a completely inappropriate situation.'

Annika sat back, looking relieved, and smiled. 'At last! You don't know how long I've been waiting to hear you say that! It's so important for you to move on. The situation with Stu, and then Ryan. You know what I think about you having time alone to work out what you need.'

No, I don't have any idea, I thought. But it felt good to know I could talk openly with Annika about the affair. 'Well, it's just wrong,' I said. 'I know I'm separated from Stu, but only just. Taking up with someone new so quickly will really hurt Vivi. Plus he's my *boss*. What was I thinking?'

'But I'm so surprised Evie,' said Annika. 'For months you've been telling me you're in love with Ryan. That you're going to tell Stu you want to take the separation to the next stage and ask him to move out. Why the change of heart all of a sudden?'

'In love?'

'Well, you told me you ended it with Stu because of how distant and inattentive he is. And you never stop talking about Ryan. How funny he is, how charming, how intelligent. How he really sees you—the real you.'

'Well, Ryan and I have been friends for a long time. We've worked together for 15 years. That's a lot of history.'

'And when his wife died, you were really there for him.'

I spat out my tea.

'What? Rebekah died?!' I looked at Annika with alarm.

'That's what you told me,' she said, suddenly looking worried again. 'Didn't she?'

'Oh poor Ryan,' I looked into my cup. Suddenly my plan to end it with him tomorrow, without any beating around the bush, seemed less straightforward. If he's lost his wife, I'll need to tread more carefully. And if he thinks I really love him, will I be breaking his heart? Maybe he loves me too.

But then, what about Stu? Hadn't I decided to try to mend things with him? Yes, he irritates me, and doesn't seem capable of communicating as much as I need him to, but it's not so bad that I want to divorce him, is it?

I was so confused, when an hour ago things had been clear cut. I now wondered if I should string Ryan along a bit longer, until I'd worked out what had been going on.

Annika was still looking at me with concern. I decided to wing it for now.

'Of course his wife died. And Stu and I are still separated. But I've been seeing Stu with new eyes lately, and I want to talk to him about trying again. For Vivi's sake I want us to have one more go at being a family. I'm ending it with Ryan tomorrow. And I'm not bulimic. My life is better than ever.'

***

It was approaching nine o'clock when I arrived home from the mall. As I searched for my house key, my phone rang. I fished around in my bag, and triumphantly pulled the phone out just in time to answer the call from an unidentified number. Breathless with this small victory, I cheerfully chirped 'Hello'!

'It's Louise,' said a distant voice.

'Lou! At last! I've been trying to reach you, but the weirdest thing's happened with my phone. For some reason I'd lost your number.'

There was silence on the other end.

'Hello? Are you there? Lou?'

After another moment, the voice on the other end spoke again. 'I thought I had made myself clear. You are never to contact me. Ever.'

CHAPTER 20

The line went dead.

'Lou?' I called into the empty phone. 'Wait!'

I half laughed as I put my phone away and retrieved my key. This was so ridiculously out of character, I must have misunderstood something. Lou was the steadiest, most sensible person I knew. Not at all into drama. I was sure it must be a small tiff, if anything. I'd call her tomorrow to sort it out.

Stu and Vivi had finished eating dinner while I was shopping, and Stu had kept my serve covered in foil on the kitchen counter, waiting for me to get home.

Let me guess, I thought, remembering the timetable I'd looked at earlier: salad and fish. I lifted one edge of the foil and looked. Yep, salad and fish. I sighed. I guess it keeps things simple.

I carried my dish to the living room and sat next to Stu on the couch. He had a sports channel playing on the TV but was also looking at his phone.

'Thanks for dinner,' I said, holding up my plate.

He grunted and didn't look up from his phone. 'No worries.'

I tried to eat slowly, but the small portion was gone in a few bites. As usual I was very hungry. Norman had been banging the sides of my belly since an hour after lunch.

My hunger was augmented by that unsettling call from Lou just now. She had been so formal, referring to herself as Louise, like that. And she sounded like she really meant it when she said not to call.

'So, I just had a call from Lou,' I said, as Stu squinted at something that required him to rotate his phone horizontally.

'Who?' he asked absentmindedly.

'Lou, my sister.'

He looked up from his phone and stared at me. 'Your sister? Are your parents OK?'

'Why wouldn't they be?'

'Well, why else would she call you?'

'Because she's my sister?'

'Some sister,' he said, shaking his head. He paused and looked at me again. 'Are you sure everything's OK, Evie? You've been acting really strange the last few days. It's like, well, I don't know. Just…'

'What do you mean by "some sister"?'

'OK, I guess that's a bit unfair,' he said. I relaxed slightly. 'I mean, the hate is probably shared equally by both of you.'

'What? I could never hate Lou!'

'OK, now you're seriously freaking me out,' said Stu, putting down his phone and looking concerned. 'Evie, we got together 12 years ago and I've only met Louise a handful of times. You didn't invite her to our wedding, remember? She's never even been to this house.'

My mind was reeling. Yet another difference between this skinny life and my old fat one. But this one was alarming. Potentially a game-changer.

Angelica had said all the major things in my life were the same. Only small day-to-day decisions were different on this side of the mirror. In what universe was cutting your own sister out of your life a small decision?

This was huge. My Lou. My big sister. My rock. My protector. My confidante. My truth teller. I felt sick.

***

I stood before the mirror in my closet after cleaning my teeth. I'd just gone through some old Instagram posts and found one focusing on 'toxic relationships'. The piece didn't name Lou, or talk specifically about our falling out, but it did talk about enablers and saboteurs and taking control and setting boundaries, and the lie that blood was thicker than water, and so on.

I didn't like my tone of voice in the post. It was so hard, unyielding, unforgiving. It didn't sound like the person I thought I was.

In the mirror my reflection looked lovely in brushed cotton pajamas with a delicate lace trim. My body was still perfect, but my face was frowning.

So many things to process. The affair with Ryan, the separation with Stu, lying to Renae, Vivi's unhealthy focus on calories, my apparent bulimia, and now this fight with Lou.

The only plus I could think of (apart from my weight loss) was that I'd found a new friend in Annika. But even that was stressful as I tried to carefully navigate the many unknown aspects of our shared past.

I looked at the outfit I'd pulled together for the office tomorrow. For my meeting with Ryan. To dump him. I'd planned to wear my old uniform of black trousers and the dowdiest top I could find.

I was dreading our meeting. I'd always hated confrontation in the best of circumstances. And having only some of the relevant information needed for the conversation put me at a distinct disadvantage.

My tummy fluttered with nerves and then rumbled with hunger. Maybe a glass of wine, or a piece of buttered toast would help take my mind off things.

'Mom,' said a small voice behind me. I turned around and Vivi was standing in the doorway to the closet. She was holding her iPad. 'Dad told me to come and say goodnight,' she said.

'Oh,' I smiled. 'Do you want me to read to you?'

She scowled. 'You stopped reading to me ages ago. I'm too old for that.'

'What? I still like being read to, and I'm thirty-nine.' I looked back at the mirror, at the reflection of Vivi standing in the doorway behind me. But something was different. The Vivi in the mirror was holding a book. I whipped around—no, it's an iPad. I looked back to the mirror. It was definitely a book.

As we made eye contact, Vivi-in-the-mirror raised her arms, as if asking for a hug. I touched my hand to her reflection. I could swear I felt a pulse of something flow through to my arm.

Turning around again, the Vivi in my skinny world was still holding her iPad tightly across her chest. Definitely not gesturing for a hug.

'Well, you're a bit of a weirdo then,' she said. She turned and walked off, calling 'Night!' in a dismissive voice over her shoulder.

I looked back into the mirror. Vivi-in-the-mirror had left too.

My chest cramped with guilt. In all the time I'd been on this side of the mirror, I hadn't once remembered story time. Every night before bed, it had been a ritual for me and Vivi to snuggle under the covers for a story. It was our special time. The story always launched us into talking about other things. It kept us connected.

How could I have forgotten that? How did I let that habit stop? I'd wanted to keep that tradition alive for as long as possible. But I'd been so distracted by everything in this exciting thin world, I'd forgotten about it.

An inconceivable thought nudged into my head. What if I go back?

Having let a chink of the thought in, my mind was suddenly full of compelling reasons to leave this skinny world.

My marriage would be restored. It would solve the Ryan and Lou problems, it would mean Vivi was back to her normal Nutella-loving, carefree kid self. There would be no more stupid 5am running club.

Yes, I'd be fat again, but I was never actually *that* fat, was I? I was only a little bit fat. I wasn't disabled by it. Just dumpy, really. And I could easily lose a few pounds if I put my mind to it, especially now that I knew all the tricks. I could just follow Skinny Evie's routine, and surely Skinny Evie's body would follow, eventually. I'd just have to be patient.

And this experience had been great motivation for knowing how amazing I could look if I really worked at it. I could have the best of both worlds if I really tried. Everyone back to normal. Everything back to normal. Me back to normal.

Without waiting to change my mind, I pressed both hands on the glass and whispered 'Mirror, mirror, let me out. I don't care if I am stout.'

There was that pulling sensation again. This time I didn't resist. I pushed through the mirror and into the world beyond.

CHAPTER 21

I sat up on the carpet. I was back. I lifted one arm and stared at it. Shook it. Watched its pendulous swing. Yep, definitely fat again.

My body felt heavier than I remembered. Like the feeling you get climbing out of a swimming pool. The buoyancy of my small frame had well and truly evaporated. And, judging from the racks in my closet, so too had a fair portion of my skinny clothes. Back again were the safe black trousers and the baggy tops in distracting colors and prints. Back again were the flat shoes.

And back again were Stu's clothes, hanging in the corner. No more separation.

I rolled myself onto all fours, then slowly raised myself to standing, clutching the closet joinery for balance.

I walked down the hall to the living room. Stu was on the couch, with the same sports channel on, still scrolling through his phone. But now there was a wheel of camembert, a box of crackers and two glasses of red wine on the coffee table in front of him.

I leant over to pick up a cracker and a wedge of cheese. The taste was exquisite. A wave of pleasure shot through my mouth. I moaned, 'Oh, this is good!'

Stu leaned over to the table. He didn't comment on my size. He merely took a slice of cheese and poked it with his finger. 'Is it room temperature yet?'

All was as before. Our old routines. Our old habits. Our old bodies. I smiled with relief. Maybe I just imagined the past few days. Some strange dream or hallucination.

After a few crackers I stood up and brushed the crumbs from my lap. 'I'm just going to read Vivi a story,' I said, walking out of the room. 'Save me some more of that.'

***

Dressing for work the next morning, I sighed at my reflection. It was hopeless. No matter how many scarves I layered around my face and shoulders, no matter how many large earrings or brightly colored spectacles I accessorized with, I still looked fat. All the accessories did was make me look older.

I pulled off the scarf I'd been trying to hide behind and stuffed it in a drawer. Matronly. That's how you look, and that's what you are.

Oh, hello negative self-talk. It's been a while. Not sure I missed you, actually. Are you finished? No, didn't think so.

The memory of my slender self seemed more far-fetched than ever. The thought that any man, even my husband, could find me attractive, was ludicrous. I am a middle-aged mom. And I look it.

Hang on, my inner voice rallied. You're also a smart, kind and ethical person. Well, maybe not as ethical as you'd previously believed. But still, the point is, you are so much more than how you look. Get a grip, Evie, get a grip. And get to work.

After this pep talk, I hustled Vivi into the car for the school run, determined to resume my normal life. The mirror thing had been a fun diversion. Thought provoking and eye opening. But it hadn't been real. This was real life. And my life was OK. I was OK.

As soon as I sat down at my desk, I picked up my phone. I'd been impatient to make this call, and intended to do it first thing, before the day got away from me.

After three rings a breezy 'Hello?'

I tentatively responded, 'Hello, Lou.'

'Howdy stranger!' said Lou warmly. 'I've been trying to get in touch with you for days. You just weren't picking up!'

'Oh really? Sorry! Busy, busy!' I fibbed.

'So how are things?'

'Oh, you know, just the same. Nothing to report really. Just wanted to hear your voice.'

'That's nice. Well, I can't really talk, sorry. Noah is home sick today. Mario's away for work, so it's just me home with the boys this week. And we're currently in the bathroom, hovering over the toilet. Food poisoning. Noah didn't eat his chicken sandwich on Wednesday. Decided to leave it in his school bag instead of throwing it away. Then thought it would be a genius thing to eat on Thursday.'

I laughed, 'Oh dear! Well, I'd better let you go then!'

'Let's do dinner soon! I need a night off from this literal shitshow.'

'Ok, I'll text you. Bye!'

'Bye!'

I held the phone to my heart. Lou was back.

***

After a busy morning, where everyone at the office was occupied and thankfully didn't need to bother me about anything, I was able to plough through my work. Suddenly, at noon on the dot, my tummy grumbled.

I wandered across to the Daily Grind. I saw and smelled the glistening chicken rotisserie waiting to be sliced into a delicious kebab. My mouth watered. 'The usual then?' smiled Joe.

I nodded and cast my eyes down to my bag to look for my purse. As I did, the array of sushi, salad and sandwiches, neatly rowed in the glass cabinet beneath me, broke across my field of vision. *Nothing changes if nothing changes*, I thought. A cheesy weight loss mantra I'd seen meme-ified many times online. But possibly true?

'Actually Joe, I think I'll have the sushi today.'

'This?' he pointed at the one he thought I'd chosen. 'OK,' he shrugged. 'Keeping me on my toes, eh?' He laughed and placed the carton of sushi on the counter.

'Something like that. Thanks.' I paid and walked away, thinking about Joe's surprised reaction to my different choice. People say they want excitement. But really, humans prefer routine. We want predictability. In ourselves and in other people.

Maybe that was why my weight loss efforts had failed to date. I was just too comfortable in my routine. The habits that calmed me were inconsistent with thinness.

Maybe when people did manage to lose weight—the usual way, not the deluded magic mirror way—maybe they were so often unsuccessful at keeping it off because it disrupted other peoples' expectations of who they were and what they should be. They had dared to break out of the box everyone knew. The box labeled fat.

Maybe that's why I came back from Skinny Evie's world. It was too much change, too soon. I couldn't process it.

My lunchtime brooding on the psychology of weight loss reminded me of Annika. I wanted to talk to her about it. Get her take on my mindset. Maybe she could help me understand myself better.

I decided to try to befriend her on this side of the mirror. Manufacture some kind of natural, not at all creepy or stalkery accidental meeting, after which we could become best buddies.

Or else I could just knock on her door and say hello.

***

146

As usual, I was planning to eat 'al desko'. No inconvenient lunchtime gym visits in this world.

Jeremy, our junior solicitor, had tried to get me moving at lunch. He'd invited me to go on lunchtime walks with him, but I always professed busyness.

The truth was I couldn't be bothered lugging active wear and sneakers with me to the office. Too complicated. Too much planning required. More emotional labor, on top of everything else I had to think about. Plus it would either be too hot or too cold on the walk. I didn't want to work up a sweat and melt my makeup. And I hated the flies.

I was very skilled at finding excuses. The simple truth was I preferred to be comfortable, and exercise made me uncomfortable.

But now, after several hours back in my fat body, I laughed inwardly at the irony. Comfortable was not the right word to describe how I felt in this fat, unfit frame.

I cracked open the clear plastic cover on the carton of sushi, pulled apart the disposable chopsticks, and drizzled some soy sauce onto the first piece. On the end of the chopstick, I examined the morsel in the same way Vivi had interrogated her lasagna. I scrunched up my nose and took a bite.

Ugh. The sushi was not great. I'd never been a fan of nori, the strong-tasting seaweed that encased the rice. And this experiment confirmed I was still not a fan.

How many years of lying to myself in the skinny world about this taste did it take before sushi became palatable,

I wondered. Or did I just suffer through eating it until I got used to it, because it was an easy healthy option? I thought about the delicious chicken kebab I hadn't bought.

As I held the second piece of sushi up to my mouth unenthusiastically, Ryan stuck his head around my office door. 'Hello!' he chirped jovially. I blushed and dropped the sushi roll onto my lap.

'Oh, um, hi Ryan!' It was the first time I'd seen him since the kiss. I grabbed a serviette and wiped up the mess of soy sauce and rice from my trousers. Lucky they were black.

Ryan tapped his wristwatch at me. 'We still on for 2pm?'

'Er, sorry, can you remind me...'

'You sent me a calendar invite for a meeting at 2pm. I said I'd get back to you. Well, my afternoon's clear, so it's a date!' he winked and walked away.

My throat seized up and my hands started shaking. Had the affair begun in this world too since I was away? I was only gone a few days. Surely not.

I clumsily scrambled for my mouse and opened my calendar to check the meeting notes.

Oh, thank God. I instantly relaxed. The meeting was just to follow up on some building quotes I'd obtained to have the bathrooms in the office renovated. I remembered Dan the builder was one of the tenderers for this job. So my meeting with Ryan today would be perfectly benign and safe. I needn't worry. And if Dan got the job, maybe that meant I'd run into Angelica too. Good. I had a few questions.

The rest of the work day passed uneventfully. Ryan was his normal friendly self. He looked at me with kindness and professionalism. And that was all. I felt relieved.

And a tiny bit disappointed.

***

The twilight sky hummed neon orange as I pulled into my driveway. I lifted out a bag of groceries I'd bought on the way home, including a now empty pack of potato chips—chicken flavored—that I'd devoured in the car while driving, to fill the space the sushi had not.

I squashed the empty packet into the bottom of my handbag—I'd hide that evidence later—then looked across the park at the magnificent sunset.

It was one of those breathtaking panoramas that happen a few times a year. The kind that causes people to stop what they're doing and just stare. There was something comforting in the largeness of it, the peacefulness of it, and the certainty that, while such beauty was short-lived, it would undoubtedly come back again one day.

For a few glorious moments, the light entered and expanded every pore of my body. Deeply inhaling the sweet smell of the damp lawn around me, my hunger took a back seat to my other senses for once.

The temperature was perfect—not hot, not cold. And the sound of the neighborhood was at this moment perfectly still. No cars coming down the street, no planes flying overhead.

Then footsteps and heavy breathing broke in on the stillness. I opened my eyes and saw Annika striding up the hill in the park opposite our houses, doing her evening laps.

Why do I feel shy to meet her, I wondered? I know she's a nice person. I've spent several hours with her. She's kind. And she's a psychologist who hates labeling people or their 'problem' behavior. She finds peoples' quirks interesting. Unlike me, judging her for being skinny, she won't care two hoots if I'm fat. In fact, she probably won't even notice.

But it felt awkward to just knock on her door and welcome her to the neighborhood when she'd been living here more than a year. I thought about crossing the road and saying 'hello, it's nice to see you again,' like a normal person. But then I'd be interrupting her exercise. If there's one thing I remembered from that fever dream of skinny, it's how annoying it was to be interrupted in the cardio zone.

Annika must have seen me watching, because as she approached the house at the top of her circuit, she raised a hand to wave and smile. I smiled back, then looked up at the sky as she retreated down the hill again.

The orange glow was gone now, dwindled to a sharp yellow line across the horizon. Above me was a deep bowl of purple. But small puffy clouds, still reflecting golden light on their undersides, carried the memory of the sunset a while longer.

I picked up my shopping and went inside.

CHAPTER 22

Wednesday. Lunch with Renae at Noodles and Strudels in the city, close to our respective offices. This hipster café, run by a German pastry chef and his Malaysian boyfriend, made no apologies for its carbohydrate-laden menu.

The eatery was wedged between smoothie bars and paleo places in the trendy advertising district. It was ironic placement, given the likely wellness preoccupations of the passing foot trade. The smell of butter wafting out the door had been what first drew Renae and me in to try the food, and we'd been hooked ever since.

Maybe Noodles and Strudels thrived not despite its health-conscious clientele, but because of them. It was their guilty treat—the 20 in their strict 80/20 regimes.

Renae was looking resplendent, with primary red hair in a Veronica Lake wave, and a dark green rockabilly dress with large colorful butterflies flying across the skirt. A cropped turquoise cardigan with orange buttons, and stripy blue pantyhose, completed the look.

I sighed inwardly. I'd been relatively happy with my outfit when I got dressed that morning, pairing my cardigan with a pale pink and blue top and grey pants. And I did look OK. Just a bit boring compared to my flamboyant friend. I reminded myself what I regularly told Vivi and tried to take my own advice: don't compare yourself to others, just compare yourself to yourself.

But my mood had been low ever since I'd come back through the mirror. Being fat had always been hard, but it was even harder now, after that brief taste of skinny. And my mood was getting lower with each hour that passed. The reality of being back in this intractably large body was sinking me.

Renae, by contrast, was in a good mood. She had a sparkle in her eye.

'So, have you started planning what you're going to pack?'

'For the Gold Coast?' I asked, already knowing the answer, but checking, since the invitation had been rescinded in skinny land.

'Of course! You're not going to bail on me are you?'

'No, I'd still love to go. But it's OK if you change your mind about inviting me. Did you think about asking Lucy?'

Part of me was now dreading the trip, and the prospect of wearing a bathing suit in public. Why had I said yes? I loved the idea of the beach. The reality though— not so much. I secretly wished Renae *would* invite someone else.

'My sister? My long-legs-flat-tummy-looks-better-than-me-in-a-bikini-and-kind-of-annoying sister Lucy? Hell, no!'

I knew Renae didn't mean to insult me, but I was feeling particularly fragile.

'Oh, so that's it!' I faux laughed. 'You just want me to come 'cause I'll make you look good in your bikini!'

As soon as I said it, I regretted it. I had meant it to sound like a joke. But it missed the mark. I sounded bitchy.

'What?' screeched Renae. 'No Evie, that's not why I asked you! Besides, you're gorgeous! Look at that face of yours. Lucy's nowhere near as fun as you. And you're not even that fat anyway.'

That last bit sounded hollow. I raised an eyebrow. 'It's true, though. I won't look as good as you in my swimsuit.'

'What rubbish,' said Renae, looking worried. 'Evie, have I done something to upset you?'

I sighed. 'No, not at all. Look, I'm sorry. There's a lot going on with me at the moment. I'm just, I dunno, frustrated at myself, I guess.' I made eye contact, trying for reassurance. 'It'll be really good to have a holiday. I'm looking forward to it. Truly.'

I raised my water glass in a half-hearted toast. Renae returned the gesture, but the mood was ruined. Neither of us could enjoy a relaxed lunch now. We'd both become tense.

We perused the menu in silence. The list of comforting stodgy food now felt embarrassing, a reminder of my stupid comment, rather than the joyful indulgence we'd been looking forward to sharing.

The server came and we carefully ordered the healthiest options possible. When our salads arrived, we pretended they were just what we wanted, rather than the double bacon cheeseburgers and onion rings we'd talked about getting before I said what I said.

Renae found an excuse to wind up lunch earlier than normal. She said something vague about a post-lunch meeting and headed off in the direction of her office.

Watching her walk away, I felt terrible. I was probably wrong about why she'd invited me to the Gold Coast. This obsessive preoccupation with appearance was probably something I experienced to a greater degree than other women. It was possible Renae hadn't given any thought to our comparative attractiveness, and just wanted my company.

But maybe it was easy for Renae to not think about my size on this side of the mirror because it was just an objective fact that she outranked me on the beauty scale.

On the other side of the mirror, where Renae—despite her quirky and appealing personal style—conformed less to the standard of ideal beauty than I did, things had felt different. On that other side of the mirror, she would surely be aware of the unfavorable comparisons that would be made, if not by anyone else then at least by herself, as we lay side by side at the pool.

If I hadn't said anything, we could have gone on holiday with our usual pattern of shared self-deprecation and praise for each other. We could have overlooked or laughed at each other's insecurities. We could have just had fun without things getting weird.

But it was going to be awkward now, after this ruined lunch. I had breached the trust we'd previously placed in each other. Before, we'd found unity in diet culture; it was a shared problem, a shared struggle. But now I'd made it a competition.

No wonder Renae had wanted to escape. She no longer felt safe from scrutiny in a relationship that had previously felt equal.

***

Because of our shorter lunch, I found myself with twenty minutes to spare before I was due back at work. I could go back early, but I wanted to stay out of the office. It, too, had unpleasant connotations with Ryan that I was also trying to avoid.

The route back to work went past a department store—a different branch of the same one I'd been to with Annika. I remembered seeing Annika last night, bouncing up and down the park in the golden sunset, looking so healthy. So balanced. So adult.

I'd wanted to go over and confide in her then.

And now, after my disastrous lunch, I wanted to confide in her even more. It would probably be easy to talk to a skinny woman like Annika about my weird who's-the-fattest competition with Renae.

I turned into the department store and searched for the active wear section. Of course, the leggings and sports bras in this part of the store did not come in my size. I was referred to a small concession down on the Real Woman level. While the garments there were made in the style of proper active wear, they lacked the high-tech fabrics and fancy construction that thinner people could wear in their quest to look like proper athletes.

But these clothes would still be more comfortable than my fleecy track pants, if I was going to honor my commitment to myself to start exercising.

I selected two pairs of leggings and two singlets that could be mixed and matched. I decided against a sports bra, because I was quite small-chested anyway and there was no way in the world I'd be attempting any jogging. Just a brisk walk to start with, and my normal bra could handle that. A pair of sneakers, I thought, would also be necessary.

After looking at the bewildering range of sneakers that, to my untrained eye all looked identical, I grabbed a random pair for the sales clerk to retrieve from the stock room. When she handed them to me to try on, I was shocked to find myself getting breathless as I bent over to do up the laces. I realized, with alarm, that all my shoes these days were slip-on styles. I hadn't tied laces in years. I felt shame that even this simple task was a physical challenge.

Regardless of whether I went through the mirror again, I resolved yet again to stop this express train speeding toward Being Really Fat. It was one thing to look frumpy and get puffed out easily when I had to exert myself. It was another thing entirely to find that everyday activities—tying shoelaces for God's sake—were also being affected.

As I paid for my purchases, I vowed to make this money count; to not have these items sit unused in my closet like all those beautiful small dresses.

I returned to the street and headed back to work, remembering the enthusiastic sales clerks who had clung to Annika the other day when we'd been shopping on the top floor for designer suits. And how, just now, making these purchases, someone had retrieved shoes for me in the size I requested but, apart from that, for the entire time I had been left completely alone.

When I arrived at the office, Jeremy spied my shopping bags. 'Ooh, did a spot of shopping? What did you get?' My instinct was to make up a lie, say the shopping was a gift for someone, and keep my efforts at getting fit a secret.

But then I wondered if I'd be more likely to stick with my commitment to exercise if I made myself publicly accountable. I took a deep breath and swallowed my embarrassment.

'I decided to follow your advice. I've bought some walking shoes and gym clothes.'

'Good one!' Jeremy smiled. 'I expect you to join me for a lunchtime walk at least once a week now. No excuses!'

'Ok, ok, you've worn me down,' I laughed. 'How about Monday lunchtimes? That will get it over and done with, and I won't have to listen to you hassling me for the rest of the week.'

'Deal,' said Jeremy, extending his hand to shake mine.

'Careful,' said Chelsea, watching from her desk, 'I exercised with him once and he took no mercy on me. Made me run the whole way.'

'That's OK,' I said smiling. 'If he tries any nonsense like that on me, I'll just fire him.'

'Fair enough!' laughed Chelsea.

CHAPTER 23

I stood in front of the mirror again. My memories of the world on the other side had started to feel dream-like.

Now, standing in my newly purchased exercise clothes, I felt a strong compulsion to step back through to the other side and skip the whole Getting Fit business.

But then I'd have to deal with the Breaking Up With Ryan business, the thought of which gave me a nervous rash. And the Not Talking To Lou business, which made me feel desperately sad. And the Salad-Loving Child business, which made me feel uneasy.

Besides, I wanted to get to know Annika on this side of the mirror, so I could have her friendship no matter where I eventually decided to settle. I was going to stay Fat Evie for a while longer.

I pulled a singlet down over the leggings and sucked in my tummy. I knew, objectively, that I wasn't so fat that people would stop and stare at me. Most people would not see me at all. I'd be another anonymous middle-aged woman taking a walk around the block.

But in these tight-fitting clothes I felt exposed. Everyone would know my secret. Evidence that I chose to eat more than my body needed was on display for the world. Everyone knew that eating too much was a bad choice, and people who make bad choices are bad people, aren't they?

I shook my head. Since when had the shape of my body become a moral issue? Well, screw that, and screw them. I took a deep breath and went to the kitchen. It was Stu's turn to cook and he was at the sink chopping onions. He looked up and didn't seem to register that I was wearing exercise clothes.

'I'm just going for a walk around the block while dinner's cooking,' I said.

'Oh, OK,' he said. 'It'll be ready in about 30 minutes.'

'Cool, I won't be that long.'

I couldn't see Annika in the park when I stepped outside, so I decided to go around the block. Hopefully she'd be running laps by the time I got back, then I could 'accidentally' meet her and get my new friend back.

I took off along the footpath. The bounce from my new sneakers reminded me of the times not long ago when, in that skinny body, I'd run around the neighborhood. I could almost imagine being back there doing a warm-up amongst the Wednesday morning running group. Out of curiosity, I tentatively sped up to a very slow run. In an alarmingly short amount of time, perhaps only 30 seconds, my lungs were burning and I was gasping for breath.

The feel of my body in flight was also quite different now from when I'd been skinny. In addition to my lack of endurance, the lift and drop of my bust, abdomen and buttocks was an uncomfortable distraction. I remembered the fat walker Sally had said mean things about. If Sally were here she'd be saying those things about me.

I thought again about the time I'd successfully lost weight in my twenties, before it crept back on. I tried to reassure myself that if I'd done it once, I could do it again.

But I'd been in a funk since lunch with Renae, and my old foe, Miss Negative Self-Talk, had taken up residence in my head.

She took no mercy on me.

She told me I needed to be honest with myself. The weight didn't just passively creep on. I *let* it come back. I made a decision to let it, with every mouthful. I made a decision to get fat again by never exercising. It wasn't like I consciously chose to be fat. But I did consciously choose not to exercise every day. I chose to eat All The Things. I made those choices knowing the consequences.

I wondered if I'd made those choices for some subconscious reason. I must get something out of being fat. There must be some pay-off for me, beyond the obvious ability to eat whatever I want. Maybe I'm secretly in love with Ryan, and staying fat protects me from acting on those feelings? Or maybe that's just another excuse. Stupid, stupid, stupid.

My anger with myself spurred me on. I leant in aggressively to my brisk walk, enjoying the sensation of sweating and breathing heavily. Fuck this body. Fuck this body. Fuck this body.

161

After looping around the block, I was soon heading back toward my house and the park opposite. And there in the twilight, sure enough, was a solitary figure clad in black, running up and down the hill.

Up and down, up and down. Not fast, not slow, just steady.

She looked so strong and healthy. I looked down at my own thighs and calves, so wide my feet splayed apart when I stood with my knees together. I almost lost my nerve to approach her.

C'mon Evie, don't be shy. She won't care what you look like. She'll be too distracted by how rude you've been for not welcoming her to the neighborhood for a whole year.

I stopped on the footpath across from our houses. This was also the high point where Annika would turn and start a new lap of the park.

Right now she was at the bottom of the hill, working her way up. I did some stretches while I waited. As I bent forward to touch my toes I looked through my legs and saw her getting closer. I stood up and waved shyly. She saw me and smiled. At the top of the hill she slowed to a stop.

'Hi,' I said. 'I don't know if you remember me. I'm your neighbor from number 63.' I pointed at my house.

Annika looked over at the house then back at me. She smiled, wiped her hand on the bottom of her t-shirt, and extended it to me. 'Hi, I think we did meet once. I'm Annika.'

'Evie.'

'Nice to meet you. Well, as you know, I live at 61 with Charlie.'

'Is that your partner?'

'Yeah. Together 18 years now. Hard to believe. And I think I remember meeting your husband?'

'Yes, Stuart—Stu—he works in logistics. Quite a few early starts for him, but that means he gets home early, so I get out of cooking dinner most nights.'

I could hear myself babbling, talking too much. I always did that when I was nervous. But Annika didn't seem to notice.

'Winning!' she smiled. 'And I think I've seen your daughter around?'

'Yes, Vivi. She's 10.'

'Nice. You sound really settled.' She said this in a natural, friendly way, as if she was genuinely happy to come across someone leading a good life.

I blushed, knowing the mess inside my head. 'I don't know about that. I think I might be going through a mid-life crisis, actually.'

My heart sped up a bit. Was it appropriate to venture into intimate confessions with a total stranger so quickly? But Annika didn't seem fazed by this self-diagnosis. On the contrary, she responded with enthusiasm.

'Oh, me too! D'you know, I read somewhere recently that humans across all countries and all cultures are at their most unhappy at age 47.'

'Oh great, that doesn't bode well for the next 8 years!' I laughed.

'Me either. I'm 43, so I'm bracing for things to get worse. And I've been through some pretty rough shit already! But the good news is that if you can get through 47, things start to get better from there. You just gotta hold on. Gotta keep your eye on the long game!'

'Well that's really motivating! Thanks!' I gestured at my workout clothes. 'I've been thinking about doing a bit more exercise too. Part of the mid-life crisis, I guess. Maybe I'll see you out here again.'

'Yeah, that'd be nice. I do this most evenings.' She used the hem of her t-shirt to wipe her forehead.

'Do you ever run in the mornings, before work?' I asked.

'Oh God no!' said Annika. 'I'm far too much of a night owl for that. I can't bear exercising first thing. I need to have been up at least three hours.'

'Me too!' I laughed. Suddenly I felt lighter. Like I'd been shown a different path. Maybe it wasn't necessary to adopt awful dawn running habits to be fit and healthy.

There was an awkward silence. I longed to ask Annika how she was feeling about the new job, but I didn't want to confuse her by discussing things I shouldn't have known.

I looked at my watch. 'Well, I should probably get back. Stu's probably finished cooking by now.'

'OK, it was nice to meet you, Evie. Might see you again tomorrow?'

'Yeah, that'd be nice!' I said. 'See ya!'

I jogged across the road to my house, feeling warm. That whole conversation had made me feel good. Better than I'd felt since I came back through the mirror. I'd totally forgotten about the awkward lunch with Renae or the hatred I'd been piling on myself when I was exercising, or the insecurity I'd felt when I approached Annika. I just felt a nice glow.

CHAPTER 24

I was still glowing the next morning, when I walked into the office. Everything felt a bit brighter. Why am I happy, I wondered? I decided that making a new friend felt a bit like falling in love. I really wanted her to like me. She was so cool. And so self-assured, but not at all intimidating like I'd spent the past year assuming she would be. It was easy being around her.

I smiled to myself remembering her horrified reaction to the suggestion of early morning exercise. A true kindred spirit.

Still smiling, I looked up and noticed Ryan sitting at his desk, watching me. His office door was open and he had a clear line of sight to the open plan space I was walking through. I felt myself blush but called out, as casually as I could, 'Morning.'

'Do you have a minute?' he said, gesturing me over.

I hesitated. The last time he'd done that, I'd been groped. I put my bag in front of me and walked to the doorway of his office, but didn't go in.

'Everything OK?' I asked, expecting him to request a work task.

'Yeah, yeah, come in. Take a seat,' he gestured to a chair at the side of his desk.

I went in reluctantly, and sat on the edge of the chair, with my bag protectively on my lap.

'Seeing you just then, smiling like that, I was struck by how unusual it was. Lately I've gotten used to seeing you scowl. I haven't seen you look happy since, gosh, since the Law Ball.'

At the mention of that event, I blushed, remembering my wardrobe malfunction. 'I just wanted to check everything was OK,' Ryan continued.

He was speaking in a faltering, embarrassed way. I knew he must hate conversations like this. It was excruciating for me too, but I was grateful to him for checking in. He genuinely cared for my wellbeing. That's why I'd stayed working for him for so long.

'Um, yeah, just...you know. Life. Always chasing my tail,' I mumbled. 'Everything's fine.'

Ryan lent over and squeezed my hand. I felt an electric jolt as he did it, and instantly remembered his hand squeezing my breast. His mouth on my mouth.

He must have sensed something in my reaction. He looked in my eyes and held my gaze longer than he normally would.

'I just, er, well, you're so important to us here. We need to make sure we take care of each other.'

I moved my hand away. 'Thanks, Ryan. I appreciate it. But everything's fine. There's nothing to worry about.'

***

'Well it's about time!' I squealed, hugging Lou close. I was standing in the doorway of her house, having finally arranged to drop in for a visit. 'How's Noah?'

Lou laughed. 'He's fine. It was a 24-hour thing. But he's certainly learnt his lesson!'

'No more chicken sandwiches?'

'Not for a while. We're going to stick with peanut butter for the foreseeable future.'

'So you were able to go on your trip then?'

'Yes! Thank God. It would have been expensive to cancel at the last minute. But Mario could've coped without me, so I would've gone anyway.'

Lou was a professional photographer who was on the road a lot, hiking and camping and taking amazing landscape photos, which she sold in a digital gallery that had proved surprisingly lucrative. What had started as a hobby had accidentally become a job. She'd been able to leave her career in recruitment to pursue this new business. But it meant she was away a lot, much to my disappointment.

'When did you get back?'

'Wednesday. Wanna see?'

She led me to a corner of her living room, where a desk was set up with a computer and a massive monitor. Lou scrolled through her latest images. It was a series of photos of an ancient lake, sitting like an enormous puddle in the crook of two mountains in the wilderness somewhere. The water was calm, and reflected trees were slanted and elongated across the surface, a phantom forest in reverse.

'Oh Lou, they're beautiful.'

'Yeah, I'm pretty happy with this lot. It was a good trip. So how are you? How's Vivi?'

I felt guilty. With my recent adventures in the forefront of my mind, I felt I'd been neglecting Vivi lately. I resolved to have some girl time with her soon. 'Oh, fine. You know, school dramas with Lily, but loving her classes. She's doing well.'

'And how's your diet going?' Lou raised an eyebrow.

'What? Don't tell me it's been that long! I've seen you since my birthday, haven't I?'

'I don't think so, hon.'

'Well, that diet didn't last too long, as you can see.' I twirled in a circle as if I were modelling a dress.

'I was worried I offended you.'

'No, of course not.' I sat on the couch. 'I often think the same thing. You know, about the futility of losing weight. It's just too hard. I should give up trying and work on accepting myself. I dunno…' I shrugged.

Lou laughed. 'So is it safe to offer you cake today, or would you prefer mineral water?'

I hesitated. It was the first of the month. Even though I'd just told Lou that my birthday resolution to diet had been abandoned, I'd actually decided that very morning that this was it: a new month, a new start. Only healthy eating from now on. I'd show that skinny version of myself that I could do it too.

Besides, why risk going back through the mirror, and all the uncertainty that involved, when I had all the tools I needed right here to get the same result. I knew Skinny Evie's secrets. I just needed time and resolve to implement them.

But I was too embarrassed to tell Lou I was starting over again.

My old internal bargaining voice returned, trying to convince me that dieting was unnecessary. Counter-productive, even.

Lou is right, the voice said, you need to accept yourself as you are. Embrace your curves. Besides, one slice of cake is probably about 300 calories. You can just skip dinner to compensate. Lou won't know you're dieting, and it won't really count as a cheat because you'll make up for it later.

These contradictory thoughts flashed through my head in a split second.

'Yes, it's safe to offer me cake,' I laughed. 'And actually, the mineral water is pretty tempting too. Can I have both?'

We settled in for a long, intimate chat. We started with our parents, comparing notes about Brian and Helen's respective new health issues, and the various age-related anxiety quirks we'd observed in each. Then I told Lou about meeting Annika and about my trip to the Gold Coast.

All the while, I longed to confide in Lou about the magic mirror. She'd known me longer than anyone, and knew I wasn't crazy. But maybe I was. Telling Lou might help me to understand whether I was delusional.

'So, um, speaking of trips,' I said.

'Hmm?' Lou was distractedly pulling crumbs off her jumper.

'Well, the weirdest thing happened while you were away. I don't think you're going to believe it, because I don't believe it myself, and I experienced it.'

'Oooh, how intriguing...'

'Well, when the builders were at our house, they talked us into putting a mirror in my closet.'

'Yeah.'

'Well, the woman—Angelica—she told me a spell. For the mirror.'

Lou looked at me, puzzled. 'What do you mean?'

'You know...oh, jeez, this is dumb. It's like a magic mirror.'

Deadpan, Lou replied, 'Are you telling me you've turned into Snow White?'

'Well, maybe the wicked stepmother.'

'Huh?'

'It worked, Lou. I said the spell, and I was sucked through the mirror.' I looked at Lou with an urgent conviction my sister hadn't seen before.

'You went through the mirror? Through it? Through the solid glass?' I nodded. 'Into what?'

'Into my house. Exactly the same. Stu. Vivi. All the same. Everything there was normal. Except...'

'Except?'

'Me. I was different. I was skinny. It was unbelievable, Lou. I looked like a model.' Suddenly my face lit up as I rushed to describe how perfect my body had been.

'And it was so easy to move around. Just getting up and down from a chair. I couldn't believe the difference. And no chafing Lou, no chafing! It felt miraculous, actually. And the clothes. They were so beautiful. And everything fit me. It was like nirvana!'

Lou smiled, reached over and sniffed the glass of mineral water I'd been drinking. 'So tell me,' she said, 'if it was nirvana, and you were so skinny, what happened?' she gestured to my body.

I looked down at my lap. 'Oh, well, I came back. It's a two-way mirror. There's a spell to come back too.'

'What's the spell?'

'Oh, no, it's silly, I don't want to say.'

'C'mon, you've told me this much. Tell me what it is!'

I exhaled and stared at Lou, who was smiling, clearly enjoying this ridiculous made-up story.

I covered my face with my hands and said, very quickly, 'Mirror, mirror let me out; I don't care if I am stout.'

'Stout?' she laughed. 'What century was this mirror produced?'

I watched her uncomfortably. 'I knew you wouldn't believe me.'

Lou noticed my expression. 'I'm sorry, Evie. It's just so unlike you to tell such a fantastical story. You're usually so rational.'

'But it's really true, Lou. I'm not making this up.'

She stopped laughing and looked at me. She could tell now I wasn't kidding. In fact, she looked a bit worried.

'OK, for argument's sake, let's say I believe you. Why did you come back? You've always wanted the perfect body, and you finally got it. What made you come back?'

'Well, most things were the same, but not exactly everything.'

'What was different?' she asked, genuinely interested.

'Well, you were.'

'I was different?' She wasn't expecting that answer. She hadn't projected herself into this ridiculous story.

'Well, not you. Us. We were different. We were fighting, Lou. Estranged. In that other place you hadn't even met Vivi. Ever.'

'That's even more crazy than this cock-a-mamy mirror story!'

'I know. But that's one of the reasons I came back.'

'Oh you silly sausage!' she said affectionately. 'That's really sweet, in an alarmingly deluded way.' She looked at me thoughtfully.

'What?' I asked.

'Well, it just proves what I've always told you. Skinny doesn't equal happy.'

'Well, I don't know,' I said, looking down at my lap. 'It certainly had its benefits.' I suddenly remembered Ryan gazing at me lustily.

'So are you going to go back? Can you go back?'

'Angelica said I could go there three times. But the third visit is the last. If I come back after that, the mirror stops working.'

'How many times have you been through?' Her skepticism had waned and she seemed genuinely interested now.

'Only once. I spent a few days there. I came back after I found out you hated me. I decided to just try to lose weight myself on this side. In the real world. It was OK on that side, but things were a bit off kilter. It was unsettling, to be honest.'

Lou looked at me for a minute. 'You have to go back,' she said.

My eyes widened in surprise. 'Why?'

'I have to know why we were fighting. I just can't imagine what could possibly tear us apart.'

'I'll think about it,' I said.

The truth was, I hadn't stopped thinking the same thing since the moment I came back.

CHAPTER 25

Renae looked sheepish, and I felt embarrassed, when we met for lunch the following Wednesday. I broke the ice with an apology.

'Can we just forget about what I said last time? I was in a weird headspace. I know you had no ulterior motive for asking me to go on the trip. It was stupid of me to project my own insecurities on you. Forgive me?'

I made puppy dog eyes and gripped my hands together in what I hoped was amusing supplication.

'Oh, don't be silly,' Renae responded immediately, pulling me into a relieved hug. 'There's nothing to forgive. One of the benefits of a long friendship like ours is we know how messed up each other is. Which is why I know *you'll* forgive *me*, when I tell you my news.'

'Ooh, that sounds intriguing. But hold that thought. Let's attend to the important business of ordering, first. They look like they're busy here today.'

'D'oh! OK. But I'm not sure how much longer I can hold it in.'

We settled into a booth at the hipster Mexican eatery I'd seen reviewed in the paper that week, and I focused on deciding between the quesadilla and the chimichanga. The latter sounded most tempting.

'So what are you gonna get?' I asked.

'The fish tacos. I've heard they're amazing here.'

'They do look good. I'm gonna try the chimichanga I think.'

The waiter arrived right on cue and took our order. After he'd left, I settled back in my seat. I smiled at Renae and said nothing further. I could tell she was bursting to share, and I couldn't resist teasing her with my silence. She couldn't wait any longer.

'I'm in love!' she blurted out.

Ah-ha—so that's what it was. I sat forward, eager to hear her story.

'But you just broke up with Dean. Who is it? When? How?'

Renae launched into an animated update about her love life, which I'd learned over the years was as colorful as her wardrobe.

'His name is Curtis. He's an aeronautics engineer from Singapore, doing his PhD here. So smart! Can you believe it? He asked me for directions on the street the other day, and I thought he was cute so I offered to walk him where he needed to go, even though it meant I'd miss my bus. Anyway, one thing led to another and… Oh my God, Evie, he's perfect for me. He loves vintage style and old movies and he's so funny and not at all interested in football like every other loser I've dated.'

I laughed, remembering all the times Renae had rolled her eyes at me when her various suitors came to barbecues at my house and ended up in intense conversations with Stu about the latest injury list or refereeing scandal, completely ignoring the women-folk.

'Wow, he's sounds like a keeper!' I laughed.

'Oh Evie, he's just perfect.' She paused, reddened a bit. 'So, um, that's what I wanted to talk to you about.'

I realized immediately what she was going to tell me.

'You want to take Curtis to the Gold Coast instead of me.'

'Would you mind? I feel terrible asking, especially after our conversation last week, but this has just come out of the blue. It's been such a whirlwind, and it would be so romantic to take him.'

I smiled, completely unfazed by her request. 'Of course I don't mind, Renae. The heart wants what it wants! Besides, you and I can go on a trip any old time. I can see how much this means to you.'

'Oh, thank you Evie, thanks!' She squealed, and shuffled around the booth to give me another hug. 'You're the best.'

Our lunches arrived soon after, and the conversation moved on.

Now that the decision was made, I felt relief for myself and happiness for my friend. It seemed like my trip to the Gold Coast was just not meant to be.

I bit into the chimichanga. It hit the spot.

***

At lunchtime the following day, I sat in BTL's conference room eating a boiled egg and lettuce sandwich, reading a novel. I was engrossed in the story when Ryan came into the room.

'Do you mind if I join you?' he took the lid off a plastic container full of curry and rice.

'Of course not. Please do.' I looked at his lunch. 'That smells nice.'

'Anything smells nice compared to egg sandwiches,' he said, wrinkling his nose at my meal.

'Oh, sorry!' I laughed, 'I wasn't thinking. I just had a craving for one today. I should have eaten it outside.'

'No, that's OK, I'm just teasing.' He stuck his fork into a piece of green chicken.

'Leftovers?' I asked.

'Yes, Rebekah usually makes too much when she cooks.'

I had a flash of memory from the skinny side of the mirror, where Rebekah was apparently dead. 'Um, how is Rebekah?' I tried to keep my voice casual.

'Busy with her studies. I hardly ever see her these days.' I thought I saw the barest hint of a frown.

'Oh?' I hoped he'd tell me more, but instead he asked how Stu was going.

'Same old, same old. He's well.' I didn't want to think about Stu. I wanted to hear about Rebekah.

Ryan and I ate in silence for a few minutes.

'So, ah, what is Rebekah studying?' I was keen to find out what I could while I had a chance.

'Interior design,' he said, looking at me with a slightly embarrassed look.

'That's quite a change.'

He laughed. 'Yes, a bit different from being an actuary.'

'I'll say! A bit like my sister becoming a photographer after working in corporate recruiting. So what brought that on?'

Ryan looked at me again. He seemed to be weighing something up. Finally he spoke. 'Well, actually, it's kind of down to you.'

'To me?'

'Well, this is awkward to explain. Maybe I shouldn't. I won't say it right and you'll get offended.'

'No, that's OK,' I said, not entirely sure it was.

'I don't want you to take it the wrong way,' he said.

'I won't. Don't worry.'

'Well, ah, about four years ago we… Do you remember we had the firm's Christmas lunch at the dock?'

'Yeah, I think so.'

'And you and Rebekah sat together.'

'Uh huh.'

'Well, later she was looking at photos from the lunch and… Well, she got a bit of a shock when she saw herself. She thought she looked a bit, um, heavy.'

My heart beat a bit faster. 'Heavy? You mean, she thought she looked a bit too much like me?'

Ryan grimaced apologetically.

'Does this story get better?' I asked, with an edge of anger. It was one thing to call myself fat. It was quite another thing for my boss to do so.

'Oh yes! Yes, that's why I'm telling you. I didn't, I don't, I mean I don't think of you like that. At all. I think you're quite beautiful actually.'

'Ryan, please. Spare me. Just finish your story.'

'So anyway, Rebekah was worried that she'd, as she put it, "let herself go".' He put air quotes around that last bit. 'So she made an appointment to see her doctor. She wanted to get some advice about the best way to address the, ah, problem. You know, typical actuary, she's always looking for data to inform how she approaches things. Anyway, at the appointment, the doctor takes her blood pressure, and when he takes off the cuff, he notices a mole on her bicep.'

'Uh-huh.'

'Anyway, long story short, it was melanoma. So, if she hadn't been in that photo with you, and hadn't been so god-damned neurotic about getting fat, she wouldn't have found the cancer and would probably be dead by now.'

'Gee. Thank God I'm fat then, hey?'

'Yeah, I know,' said Ryan, biting into his curry. He stopped mid-mouthful and looked over to me. 'God, sorry, that sounded bad. What I meant was, it's lucky how things turned out.'

I blinked and tried to keep my face neutral as I put the rest of my sandwich back in my lunchbox and closed the lid.

'And now she's doing interior design?'

'Yeah, the brush with death made her re-evaluate things. She realized she hates being an actuary.'

I smiled politely. 'Good for her.' I leaned across the table, looking directly at Ryan. 'Now tell me the important bit, Ryan,' I said crisply. 'After all that, did she manage to lose some weight?'

He heard the change of tone in my voice. He looked at me and shook his head, clearly annoyed at himself. 'I'm sorry I told you that story. I shouldn't have. I've made you feel bad.'

'No, not at all,' I put my hands up in protest. 'I know I'm fat. I don't need you to tell me that. I'm not blind. But still, I guess the chemo must have helped a bit with weight loss, hey?'

'Evie.' He looked at me, a bit wounded, a bit disappointed. I regretted saying it.

I stood up to go back to my office. 'I have to go.'

'I meant what I said,' Ryan said as I reached the door.

'Which bit?' I asked, hoping the tears filling my eyes wouldn't show.

'I think you're beautiful. I always have.'

I turned and walked away.

Back in my office I punched out an email to Ryan and Melissa, telling them I was working from home for the rest of the week.

Thirty minutes later I stood in front of my pantry, looking for something to eat. I wanted cookies like I'd never wanted cookies before.

As I searched the pantry I thought about my skinny self and wondered how the affair with Ryan had started.

I wished I'd kept a diary on that side. The Instagram posts were somewhat helpful. But despite the pseudonym, they rarely ventured into my secret life. And certainly not into the realm of down-low workplace liaisons.

If I went back, I could be straight with him. Tell him about the mirror, like I told Lou. Get him to help me understand. That would help me know how to end things with him in the least damaging way. Although after what he said to me today, I felt inclined to make him suffer.

There were two cookie choices before me—salty cheesy crackers, or chocolate-covered mint.

I couldn't decide, so I had both.

CHAPTER 26

The following week I developed a heavy cold. At first I was relieved, as it was an easy way to keep my distance from Ryan.

But by the fourth day, I was feverish and getting worse, so I made a doctor's appointment. I sat in the waiting room ignoring the dog-eared trashy magazines. The cruel paparazzi shots and bitchy 'who wore it best' features no longer amused me.

'Evelyn Swan.' I looked up and saw a doctor smiling at me from the hallway leading to the consulting rooms. He was a doctor I hadn't seen before. My usual physician, Dr Adichie, worked part-time and I hadn't been able to find a suitable appointment time with her.

I followed the unfamiliar doctor down the hall to his room. He gestured to the chair next to his desk, then sat down and smiled at me.

'I'm Dr Park. How can I help you today?'

'Hi, nice to meet you. So, I got sick over the weekend. I think it's just a cold, but I started feeling worse today, and wondered if it might be a secondary infection. I just wanted to check I don't need antibiotics?'

The doctor nodded and smiled. 'Let's take a look, then.' He took my temperature, examined my throat and my ears, listened to my chest.

When he was done he sat back down, typed a few notes, then spoke. 'It's just a virus. Antibiotics won't help. You need to rest, stay hydrated, and take some paracetamol.'

I felt reassured, but also annoyed I'd wasted money on an unnecessary check-up. I was about to grab my bag to leave, but the doctor kept talking.

'So what is your weight?'

'Oh, I'm not sure,' I lied. 'Why do you need to know that if I don't need antibiotics?'

'I'm just checking our notes are current. We don't have a weight recorded here for you.'

'Oh, well, I'm usually very healthy. I generally only come in for pap smears and contraception. Or when I have a really bad cold, like today. Dr Adichie has never weighed me before.'

'Well, I think we need that information so we can give you the best care.'

'Oh, really? I can't see...'

He cut me off. 'How often do you exercise?'

It looks like we're doing this then, I thought, suddenly feeling like a child sent to the principal's office. 'Um, I try to do a brisk walk every evening, for 30 minutes.' I jutted out my chin, glad to have a ready answer.

'And how long have you been doing that for?' he looked at me seriously over the rim of his glasses.

I felt chastened. 'Well, it's kind of a new thing. I just started. But it's been going well…' He kept staring at me. 'So, about a week now, I guess.'

He typed into his computer.

'And your food? What's your diet like?'

I pulled my cardigan in front of me. 'Well, it's OK. I don't eat much junk food. We mostly have home-cooked meals. I hardly ever go to those fast-food places. My main problem is that I eat large portions. I've always had a big appetite. I have seconds, finish my kid's leftovers, things like that.'

'You need to stop doing that. And how about fruit and vegetables?'

'Vegetables every day,' I said. 'Sometimes I forget to have fruit.'

'Any family history of diabetes?'

'Um, a few aunts and uncles have it, I think.'

He pulled out a tape measure. 'I want to do a diabetes risk screening. Please stand.' He put the tape around my waist. As he measured me I stared over his shoulder, feeling embarrassed.

To distract myself I focused on a poster on the wall. It was a medical drawing of a human torso. It was cross-sectional, with the bones, organs and muscles illustrated in minute detail. The layer of fat drawn between the skin and the muscles was tiny. Jeez, I thought, even medical diagrams are skinny.

'Women should have a waist circumference of thirty-one inches or less,' Dr Park said.

'What's mine?'

'Yours is forty-two inches. High risk. Sit down please.'

He then took my blood pressure.

'One thirty-eight over eighty-four,' he announced, typing again.

'Is that good?'

He shrugged. 'A bit high, but OK.' He stood up. 'Follow me.'

He led me led me to the other side of his room, where there was a scale.

'Shoes off,' he said. I slipped off my shoes and stood on the base plate. He looked over my shoulder and I smiled politely. Why did I smile? Was I trying to apologize for being naughty? I am seriously fucked up.

As the numbers settled he read them out, as if I was not just fat, but also blind. 'Two hundred and forty-four pounds. How tall are you?'

'Five three.'

'Too much,' he pointed at the scale. 'You need to lose weight. You're at greater risk of heart disease and stroke.'

'But you just said my blood pressure was OK.'

'Yes, but you're clinically obese.' He pointed at a poster above the scale. 'Look,' he gestured at a red square in the upper right quadrant of a graph on the poster. 'Your BMI is here. It should be down here.' He moved his finger to point at a green band in the lower left of the poster.

'Oh, OK, good to know,' I said sarcastically, as if this was something I'd never considered before. 'I'll get right onto that.'

My surprise at this spontaneous weigh-in had worn off and I was cross now. I was tempted to ask him what his BMI was, to level the playing field a bit, but he was annoyingly trim. I didn't want to give him the satisfaction of pointing out a green square.

Dr Park headed back to his desk, and I trotted to my chair on stockinged feet, holding my shoes in my hand. The doctor rifled through some brochures in a folder while I slipped my shoes back on. Then he handed me a wad of reading material. 'Take these with you,' he said.

I looked down at the brochures. *The obesity and overweight factsheet. Obesity: your clinical support options. Understanding the food pyramid.* He sat back in his chair, smiling benevolently at me, his body language indicating the consultation was finished.

'I hope you feel better soon.'

'Thanks,' I said, standing up. I sneezed in his direction, without covering my mouth.

CHAPTER 27

My cold went away, and my anger toward the doctor turned to self-pity. I read the brochures he gave me.

Suck it up, Evie. He's just telling you the hard truth. He sees the end result of obesity every day. Patients with diabetes and heart disease and organ failure. He was just trying to help, in his ham-fisted way.

But Lou was outraged when I told her. 'It's complete bullshit, Evie,' she raged over the phone. 'He had no right to talk to you that way. To infantilize you like that. And anyway, he's wrong. Studies show that skinny people are not necessarily healthier than fat people. In fact, being slightly overweight may protect you from some illnesses.'

'That's hard to believe,' I said.

'It's true. I read somewhere that about one-third of obese people are actually metabolically healthy and about a quarter of thin people are unhealthy.'

'Well, that doesn't make me feel better,' I said.

'Why not?'

'Because it means that two-thirds of obese people are metabolically *unhealthy* and three-quarters of thin people are healthy. That's not great odds for me.'

'But those are averages, Evie. You need to focus on yourself and your health on an individual level. Didn't the doctor say your blood pressure was fine? And you don't have diabetes?'

'Yes. But I can't tie my own shoelaces. Look, I know for a fact that I'll feel better if I lose weight, because I've experienced life in a smaller body.'

'You're not referring to that crazy mirror business, are you?' Lou didn't really believe my story, despite encouraging me to go back. And why would she?

'It's not just that. I remember how I felt, right before I met Stu, when I'd lost all that weight. I'd never felt better. And I didn't catch a cold back then for a whole year.'

'You were childless and living by yourself. There wasn't anyone around to give you their germs.'

'Well maybe. But I still need to get in shape. I want to do it before my fortieth. I'd really like your support, Lou. It would mean a lot to me.'

'Oh Evie, of course I'll support you. But can you promise me one thing?'

'What?'

'Can you just try to imagine, and possibly accept, that you might stay this size for the rest of your life, and that if you do, everyone will still love you? You can have a happy, healthy, successful life at any size.'

I could not imagine ever accepting that. But Lou was trying to meet me halfway. I made a non-committal noise.

'Just show yourself some grace, Evie. If you're hungry, eat something. Have you heard about intuitive eating?'

'No?'

'I think it's about trying to strip away all the dieting baggage and just focus on the cues your body is sending you to nourish it. From a place of acceptance. You just eat what you want, but over time, because you're not restricting yourself, what you want will change.'

I had to admit that sounded sensible. I assured Lou I would look into it. Her outrage about the doctor had made me feel better. She'd helped dial down my self-critical inner dialogue.

After our call I did as promised and reflected on whether I should change tack. This dieting caper had proven futile so far. There was a strong chance I'd be fat forever. Dare I consider accepting that fate? Would it be so bad?

But I knew myself better than that. I knew I'd only honestly face that question if the escape hatch to Skinny Evie's world was taken away.

***

I returned to work after recovering from my cold, feeling sheepish about snapping at Ryan for telling me of Rebekah's near-death experience.

Ryan must have felt bad too, because there was a bouquet of flowers waiting on my desk when I returned.

And as soon as he arrived at work that morning, he came into my office and closed the door.

'Thank you for the flowers,' I said. 'That wasn't necessary.'

'I wanted to. Anyway, I hope you're feeling better. All recovered? Make sure you go home early if you're not feeling well.'

I waved away his concern. 'I'm fine, really. It's good to be back. I was getting sick of Netflix.'

I still felt emotionally fragile and hoped my feeble attempt at humor would reassure him. I just wanted him to leave my office so I could put the whole thing out of my mind. But he sat down in the chair next to my desk and took a deep breath.

'Evie, I feel terrible about how we left things.'

'Me too. I'm sorry I exploded like that.'

'You had every right to. I can't believe I told you that story. Even as I was speaking the words I could hear a voice in my head saying "shut up Ryan, don't go there".'

I winced. 'I was angry because I was embarrassed.'

'I know. And now I'm embarrassed for being such a dick. I want to make it up to you. Please let me take you to lunch.'

'Really, there's no need. I'd rather just forget about it and get back to work.'

'Evie, I joined you in the boardroom because I wanted to spend time with you away from work. To talk to you. I like your company. To be honest, I've been feeling a bit isolated lately.'

'Is everything alright?'

Ryan sighed. 'I think so. Things are just…weird right now. I could use a friend. You'd be doing me a favor if you came to lunch.'

'Well, I can't say no to that,' I smiled. 'Lunch it is.' Ryan squeezed my hand then stood to leave. Again, my fingers burned where he'd touched them.

'Would 12pm suit? I'll make reservations.'

I nodded and he left. My tummy juddered. Was it fear? Excitement? Curiosity? All of the above? I turned to the long list of unread emails in my inbox and tried to focus on work.

Ryan took me to The Topaz Room. Fancy fine dining with a degustation menu. Wine was paired with eight bite-sized courses. I felt tipsy by my second glass, and the food was incredible.

On the third course, paired with an exquisite shiraz, I lifted my glass to him. 'What shall we toast for this course?'

'How about my birthday?' he said.

'No! It's not your birthday, is it? How did I not know that after all these years?'

'I'm sure I've told you before. Anyway, forty-seven today.'

'Uh-oh.'

'I know,' he groaned. 'Nearly 50!'

'No, it's not that. My friend told me scientists have proven 47 is the unhappiest age.'

Ryan slumped in his chair. 'Well, that sounds about right.'

'What do you mean? You seem happy enough from where I sit. You lead a charmed life.'

'You never can tell, can you?' he said.

'So what's up? And why the hell are you at work on your birthday, anyway? Rebekah should have taken you away for the weekend. If my kids had flown the coop that's what I'd do.'

'Rebekah is in New York at a trade show. She texted me this morning.'

'She texted you? She didn't call?'

'Here, look.' He pulled out his phone and handed it to me. The text said 'HBD Ryan.'

'That's it? Not even a love heart emoji?'

'Remember how I told you she reassessed her life after the melanoma? Well, I was part of that reassessment. She wants to move to New York because that's where the "design scene" is. And she doesn't want me to go with her. Not that I could, with the business and my clients here.'

'What are you saying? Are you guys separating?'

Ryan nodded. 'It appears that way.' My heart thumped.

Ryan continued talking. 'And you know what? I actually feel fine about it. Me and Rebekah—it's run it's course. Both of us feel…neutral toward each other. There's no animosity. But as empty as things were with her, what I hadn't expected after she left was the loneliness. I took her company for granted. Life was simple. I would work and I would go home, day after day, week after week, year after year, and she was always there. Whenever we socialized, I just tagged along and spent time with her friends. I never made any effort to make my own friends. I should have.'

'Is that why you asked me to lunch? Because there was no one else to ask?'

'No Evie,' he said seriously. 'I asked you because I can't think of anyone else I'd rather spend my birthday with.'

I smiled. 'Well, thanks. I'm honored.'

'Would you mind not telling anyone about my separation? I'm not ready to talk about it with other people yet.'

'Of course,' I said, 'It's in the vault.'

When we eventually returned to the office, and went to our respective desks, I texted Ryan a birthday cake emoji. He sent me back a love heart.

***

For two months following Dr Park's 'pep talk', I power-walked up and down the park each evening while Annika ran alongside me, and I joined her at her Pilates classes each Sunday.

I researched intuitive eating, and it sounded good. Logical. Sensible. I tried to tune into my body's natural hunger cues.

I ate according to the food pyramid in the brochure Dr Park had given me. I tried to balance my meals, having mostly bread, rice, pasta and cereal, followed by vegetables, dairy and eggs. I had smaller serves of meat, and I tried to limit my fat intake as much as possible. As prescribed in the pyramid, I used oils sparingly, and chose vegetable oils because they were lower in cholesterol. I bought non-stick bakeware and spritzed oil onto it with an aerosol. I had low-fat milk and cheese.

The daily walking made me feel very good—energized and alive—but it also made me hungry. I showed myself grace. I ate when my body told me to, and I ate until I was full. This meant I ate a lot.

Eight weeks after that doctor's visit, I weighed myself. I was 253 pounds. Despite all that mindful eating and all that exercise, I had gained weight. I still couldn't do up my laces without the assistance of a bench to elevate my foot. I still couldn't roll over in bed. Stu grumpily complained that my snoring was worse than ever.

I wondered if my age was to blame. Perhaps my metabolism was slowing as I approached menopause. But that was still 10 years away. Surely it couldn't be that.

I thought about the 'solutions' in the other brochures Dr Park gave me: weight loss pills or bariatric surgery. In my darkest moments I wondered if that's what I needed to try next.

But why put myself through those extreme measures when a simpler alternative presented itself? I'd tried to ignore it but found myself lingering longer and longer in front of the magic mirror each day.

Ryan and I had been spending more time together since his birthday. Lunch nearly every day, and recently we'd started to meet on the weekend for a walk or a visit to a gallery. This had been prompted by a lunchtime chat about the new blockbuster exhibition at our local art museum.

I asked Stu if he minded me socializing with Ryan. I explained Ryan's separation from Rebekah and his loneliness. I didn't mention my secret crush. Stu shrugged indifference. 'Do what you like.'

The memory of Ryan's kiss in the skinny world replayed in my mind over and over. I found myself dreaming of him. Torrid, explicit, blush-making dreams that I tried to push out of my head each morning when I saw him at the office.

Stu began to feel more and more like a roommate than a husband. I rebuffed his advances. I didn't want to be thinking of someone else when he kissed me.

It felt like ages since that first trip through the mirror, and I began to romanticize what it had been like on the skinny side. I airbrushed my worries about Vivi, and glossed over the separation from Lou. I only remembered the feeling of Ryan's hand on my body, his hot breath on my neck. I wondered how different sex would feel in a smaller body. Would I feel more adventurous, or would it be an irrelevant detail?

One night, woken breathless from a dream, I finally admitted to myself that my feelings for Ryan were serious. More than just a crush.

I was all mixed up by this realization: excited and sad and scared. Excited at the prospect of being with Ryan. Sad for the fracture this would rend in Stu and Vivi's worlds; a broken home. And scared because being intimate with Ryan meant letting him see me naked. The thought made me cringe.

Because of these conflicting feelings, I held back from telling Ryan how I felt. We continued our innocent shared lunches and our just-friends dates.

But the dreams continued, and the mirror started calling to me. I realized it was a shortcut to Ryan. If I went back to that skinny life I could avoid those awkward first fumblings of a new relationship. We could pick up where we'd left off. I would tell him I was ready to commit. Ready to ask Stu to move out.

On that side of the mirror I could try out a more serious relationship with Ryan without hurting Vivi. My Vivi. The sweet, innocent real one in this world. Not the mirror Vivi who'd already dealt with her parent's separation.

I could mend fences with Lou—surely our problems weren't insurmountable.

The only downside I anticipated was Norman, the ever-present hunger that had plagued me there. But with my now constantly intuitively full belly, the memory of my hunger on the skinny side had faded. It didn't seem that much of a big deal. It seemed a small price to pay, not only to be skinny, but to have Ryan as my lover.

I decided to go back.

CHAPTER 28

I arrived at the office in a navy suit, pencil-skirted and cleavage-boosted. I'd taken extra care with my hair and make-up, and wore fishnet stockings with my tallest stilettos.

I'd revved myself up at home. The excitement and relief that the spell still worked, that the mirror had yielded and let me through, that I would be with Ryan soon, had carried me through the morning on a cloud.

But now, in the BTL car park, I hesitated. Maybe I'd fallen in love with the idea of Ryan. Apart from that first surprising kiss, we'd only shared meaningful glances and squeezed hands. I hadn't truly tested the relationship beyond our long-standing professional involvement.

Our more recent lunches and gallery visits had been sweet and perfect. Had left me wanting so much more. But was I really ready to sleep with him? Because now that I was here, that's what he'd assume I wanted.

I suddenly felt shy. The *femme fatale* act evaporated. Who was I kidding? I was a fat, middle-aged mother playing dress-up. Faced with the reality of taking things to the next step, I suddenly missed the innocent, burgeoning flirtation I'd enjoyed with Ryan in the real world. Had I put that at risk by coming through the mirror? Only one way to find out.

I took a deep breath and stepped into the office.

And nothing happened.

The work day unfolded as usual. My aggressively sexy attire was apparently normal, or at least not noteworthy, in this place. The people around me went about their business, friendly, polite and indifferent to my physical appearance.

Ryan was tied up in meetings all morning. In the afternoon he looked up at me from his desk when I walked past his office and nodded. He looked under pressure. He was handling settlement negotiations that would escalate to litigation if he couldn't convince his client to accept the deal, and he knew that would be a disaster for the precariously financed single mother.

After all my excitement that morning about coming through the mirror, after all the build-up in my head, Ryan didn't talk to me that whole day.

I drove home feeling foolish and disappointed. Self-doubt crowded my mind. Had I misremembered the whole affair-with-Ryan business? Had I come back here for nothing, risking Vivi's wellbeing and Lou's love in the process?

I still had so much to learn here.

***

I checked my schedule on the fridge and dutifully cooked the Greek-style lamb fillets with chick pea and red onion salad that was allocated for Friday nights. As the meat was browning, I ransacked the pantry, looking for something, anything, to tame Norman. I was almost shaking with hunger.

There were no crackers or cheese to be found, but the fridge yielded some lovely fresh grapes. I popped them into my mouth one after the other as I cooked, savoring how delicious they were. Perhaps it wouldn't be hard to maintain my figure here after all, if I eschewed junk and just snacked on whole foods. I could do that.

I decided to make a list, after dinner, of every unprocessed food I could think of that I enjoyed eating. I would stock up and allow myself some healthy snacks any time Norman grew too insistent. Surely if I kept up with my daily running the odd snack wouldn't make a difference.

At dinner Vivi was her normal, happy self (apart from the fact that she ate her salad without making a fuss).

Stu was the same too. He told a long, boring story about something that had gone wrong at work. He didn't ask about my day. It saddened me to realize he treated me exactly the same in both worlds, whether separated or married, fat or thin. He didn't cherish me.

The lamb and salad were delicious but, having grown accustomed to intuitive eating as opposed to strict portion control, it took a heroic effort to stop myself scoffing Vivi's leftovers. I felt a physical twist in my gut as I scraped her leftovers into the trash. I wondered what would happen if I followed intuitive eating on this side of the mirror. I suspected I wasn't intuitively skinny. I would never be intuitively skinny.

As a distraction I locked myself in my bathroom, disrobed and stood on the scale. One hundred and four-teen pounds. Part of me was thrilled to see this number. But part of me was worried. It seemed so low. Even lower than my first trip through the mirror. And I could see my ribs well enough to count them.

I punched some numbers into a BMI calculator on my phone and worked out that my BMI was 18.98. To my amazement, the calculator congratulated me with a big green tick: 'A BMI of 18.98 is within the healthy weight category. This is generally good for your health.'

I looked in the mirror. Was I really healthy? I thought I looked a bit pale and gaunt, to be honest. I remem-bered reading somewhere that BMI measures were imprecise. But it must be OK if this official public health website was reassuring me I was a good weight for my height.

My head was itchy. Instinctively I reached up to scratch. My fingers brushed against the base of a hair extension. I'd noticed last time I was here that I had hair extensions. I'd read on my *Shrinking Violet* page that weight loss could lead to hair loss, and that my consistent caloric deficit over more than a decade had stripped a lot of volume from my scalp. 'Yeah, I was a bit freaked out at first,' my pseudonymic self had written, 'but hair extensions work wonders. It's just not a big deal.'

I'd also lost my period. Secondary Amenorrhea, it was called. In the *Shrinking Violet* discussion of this condition, Skinny Evie had shockingly dismissed it, breezily telling her readers that, oh well, her family was complete anyway, and wasn't it great to be saving so much money on sanitary products.

On my first night back in the skinny world I tried to ignore these red flags. I tried not to think about whether I could possibly stay here long-term, accepting these alarming side effects of prolonged calorie restriction.

I pulled on my woolen bathrobe—weighing myself naked had made me cold to the bone and triggered some serious shivering.

Norman roared alive in my belly.

Positive thinking, Evie. Focus on the positive. I pulled up a picture of Ryan on my phone. God he was handsome.

***

At bedtime I insisted on reading Vivi a good-night story. I wanted to start this second visit through the mirror on a better footing.

At first Vivi acted like she was humoring me, but toward the end of the chapter I could tell she was enjoying herself. She wedged her small body within the crooks and crannies of my folded frame and breathed slowly, listening without interruption. The reading also distracted me from my hunger. Finally, the day's disappointments and worries were fading in my mind.

After switching off Vivi's light, I passed Stu getting ready for bed in the guest room. I said good night and felt no pang that he wasn't sharing my bed.

I sank between the sheets, glorying in the feeling of space around me. I felt free from my marriage and free from my fat. I rolled over twice, testing my agility, smiling with relief.

Then I thought of something. I bounced off the bed and grabbed my sneakers. I bent over and tied the laces. Easy peasy. No exertion required. Vindication for coming back.

I kicked the shoes off and lay back in bed.

I didn't know what the next day would bring, but I felt more hopeful than I had when I'd left the office earlier that evening.

I started reading my book (once again the same book I'd been reading in my fat life). And then my phone beeped. A text message from Ryan.

> *Sorry for being so distracted today. You looked delicious. Wear that suit when you come to the Regent on Saturday. xxx*

My heart galloped away. I knew I'd made the right decision.

CHAPTER 29

I met Renae for lunch on Wednesday without my usual homemade macro-balanced, calorie-counted freezer meal. I just didn't feel right about expecting her to conform to my dietary strategy when I knew she'd much prefer eating out. I'd texted her that morning to let her know, so she didn't go to any needless trouble packing lunch. Besides, I'd gone to the dreaded running club at dawn, and worked up a real sweat, so I felt like I had calories to spare.

We met on our corner and decided to go Italian. I fancied a big dish of pappardelle with beef ragu. I led Renae to the fantastic Italian bistro one street away.

We settled into a booth and Renae immediately ordered a jug of Italian sangria, despite the fact we had offices to return to. 'Go on—live a little!' she urged. I didn't take much coaxing.

Renae's dress that day was typically colorful—a mustard yellow and hot pink flamingo print, with a wide collar, set off with fishnet tights and Mary-Jane heels.

I'd complimented her on the ensemble when we kissed hello, and she'd praised my red dress in return.

I remembered that in this skinny world, our awkward, awful lunch hadn't happened.

After we charged our glasses, Renae complimented me again.

'I really do love that dress,' she said. 'The color is great— you look like a *pomodoro appassionato*!'

'I didn't know you speak Italian. I'm impressed.'

'Well, all the better for perusing this menu. Yum.' She put purple glittery spectacles on. 'I have to say, Evie, I'm enjoying this recent change in you.'

'What change?'

'Well, it's like a loosening up. I don't just mean ditching the homemade lunches. You seem different, somehow. Less intense. Less driven. It's hard to explain.'

'I think I know what you mean. I feel like I was a suit-case that had been overstuffed, but now the lock's broken and the messy innards are spilling out.'

Renae laughed. 'Well? Not exactly how I would have put it, but yes, I suppose. That reminds me, actually. The Gold Coast. Lucy's had to cancel. So, I know it's a bit awks, but can you still come? I know I allegedly invited you before— I still can't for the life of me remember that, and I haven't ruled out that you've pulled an elaborate ruse to wrangle an invitation—but it would be so great to have you there.' The waitress placed an icy jug of pink wine between us. 'Think of all the other jugs of sangria we can share!'

SARAH WILBOW

I lifted my glass to hers. I had no bathing suit inhibitions in this world. 'I would LOVE to come, Renae. Thank you.' We both took gleeful sips.

I wondered if she'd met Curtis, the new boyfriend, on this side of the mirror. I'd try to find out. 'So,' I continued, 'how are you feeling about Dean not going on the trip. Are you going to be sad?'

Renae waved away my question. 'Dean was a big mistake. Ancient history.' She sighed, looking out the window.

'What is it?'

'Oh, I dunno. This will sound silly. A few weeks ago I was rushing to get to the bus because I had my drawing class after work, and I passed this hot Asian guy near the bus stop. He looked lost, like he needed directions or something. God, Evie, he was so spunky. We made eye contact for a split second and I thought he was about to ask me something, but my bus had pulled up so I kept running. After I got on and looked back out the window, I could see him watching me. Ever since then I haven't been able to get him out of my head. I feel like I should have stopped to talk to him. What if he was my soul mate, Evie, and I just ran right by him?'

She slumped back in her chair, dejected.

'Oh no. That sounds terrible,' I said.

'I know. Story of my stupid love life. Why can't I catch a break?'

'Well, maybe you'll run into him when you least expect it. Maybe he'll be at the Gold Coast.'

'It's nice to imagine, but I doubt it.'

'Never mind,' I said. 'If it's meant to be, it will be. Somewhere, somehow.'

'Do you really think so?'

'Stranger things have happened. Believe me.' I thought about the impossible twist that events in my own life had recently taken.

Renae perked up when her lunch arrived. She'd ordered the burnt butter and sage gnocchi and, as planned, I had the pappardelle.

We were at lunch a bit longer than I'd anticipated, and drank a bit more than I'd expected, but I felt relaxed and happy. I joked to myself that there had to be some benefits from sleeping with the boss. I was sure Ryan wouldn't care. And I ignored the glance Jeremy and Chelsea exchanged when I waltzed back into the office, slightly tipsy, an hour later than I said I'd be.

***

'So, ah, I have plans tonight,' I told Stu on Saturday morning, trying to ascertain our childcare arrangements without directly saying so.

'I know, I know. You wrote it on the calendar, remember? You don't have to keep nagging me. I won't forget.'

'Great,' I said, ignoring his grumpiness and setting off in search of this useful-sounding calendar.

There it was on the kitchen desk. A day planner with Vivi's movements color-coded by responsible parent. Stu's parental duties were written in green and mine were in blue. Handy, I thought, recognizing my own organizational skills at play. If anyone could coordinate a shared parenting arrangement it would be me.

The planner told me that Stu was taking Vivi to the movies tonight and I'd written 'dinner with friends' for myself.

Then I texted Ryan. 'Childcare sorted. Where shall we meet?'

He wrote back 'Meet in bar at 8.' It was the sexiest message I'd ever received.

The rest of the day seemed to pass in slow motion as my anticipation grew. I tried reading my book but was too jittery to concentrate. I had the same trouble composing the week's *Shrinking Violet* post, so I went out to the garden to pulls some weeds. It felt good to keep moving.

As I worked through the veggie patch, digging, twisting and pulling out the imposter shoots, I thought nostalgically about the first time I met Ryan.

***

The coffee machine was intimidating. Like everything else on the top floor of the glass and metal tower housing Williams, Henderson and Bligh Lawyers. It blinked menacingly at me as I approached, my small ceramic cup proffered like a pilgrim's votive.

Which button should I press?

It was yet another question in a seemingly unending stream of questions on my first day as a legal secretary at Mighty Blighty (as the legal fraternity referred to this top-tier firm).

I eventually found my way to the tearoom (incorrectly stumbling into a meeting room and broom closet along the way), feeling overwhelmed by the onslaught of information recited to me by Mrs Vukovic.

Mrs Vukovic was in charge of the legal secretaries in this division of the giant multinational firm. She was an older woman, surely nearing retirement I hoped, who had quickly conveyed, with an impressive economy of words, that she believed in tradition, discipline and deference. And formal titles. She'd scared the bejeezus out of me.

My hands shook as Mrs Vukovic showed me the fax machine and explained the DX code system and imparted what had probably been Very Important Information about a particular court registry. Very Important Information I'd instantly forgotten.

At 10.25am, Mrs Vukovic looked at her ancient, dainty wristwatch, and told me to go and have some morning tea, because she needed to go to a management meeting that was not appropriate for me to attend.

And so here I was, in the sleek and shiny kitchen on Level 23, trying to work out which coffee pod to choose, where to insert it, where to put my cup, and which button to press to release the coffee.

I closed my eyes and selected one of the buttons at random, unable to decipher their stylish hieroglyphs.

The machine gurgled awake and made an alarming snorting sound, like an old man clearing his throat.

I winced and looked around, desperately hoping I wasn't disturbing anyone in the hushed environs of Level 23. Then nothing. All sound ceased and my cup waited, empty and dry.

I stood paralyzed with indecision. What to do? Press again? Had I broken it? I started a staring competition with that incessant blinking light.

'Careful, that thing is deadly.' I jumped and turned around. Standing in the doorway was a tall, dark-haired young man. Gorgeous, suit-clad, exuding an easy confidence, half-smiling at my obvious bewilderment.

'I pressed the button but nothing happened.'

'Let me see if I can help.' He had a fiddle, reinserted the pod and pressed all the buttons. The gurgling noise repeated and we looked at each other in alarm. Then another mechanical snort, but no coffee, as we stared at the machine. Someone serious-looking walked past the kitchen doorway and frowned at us. We giggled.

'OK then,' he said. 'I think it's really broken.'

'I hope it wasn't my fault. This is my first day. Not exactly a great first impression.'

'Oh God, are you Evie?'

I looked up at him in surprise. 'Yes?'

He stuck his hand out to shake mine. 'Ryan Timms. I'm one of the Associates here. I think I'll be sharing you with Melissa.'

'Oh yes, great! Lovely to meet you. I'm still having my orientation with Mrs Vukovic.

He grimaced in sympathy. 'Not much fun, that one. But essentially harmless. Anyway, I'm back from court. Sorry I wasn't here to greet you first thing.'

'No, that's OK.'

'Well, if we're going to be working together, I guess I should confess to you my deepest, darkest secret.'

I raised my eyebrows, confused, intrigued and amused.

He reached above my head and opened a cabinet, pulling out a jar of instant coffee. 'All the coffee snobs here make me hide this away. But I've actually always preferred this stuff. There's no risk of the jar and spoon breaking down.'

He opened and inhaled deeply from the jar. 'Mmmm. You wouldn't believe how many late-night study sessions this stuff got me through.'

I laughed. 'That's so weird—and I'm not just saying this because you're my new boss—but I actually don't mind instant either. It's so much easier to make. And I think it tastes OK.'

'Let me get you one,' he said. 'How do you take it?' He took my cup from the stupid fancy machine and dumped in a teaspoon of coffee granules.

'White with one, thanks.' I liked how he smiled.

Ryan walked with me back to my desk, which was right outside his and Melissa's offices. He said he was fairly new to the firm too, so we could learn on the job together. He said it was going to be such a novelty to have a legal secretary after getting used to doing all his own filing and typing and phone answering.

'Just ask if you have any questions. Door's always open.' Then he winked and went into his office.

I sat at my desk, feeling much better. Perhaps it wouldn't be so bad working here, with kind people like Ryan to report to.

I tried to bury the thought, but I couldn't deny that I found him very attractive. Maybe it was because he'd been nice to me when I was feeling vulnerable. I glanced up and looked at him through the door, sitting at his desk. No, it wasn't just that. He was definitely, objectively, very good looking.

I wondered if he was single. Suddenly a whorl of daydreamy movie-style montages sprung into my head. Ryan asking me out on a date. Ryan sweeping me off my feet.

Stop it, Evie. You always do this. Snap out of it. He's your boss. You've known him for two minutes. Besides, you think this about every man who is vaguely attractive and vaguely nice to you.

I shook my head and opened the folder of induction notes Mrs Vukovic had left on my desk. I was soon absorbed in my reading.

Late in the afternoon, as I was packing my bag to leave for the day, my desk phone rang.

'Good afternoon, Williams, Henderson and Bligh, how may I help you?' I answered dutifully, as instructed by Mrs Vukovic.

'Hello, could you put me through to Ryan Timms please.'
'Certainly. Who can I say is calling?'

'It's Rebekah. His wife.'

'One moment please.'

I transferred the call. As I did, I looked into Ryan's office. When he picked up the receiver, I saw him smile broadly and lean back in his chair looking relaxed and happy.

Of course, I thought to myself. The good ones are always taken. Oh well.

It was a brief and sweet fantasy, but I packed it away.

***

At eight o'clock I sat in my car in a parking garage across from the hotel, watching the clock. Although I was nervous, I wasn't having second thoughts. I was waiting to make my entrance. I wanted to be a few minutes late, to make him wonder, for just a minute, if I'd show.

Part of me still felt like I was playing a game. Role-playing. Dreaming. How in the world could this truly be happening? Handsome, charismatic Ryan, and dumpy suburban me?

The surreal nature of the situation was scary but liberating. If this is just my imagination, I thought—some kind of lucid dream—then anything goes.

At seven minutes past eight I locked my car and walked across to the hotel.

The bar was nestled at the back of the lobby. I hesitated in the doorway of the dark and hushed room, self-consciousness descending upon me once again. And then I saw him, and he turned and saw me and smiled.

And everything was fine because it was just Ryan. My old, familiar friend. The gentle man who'd cared for me and respected me for so long.

I took a deep breath and walked toward him, trying to look sexy but giggling nervously. His eyes stayed locked on mine. He held out a hand to me. He pulled me close and kissed me on the mouth.

It was then I knew for certain that he was my person.

***

After one drink, and an unbroken stream of easy banter, we moved from the bar to a room upstairs. The twinkling lights of the city spread out below us.

Later, when I tried to piece together what happened, when I tried to pinpoint the moment everything went wrong, it was easy to forget the tenderness and ease I'd felt in his arms at the beginning.

The sex was even better than I had dreamed it would be. I felt like I'd arrived home. As I stared into his eyes, our faces only inches apart, I knew in my heart that we'd be together forever. He no longer needed to wait for me to be ready to commit.

It didn't occur to me to question why we were meeting in a hotel. It was sexy as fuck and I just assumed the venue was chosen to heighten the passion.

It didn't occur to me to question why we weren't already living together on this side of the mirror. All the evidence pointed to us being in love. We'd been seeing each other for some time. I was separated and he was single, his beautiful wife years dead.

Caught up in the moment, I forgot I was flying blind in this world, making life-changing decisions on the scantest of information and experience. I'd filled my knowledge gaps with what I *wanted* to be true, rather than testing the veracity of my assumptions.

In hindsight, that's where it went wrong.

I was resting my head on his chest, listening to his relaxed breathing, and he was twirling my hair in his hand. I kissed him and sighed happily. He stroked my back.

'Ryan?'

'Mmm?'

'I think I'm ready.'

'Again?'

'No, not that!' We laughed. 'I think I'm ready to take the next step.' I sat up and looked at him. 'I'm going to ask Stu to move out. I want to live with you.'

On the other side of the mirror, I'd been sharing my innermost thoughts with Ryan for months during our regular lunch dates and gallery visits. Our conversations were so unfiltered. It felt like the most natural thing in the world to be completely candid with him.

But now, at the suggestion we live together, Ryan's body tensed slightly. He sat up, unsmiling.

'What do you mean?'

I fell into a chasm. Dark and confusing and scary.

'Well, I mean I want to be with you. Like this. Every day. I want everyone at work to know we're a couple. I don't want to keep it a secret. I love you, Ryan.'

He dropped his head to his knees.

'Oh Evie. Oh babe. I had no idea you felt that way.'

'You didn't?' I heard my voice ricochet up in panic and embarrassment.

'I'm so fond of you Evie.'

'Fond?'

'I thought we'd agreed this would be a casual thing. A friends-with-benefits deal. You said you didn't want to be tied down after a failed marriage. And then there's Vicky.'

My stomach dropped. 'Vicky?'

He looked at me like I was a simpleton. 'Vicky. My girl-friend. You've met her, remember? The pediatrician?'

'Oh,' I whispered. 'I just thought that after tonight… After what we just did… Doesn't it change things? I thought it meant something.'

Mortification crashed over me as I realized I was just his fuck buddy. No more, no less.

And who was this Vicky person?

'Meant something? That's not fair, Evie. You're the one who made it clear you wanted an open relationship. You're the one who insisted on living with your ex-husband. You're the one who encouraged me to ask Vicky out when she moved in next door. You can't make me out as the bad guy.'

His voice was rising too, and I could feel my embarrass-ment morphing into anger—an easier emotion to access and discharge.

We stood up, facing each other on opposite sides of the bed, clutching clothes and sheets against our naked bodies as armor.

'I am co-parenting with Stu. I don't want him there, but I'm putting Vivi's needs before my own!'

'And what about my needs?' Ryan's voice raised to match my own. 'I risked my professional reputation when I let you seduce me. I am your *boss*. Do you realize how much trouble I could get in if people found out? Melissa would dissolve the partnership. Even if it is above board and we both consented. Mud will stick. We work in family law, for God's sake. And now you want to just announce it to the world? People will accuse me of sexual harassment.'

'Do you think so little of me that you believe I'd let that happen?'

'What I *thought* of you, Evie, was that you were a hard-working, sensible person. But all of a sudden you're coming and going, seemingly never in the office, and when you do grace us with your presence it's only because you're fitting us in between boozy long lunches. You don't seem to be getting any actual work done anyway. You've been setting a terrible example for Chelsea and Jeremy.'

'Are you giving me a performance appraisal now? Really?'

'To be honest, I don't know who you are anymore Evie. You've been acting very unlike yourself lately. I thought we were just going to have some fun tonight, like we usually do. But you're acting like I've broken a promise to you.'

'Well don't let me stop you having fun!' I shouted, pulling on my clothes. 'I'm sure *Vicky* will be very willing to pick up where I left off.'

I stepped into my shoes, grabbed my bag and walked out of the room.

CHAPTER 30

It was ten thirty-nine when I restarted my car in the parking garage. It had taken just two hours and thirty-two minutes to find and lose the love of my life.

Norman disturbed my thoughts. He reminded me that between the drinks in the bar and the sex in the hotel room I hadn't eaten any dinner.

I was tired of fighting this incessant hunger. I was emotionally exhausted; tortured by Ryan's rejection and ashamed that my soft-focus fantasy was so off the mark. I wanted to feel better. And quickly. I needed comfort. I became obsessed by the idea of a big, greasy burger and fries.

'Fuck it,' I said to no-one. 'Why not.'

I could get fast food on the way home, I thought, reversing out of my car space. But one burger might not be enough to fix this emotional wound. And my skinny body, with its shrunken stomach, could probably not tolerate anything more than one. I might only manage half a burger.

I also didn't need Stu lecturing me about purging tonight. And I didn't want to risk Vivi seeing or hearing that. Besides, it was Ryan's fault I felt compelled to gorge myself, and I'd be damned if it was me who wore the consequences of his cruelty. Why should I be the one to suffer, when this pain was his fault?

I thought of a solution.

As I drove home, a quiet voice in my head pleaded with me to resist the impulse to self-destruct. Stop Evie. Think. But that valiant little voice just made me more frustrated and angry. Self-awareness morphed into self-loathing. Why does my stupid mind always go to stupid food?

It annoyed me to think Ryan would not be driven to comfort eat in this moment. He'd probably be sitting alone, getting drunk. It also annoyed me that, even if he did resort to eating his feelings, it wouldn't make a lick of difference to his waist. Unlike me. If I so much as *smelled* a burger I'd gain five pounds.

It was so fucking unfair. For the millionth time in my life I cursed the gods of body shape, the gods of metabolism, the gods of appetite. Why did they make me this way? Even in this skinny body I couldn't escape their grip.

Well I'd show them. I'd have my burger and eat it too. What was the point of having access to a magic mirror if I didn't use it? I'd sworn to myself I'd only go back to being Fat Me in a crisis. This felt very much like a crisis.

I pulled into my driveway feeling calmer. I'd made my decision.

Stu's car was in the driveway, which meant he and Vivi were back from the cinema. There was no need for my ex to know things had not gone well with my new lover (if he suspected that's where I'd been). I put on a happy face.

'How was dinner?' he asked, when I let myself in.

'Fine thanks. How was the movie?'

'It was OK.'

I wasn't interested in hearing any more details, even if he had been inclined to tell me (which I could see he wasn't, from the way his eyes had already refocused on the TV).

I kept walking down the hall and stopped at Vivi's doorway. She was watching something on her iPad in bed.

'Hi honey, I'm back from dinner now.'

She barely looked up from the screen. 'Hi mom.'

'I'm just going to take a shower, then I'll come and read to you for a bit and tuck you in, OK?'

She rolled her eyes. 'I don't need to be tucked in.'

'I know. Just humor me.'

I continued along the passageway to my bedroom. I quickly showered Ryan off me, then made a beeline for the mirror.

Despite being freshly washed, I looked disheveled. My eyes were swollen and my face was blotchy. But for once I wasn't there to critique my reflection. I was on a mission.

I placed my palms on the mirror and said the words.

CHAPTER 31

I melted through the glass into my old closet. Fat Evie again. Back much sooner than expected.

The bedroom was empty. I was wearing sweatpants and fleecy slippers. I kicked those off my feet and stepped into my Birkenstocks. Sturdy, broad and comfortable.

As I headed to the front door I passed Vivi in her room, still in bed, but now reading a book instead of watching her iPad. She didn't look up as I passed.

From the foyer I could see into the living room. There was Stu, slumped on the couch, watching the same sci-fi series as before, looking slightly more paunchy than his skinny-world self.

I cleared my throat to get his attention. 'I just had a weird craving for a burger, so I'm gonna get one,' I said. It was late to be going out for food, so I felt the need to explain myself. Besides, we weren't separated on this side of the mirror, and there was a greater expectation for marital communication. 'It's this intuitive eating thing—it works best if you listen to the signals your body sends, and I'm getting major Big Mac vibes.'

'Oh, OK. Can you get me one too?'

'Sure can,' I said, pleased to not be alone in my bad choice. 'Won't be long.'

The nearest drive-through was six minutes from my house. I ordered a burger and large fries, a large choco-late thick shake and a caramel sundae for both of us. The aroma in the car as I returned home was heavenly.

I left Stu alone with his meal in the living room and took mine to the closet. Adrenaline was charging through me. My whole attention was focused on the anticipation of that first bite. My mouth watered thinking about the sweetness of the bun, the slightly sour tang of the sauce and the cool crunch of the lettuce contrasted against the warm softness of the beef. I hadn't wasted any time thinking about my re-fattened body. I just wanted that food.

I sat alone, with my back against the mirror. I ate quickly at first, demolishing the burger in five bites, licking the sauce off my fingers with exacting attention, determined to not miss a single drop.

I slowed down once the initial rush of pleasure began to diminish, sighing with relief as I started on the fries, shake and sundae. I closed my eyes, enjoying the taste, the smell, the texture, the feeling of the food in my mouth, and the sensation of swallowing. And then the lazy pleasure of satiety. The feeling of fullness. A stretched belly. It felt like too long since I'd let myself overfeed like this. It was so satisfying.

I wiped my mouth with a paper serviette and stuffed the food wrappings back into the carry bag. I went to the kitchen, put the scrunched-up bag in the trash, and had a huge glass of water. I took a large, squidgy, white chocolate chip cookie from the pantry for good measure, and chewed it on the way back to my room.

I was done.

I stared at my reflection. Although I'd momentarily felt better—had felt glorious, in fact—I was now faced with the wreckage of my binge. My face was flushed. My neck was sweaty from the sudden carb overload. The pupils of my eyes were dilated from the surge of dopamine. And, despite the momentary reprieve from thinking about it while I'd been eating, the memory of Ryan shouting at me now burst back to the front of my brain.

I had no reason to stay here, moping with a tummy ache. I squared my shoulders and pictured myself showing up at work next week looking sensational. I'd make Ryan sorry.

I put my palms back on the mirror and departed the scene of the crime.

CHAPTER 32

I woke with an empty, growling stomach and the heavy feeling of my fight with Ryan throbbing in my head, before the specific memory of his words resurfaced. Then I recalled his face, contorted in anger, yelling at me. I'd never seen him look like that before.

As I lay alone in bed, I thought about my trip back to my real home in Fat Land. Stu's clothes in the closet. His phone charger on his side of the bed. Vivi giggling at a storybook rather than frowning at an iPad.

I felt lonelier on this side of the mirror than ever before. Fabulously thin, but hollowed out.

I was desperate to talk to Lou. To process what had happened—what was still happening—with the benefit of her sensible, clear-headed wisdom. But how could I confide in her about my love life and my mirror life when our own relationship was in tatters.

It was time to put things right.

I called the number she'd used when she rang me that night in the driveway on my first visit to Skinny Land.

No answer.

I sent her a text instead.

Lou, I'm sorry for whatever it was that caused us to stop talking. I need you. Can we please talk? It's important.

I hit send and hoped she'd accept this as the fig leaf I intended it to be.

Fortunately, weekend chores filled my day with mindless activity until my Pilates class with Annika. I was grateful, for the millionth time, for my new friend. She would listen. She wouldn't judge.

After our class I recounted the events of the night before, seeking Annika's affirmation and support. She was kind and gentle, and listened carefully. She didn't criticize or diminish my feelings, and expressed sorrow for my sadness. But I could tell she was holding something back.

'Please,' I said, 'tell me what you're thinking. Nothing you say will make me feel worse than I already do. I just need your honest opinion. Do you think I over-reacted?'

'Oh Evie,' she said.

I could tell she felt uncomfortable, but at last she spoke. 'Relationships are so complicated. What people think they want, and what they really want, can change over time. Maybe you've both just moved in different directions.'

'But don't you think he misled me? He should have mentioned Vicky at the start of the night. Checked I was still OK with the arrangement. He took me for granted. He made me feel like nothing. Like a piece of meat.'

'I can see why you'd feel that way.'

From her tone of voice I sensed a 'but.'

'Go on,' I said. 'Say it.'

'Evie, based on everything you've ever told me, I always thought it was *you* who wanted to keep things open. I know your feelings for him became more serious over time. But in the beginning you made it really clear to him you wanted to keep things casual. I hate to say it, Evie, but I'm not surprised he doesn't see you as a long-term partner. You presented yourself to him as a sex object. Is it a surprise that he treated you as one?'

***

I went to work on Monday as planned. I'd toyed with the idea of working from home, but my pride wouldn't let me. I didn't want Ryan to know how much my heart was breaking; how much power he had over me.

Despite my vow on Saturday night to make him regret letting me go, I couldn't face the sex kitten look. I rifled through my clothes to find plain trousers, which I paired with a dark green blouse. I found some old black ballet flats behind my pairs of shiny heels. Rather than blowing out my hair, I tied it back in a ponytail. It felt perversely good to be back in my old work uniform.

Ryan was at his desk when I arrived. I ignored the anxious churning in my stomach and didn't make eye contact with him. I went straight to my desk.

Through the day we kept our distance as much as possible. There was some inevitable but polite discussion of work issues, but no chit chat and no allusion to the events of Saturday night.

Late in the afternoon, Ryan sauntered over to Jeremy's desk, just steps from my door. I could hear every word of their conversation, which I quickly realized was the whole point. He had his back to me. I could see Jeremy's face if I looked up from my screen, but I pretended to focus on my work. I kept my eyes glued to my monitor while I listened to them talk.

'Jeremy, I was thinking we should include some photos from the Law Ball in our quarterly client newsletter. Could you prepare an article for that please?'

'Yeah, no worries. When do you need it by?'

'Oh, no rush, next week would be fine. We can mention how much money we raised for the shelter.'

'Great idea. I could include their contact details and encourage people to make further donations,' said Jeremy.

'Excellent suggestion.' Ryan paused, and I sensed him turn his head slightly in my direction. 'That was a great night, wasn't it? But kind of a shame the ball wasn't held *this* month.'

'Why's that?' asked Jeremy.

'Well, it would have been a great opportunity to introduce everyone to Vicky.'

Jeremy's voice was full of good-natured interest. 'Have you started seeing someone, boss?'

'I have,' said Ryan, purring like the cat with the cream. He spoke a bit lower, as if confiding a secret. 'We've actually been together for a while now, but I've been keeping it quiet. Haven't wanted to deal with gossip, you know, in case it didn't work out. But it's getting more serious now. We've decided we're ready to go public.'

'Man, that's great. Congratulations,' said Jeremy, and I could see them shaking hands in my peripheral vision.

I scoffed. It was beneath Ryan to use Jeremy like that, as a prop in a juvenile effort to hurt me. I wouldn't dignify it with a response.

I sat up straight in my chair and put my headset on. I started a video call with our payroll contractor while they kept talking. I wouldn't give Ryan the satisfaction of seeing me upset when he turned around (as I was sure he would) to gauge my reaction.

CHAPTER 33

Over the coming days, my anger morphed into sadness and regret. My dreams of a future with Ryan had suffered a setback, but our fight had only reinforced to me how deep my feelings for him truly were.

Now that we were no longer together I wanted him even more.

True, I didn't know what 'together' had ever meant, given the strange amorphous arrangement we'd shared in this skinny world. But the implosion of that arrangement grieved me.

I missed the innocent happy lunches we'd become accustomed to in the fat world. I hoped, over time, we could get back to that place, and then, maybe a bit more slowly, a bit more publicly, we could take things to the next level.

I ignored the fact of Vicky. I ignored the fact of Stu. I channeled Scarlett O'Hara and decided to worry about those things another day.

Besides, I had other important problems to solve if I was going to stay on this side of the mirror. First, I needed to get my sister back.

Lou hadn't responded to any of the texts or voicemails I'd left for her.

I called our mom for advice. She sighed over the phone. 'Darling, I promised both of you I wouldn't get involved. But I wish you *would* work it out. Christmas just hasn't been the same since you girls had your tiff.'

'Do you remember how it started?' I asked, too tired to pretend I knew what was going on.

'Oh gosh, it was such a long time ago. I think it had something to do with your diet, sweetheart, but I don't remember the details I'm sorry.'

'Well that doesn't sound like anything that would justify a decade-long estrangement. Why wouldn't she be happy for me losing some weight and getting healthy?'

'I don't know, darling. I think there may have been an important party you missed or something. It's all very hazy I'm afraid.'

'Don't worry, mom. It actually doesn't matter why we're fighting. What matters is that we stop fighting.'

'It would mean the world to me if you could do that.'

'Well, I can't promise Lou will come around, but I really want to make things up with her,' I said.

Despite my pleading, though, mom wouldn't give me Lou's number. She said she'd promised not to, unless it was an emergency. So I resorted to good old-fashioned cyber-stalking. A simple Google search quickly told me where to find her.

To my surprise, the Lou on this side of the mirror didn't operate her photography business from a corner of her living room. She had a gallery downtown. In this skinny world, it appeared, Lou was a phenomenally successful photographer.

Huh, I thought, we both got what we most desired on this side of the mirror. Or, at least, what we *thought* we most desired. I got skinny and Lou achieved professional acclaim.

The following day I skipped the gym at lunchtime and drove to the gallery to talk to her.

Sitting in my car outside, I braced myself for her reaction when she saw me walk in uninvited.

I hated confrontation, and nearly drove off. But Saturday night's stupid burger binge had used up my second trip through the mirror. I was now playing my last hand. My third trip. I either fixed things in this life so I could stay, or I'd have to go back to being fat forever.

And for some reason it was important to me that Lou and I mended this rift, even if I didn't stay here. I hated the idea of our relationship being fractured anywhere in time and space, or whatever parallel universe this was.

I took a deep breath and walked inside.

The gallery was deserted. I circled the perimeter, looking at Lou's pictures. They were unmistakably her work—I was so familiar with her style—but they were more sophisticated and accomplished than I'd seen before.

Her images were predominantly landscapes, but she'd started taking portraits too. My heart swelled with pride as I took in each photograph, amazed at the subtle but powerful ways she conveyed her subjects' characters and life experience just using light and shade and composition. It was astonishing.

I heard some movement behind me and turned around. 'What are you doing here?'

'Oh Lou, these pictures are incredible,' I said. 'Really so good.'

'Thanks,' her voice was cool, 'but I'm sure you didn't come here to discuss my work.'

I cleared my throat. 'No, you're right. I want to...' I took a breath. My mouth was dry. 'I don't know how to say it, so I'll just say it. I miss you, Lou. I miss having you as my sister. I miss seeing you every week and talking to you every day. I want you back. I don't care about the past. I want to do whatever I can to fix things.'

'So you just show up out of the blue and expect we can pick up where we left off? You couldn't call to check if this was a convenient time?'

'Well, I think you blocked my number.'

Lou was quiet for a moment. 'I guess that's a fair point.'

She sighed deeply, seeming to weigh up the cost to herself of hearing me out. 'Listen, I have an appointment here in 40 minutes, so you'll need to be gone by then. But I suppose we can go to my office to discuss things until then.'

My heart leapt at this glimmer of rapprochement.

I followed her to the office—a windowless room along the back wall of the gallery—and sat where she pointed.

'So,' she said, inviting me to say my piece.

'Well, it's kind of a long story, but I've recently suffered some amnesia—I'm fine—but there are still some…gaps… in my memory. When I texted you the other week, when you called to tell me not to contact you, well, I'd forgotten we'd had a falling out. I still can't remember it, actually. I just can't imagine what could have happened to make us stop talking.'

'Amnesia? Have you seen a doctor?'

'I've been talking to a psychologist,' I said, thinking of Annika. Technically it wasn't a lie, and I didn't want to complicate this delicate conversation with fantastical tales of magic mirrors.

'And you really don't remember our fight?'

I shook my head.

'Well Evie, it was your idea that we have some distance, and I'm not sure I can shed much light on what *you* were thinking. From my perspective I thought things with us were fine. I thought you were happy. You'd just got a job at that law firm…'

'I still work there,' I said.

'…and you'd lost a lot of weight. Then I started to get worried about how much weight you'd lost. The way you were talking, it sounded to me like you had an eating disorder.'

I winced with embarrassment, knowing there was no reason to feel ashamed about mental illness but feeling the stigma anyway.

'At first you were fine. But then you became obsessed. It was literally all you talked about. It became boring. Then it became tedious. And then it became pathological. You wouldn't relax your rules for anything. I mean anything. Not for my wedding, not for mom and dad's fortieth anniversary, not for your own birthday. And you were so sanctimonious and judgmental about everyone else's eating. You sucked all the fun from our lives.'

I didn't know what to say, so I said nothing.

'And the thing was, if I thought it made you happier, being skinny, then I probably would have been OK with it. But you seemed miserable. Always cranky. And you didn't look healthy to me. You became so drawn and grey. Your hair started falling out. Everyone else congratulated you about losing weight, but I never did. I challenged you about it. I think that's why you pushed me away.'

'For challenging me?'

'Yes. I think you knew I was right and you didn't want to hear it. I was worried you were losing weight for all the wrong reasons. Not because you wanted to, but because you felt obligated to.'

'Obligated? By whom?'

'By society. By mom and dad. Though they'd never say so, they're very preoccupied with good health. Maybe you felt like you'd disappointed them by getting fat. And obligated by your profession too, and its expectation that you need to look a certain way to project success. Even by me, maybe.'

'By you?'

'Well, subconsciously at least. When we were at school, I was embarrassed you were fat.' She looked at me sadly. 'In my defense, I was just a kid myself. But still, you must have sensed that. It couldn't have been good for you to sense that.'

A feeling of panic suddenly rose in my belly. An event I hadn't thought about for decades surfaced in my mind. I blinked it away. I wanted Lou to finish saying what she had to say.

'Anyway, I kept challenging you about picking at your food like a bird, and doing two hours of cardio a day, and never accepting my invitations to lunch or dinner. You became obsessed. Single-minded.'

I nearly interrupted her to say 'You have to be single-minded if you want to lose weight,' but I didn't want to prove her point.

'So we started to drift apart. And then you decided to skip my thirtieth birthday so you could run a marathon.'

'I did?'

'You don't remember? We had a fight about it beforehand. I'd booked a weekend away for all of us to go skiing. You wanted to do this stupid marathon that was on the same weekend, because you'd set yourself a challenge of running one race each month for a year. I suggested you could run it on a different day, on your own, without other people or time-keepers, but you said it wouldn't count. By this time we'd been fighting about your dieting for a long time. That was the last straw. So I gave you an ultimatum, and you chose the marathon. It was a pretty bad fight. We both said ugly things.'

Lou stopped. She didn't sound angry. It seemed like she had processed her feelings about my rejection years ago.

'And we haven't spoken since?'

'Barely.'

I sat back in my chair, thinking about how to respond. Finally I spoke. My heart was hammering in my chest.

'I agree I have an unhealthy focus on my appearance, and that I've been more rigid about food and exercise than I perhaps intended when I first tried to lose weight. As for *why* I wanted to lose weight, the simple truth is I got sick and tired of feeling sick and tired. I know that's a cliché, but it's true. I felt lousy. And I was scared I'd never attract a partner. And I was so sad I couldn't wear the nice clothes my friends were wearing. It sounds shallow when I say it like that. But I was miserable when I was fat. It was on my mind constantly. Every single day. Even when I was focusing on other things it was always there, like my shadow. Any time I walked into a room I'd automatically check to see if I was the fattest person there. Random strangers said horrible things to me. I couldn't enjoy simple things like wearing a sleeveless top on a hot day. It was awful. For years it was awful. And then by some miracle I managed to lose weight. It was so hard, but the thrill of getting smaller kept me going. Then, once I lost it, it was even harder to keep it off. It felt like I had to exercise more and more *and* eat less and less just to stay in the same place, to maintain what I'd lost. It was exhausting. I felt so tired and grumpy.'

'Hangry,' said Lou.

'Yes, exactly. What I'm saying is, it took every ounce of willpower and self-discipline to get this body and hold on to it. I *had* to become rigid. I couldn't afford to expose myself to any temptation. If I relaxed my resolve for one moment, I might never get it back.'

'But so what if you never got it back? Why does it even matter if you're fat?' she said.

'That's easy for you to say, in your thin, easy body. Didn't you hear what I just said about how hard things were?'

'But those hard things were because of other people's reactions to you. Couldn't you put your energy toward fighting them about their attitudes instead of fighting yourself about the body shape you were born with?'

'But I wasn't born that way—that's the point. I can control being fat if I work at it.'

'At a very high cost. That's a steep price to pay, to ensure strangers are kind to you.'

I could feel myself getting angry. This was just a theoretical argument for Lou.

'You must understand why I was embarrassed about myself. You just said *you* were embarrassed about me too.'

Lou flushed and looked at her lap. 'Well, that was a long time ago. But I'm still sorry. I should have had your back.'

'What do you mean? You never let me down.'

Suddenly Lou looked away, and I realized she was getting emotional. She said quietly, 'You don't remember Mr Dunn?'

That flash of panic came back to me. Mr Dunn. 'Oh my God,' I whispered, 'I'd forgotten. I must have blocked it out.'

***

Coopers Creek School. Two hundred and fifty children stood in rows of varying uniformity under the sun. It was Monday, nearly lunchtime. Half assembly day. Full assembly happened once a month in the school auditorium. But every other Monday we stood together for a shorter reading of notices and sports results.

For a kid not interested in sport, or in need of reminders to return permission notes, I tended to tune out during these deadly dull convocations.

On this particular day when I was 10 years old, I'd stopped listening even though it was Mr Dunn's turn to host the proceedings.

Mr Dunn was very old—maybe 50—and was Santa Claus fat. But there was nothing jolly about him. He was the scariest teacher at school. He had a few strings of frizzled grey hair slicked down on his bald head. His skin was red and mottled. His neck was like a pelican's gullet. His eyes were small but magnified by the thick lenses of his square plastic spectacles. He wore dirty white button-down shirts with brown shorts, long white socks and sandals. I remember the shirt buttons from his naval to his belt gaping apart, exposing a stained greyish singlet beneath.

Looking back now, Mr Dunn's red face was probably caused by a mixture of alcohol, sunburn and depression. But back then, we attributed it to anger. He had the shortest fuse of any adult we'd ever known. And although limited in our experience of the world, we, the children of Coopers Creek, were adept at sensing danger. Mr Dunn reeked of danger.

I should have been paying more attention.

My lack of focus became apparent a few minutes into assembly, when Mr Dunn told everyone to sit down. I remained standing, daydreaming about going for a swim after school.

Everyone stared at me, and a few kids giggled. I could hear Lou's voice somewhere nearby, hissing 'sit down Evie.' But it was too late. Mr Dunn had noticed.

He must have been having a bad day because this should have been treated as a minor lapse from an otherwise obedient child.

But he reared back with affected shock and outrage.

'Just what do you think you are doing, Evelyn Swan?' he shouted. 'Are you special, are you? Do the rules not apply to you?' He wielded his sarcasm like a whip.

I quickly sat down with my classmates, but he wasn't having it.

'Oh no you don't!' he yelled. 'Get up this instant.' I stood again, heart racing, face aflame. 'Come here. You will stand by this wall so I can see you're paying attention.' He pointed to the brick wall of the classroom behind him.

Assembly continued, and Mr Dunn continued with his list of announcements. I was blinking back tears, determined not to cry in front of my classmates. But it was so hot. Gradually my feet shuffled backwards until my back was pressed against the wall. And then I was leaning on the bricks.

Mr Dunn turned around and saw me not standing to attention.

'You will stand up straight, young lady,' he roared. 'Don't you dare lean against that wall. You're so fat you'll knock it over.'

He turned back to his notes, pushed his glasses back up his nose, wiped his forehead with a handkerchief and muttered under his breath. Then he resumed the litany of instructions.

The children sitting in front of me mostly stared in their laps and avoided my eyes. But some of them laughed, heads together, whispering about me. I sought out Lou's face in the crowd. She saw me, then looked the other way, perhaps trying to pretend we weren't related.

I stood there, focusing on the shine the sun was casting on my recently polished black shoes, and decided I must have misheard what he said. He wouldn't have called me fat in front of the whole school, would he? I wasn't fat, was I?

***

'I remember now what he said,' I told Lou.

'I'm so sorry, Evie,' she reached forward now and took my hand. 'I was your big sister, and it was my job to protect you. And I didn't. I wanted to punch his lights out. I wanted to stand up and scream that he was a disgrace, and everyone hated him. But I didn't do it. I didn't say anything because I was scared he'd pick on me too.'

We sat quietly for a moment. The gallery's door jingled open.

Lou looked toward the noise. 'I think that's my meeting.' She called out toward the door, 'I'll be right there!'

I kept watching her, remembering our childhood. 'Lou, I forgive you. What Mr Dunn did wasn't your fault. You were just a kid. The other teachers should have protected me. At least things have changed since then. If he did that today he'd be fired.'

'And rightly so. I know rationally it wasn't my fault,' said Lou, 'but the feeling that I let you down is still there. I guess that's why I've always been so weird about you trying to lose weight. Maybe I liked the idea of you being proud of your fat body because it would be the ultimate fuck you to the likes of Mr Dunn.'

'Maybe,' I said. 'But life isn't that simple. I'm the one who has to live in this body, and it's hard work carrying around so much fat, no matter how theoretically satisfying it might be to disrupt people's ideas of beauty.'

'But you're not carrying around fat, Evie,' said Lou. 'You did the impossible. You lost weight and kept it off. Do you know how rare that is?'

I shook my head. 'I might be thin here,' I patted my belly, 'but I'll always be fat here.' I tapped my temple.

Lou looked anxiously at the door again. 'I'm sorry, but I have to go.'

'Yes, I know. That's OK. Thank you for talking to me. Can we have lunch next week?'

'Yes, I'd like that. I'll text you.' She returned to the gallery.

CHAPTER 34

I knocked on Annika's door, not sure if she was home, but bursting to tell her about my breakthrough with Lou.

'Evie, come in!' she smiled when she saw me at her door. I followed her in, reminding myself that I needed to pretend I'd been in her house before. I wasn't sure if I had, but I should err on the side of caution. If I decided to stay—and I was still deciding—then I'd probably come clean to Annika about the mirror. But I wasn't ready for that quite yet.

Annika's house was, like its owner, beautiful and welcoming. The large spaces were painted a warm white, which reflected sunshine into the furthest corners, a natural mood booster.

'I've just put the kettle on for some green tea. Would you like some?' asked Annika, leading me to her kitchen. I couldn't remember tasting green tea before, but I knew I liked regular black tea with milk, so I didn't see much risk in saying yes. It sounded like the kind of thing Skinny Evie would drink.

Annika placed a colorful mug before me, with the pale green liquid steaming within. She hadn't offered or added milk. I blew some heat off the top and took a sip. It was surprisingly refreshing—a clean taste. I made a mental note of the brand of teabags sitting on the counter. I'd try to find some on my next trip to the market.

'So what's up?' asked Annika. 'I thought you'd be at work this time of day.'

'I was, but I called in sick this afternoon. Something amazing just happened.'

'Oh wow. Nothing bad, I hope?'

'No, just the opposite. I went to see my sister, Louise. And she didn't kick me out. We actually talked. We're going to have lunch next week. I'm just so happy, Annika. Far too excited to go back to work.'

'Oh Evie, that's wonderful!' Annika put down her mug and came around the island counter to give me a hug. 'I always knew you'd both work it out eventually.'

'I think it helped that I just decided to let the past stay in the past.'

'Still, it takes a lot of work to reach that point. I'm proud of you.'

'Thanks.'

'I hope I get to meet her. You should have a party for your fortieth and have us all get together.'

'That's a great idea! It's still ages away. Who knows where we'll be then. But I like the idea of having a party.'

Annika's dog started yapping madly and a few seconds later her doorbell rang.

'I must have a delivery, sorry,' she called over her shoulder as she raced to the front door.

While I waited for her to come back I took the opportunity to look around the kitchen, which was very neat but homely. Annika had achieved a lovely balance in her décor. It was clean-lined, modern and cozy.

But it wasn't too perfect. I was pleased to see Annika's refrigerator cluttered with magnets and papers, after-hours plumbers' numbers, emergency doctor details, a shopping list and photographs.

I examined the photos curiously. I still hadn't met Annika's partner, Charlie—he seemed to be a phantom. A workaholic, always at the office or travelling for work. I searched the photos to get a sense of what he looked like.

But there were only three pictures, and all of them were women. There was Annika embracing an attractive short-haired woman on a beach. I wondered if that might be her sister. They looked very affectionate.

There was a photograph of a cute baby, about eight months old.

And there was a photograph of an obese woman in her twenties with a very strong resemblance to Annika. I wondered if she was another sister, or a cousin perhaps.

Annika returned to the kitchen carrying a parcel. 'Oh, my day's taken a happy turn too, Evie! I found this amazing dress in an online sale. Sixty per cent off! I hope it fits me.'

'Well open it, I want to see!'

'Do you mind?' she asked, clearly keen to inspect her purchase.

'Go on!'

Annika pulled scissors from a nearby drawer and neatly bisected the tape on the plastic package. Satiny champagne-colored fabric fell out of the tissue paper within, and Annika held the dress up against her body.

'Well, I'm definitely going to need you to have a birthday party now, so I have somewhere to wear it.' She smiled and held the dress up to examine it. 'There's nothing like a pretty dress to lift my spirits.'

'Me too,' I laughed, once again understanding how well matched we were as friends. 'So, I was admiring your photos here. Who's the cute baby?' I asked, hoping she hadn't previously told me.

'Ah, that's Thomas, my godson. Isn't he divine? I went to grad school with his mom back in Copenhagen. That's where they live, so I haven't met him in person yet. But maybe next year.'

'And here you are on the beach with…'

'Charlie. That was the last time I was able to get her to take a break from work, and it's more than a year ago. Can you believe it?'

I flushed with the realization that Annika's partner was a woman. I tried to remember if I'd used male pronouns in my recent conversations with Annika, but I think I'd gotten away with it. Phew—that was a close call. Just when I'd start getting comfortable in this mirror world, I'd be reminded every now and then how little I knew.

'And who's this?' I pointed to the obese young woman.

Annika stared at me strangely.

'Pardon?'

'Sorry, my memory is so terrible. You might have told me before, but I've forgotten. Is she a relative? I can see a resemblance.'

'Evie, that's me.'

CHAPTER 35

I stifled a gasp and looked at the photo again. The woman's face definitely looked like Annika's—same eyes, nose and mouth. But that was where the resemblance ended. Her hair was much lighter and her body was even heavier than my own on the fat side of the mirror.

'Oh,' I stammered, trying to think of a way to cover myself. 'Now that you mention it, I think I have seen this before, but I must have forgotten. I'm so used to seeing you like this,' I gestured toward her, 'that I don't associate you with…being large.'

'Being fat, you mean. I'm very comfortable with that word. You don't need to use euphemisms with me. "Fat" was hurled at me as a weapon for so many years that its impact quickly blunted. It never offended me. It was a fact. What offended me more was people looking away or trying to pretend I wasn't fat.'

'Why did that offend you?'

'Because it felt like they were being polite, not authentic, as if I needed special treatment. I don't know. It's hard to explain.'

'What about your parents? Did they pretend you weren't fat?'

'God no. My dad's nickname for me is still 'Fatty,' and my mom sent me to Weight Watchers when I was 12. I think she thought me being fat made her look like a bad parent.'

'Yikes, that's tough. I was chubby as a kid too.'

'Really? I didn't know that. You'd never know from looking at you.'

'I could say the same.' We both laughed. I hid my embarrassment with a sip of tea.

'So, tell me about Louise,' Annika said. 'I want a blow-by-blow account.'

Later, at home, it occurred to me that I hadn't asked Annika how she lost all that weight. I suppose I didn't ask because the answer seemed obvious. Eat less, move more. Everyone knew that.

***

After dinner Stu and I streamed a new show on Netflix. As we settled into our adjacent couches he looked at me guiltily.

'What's the matter?' I asked, smiling.

He pulled a face. 'I know you hate it when I ask this, but do you mind if I open a bag of chips while we're watching?'

I laughed and wondered how hard it must have been for him to live for so long with my food fascism. 'Well, that depends,' I said.

'On what?'

'On the flavor. You know I'm not keen on Sour Cream and Chives.'

Stu leaped up and ran to the kitchen, returning with a bag of plain salted chips, classic and delicious, and a large bowl to pour them in.

'I didn't see those in the cupboard,' I said.

He looked sheepish. 'I hid them behind the self-raising flour. You bake so infrequently that I figured that was a safe place.'

'Hey Stu, I'm sorry I've been so selfish about my eating regime. Please feel free to eat what you want, when you want. It's not right for me to impose rules on you. Especially now that we're, you know, separated.'

Stu looked at me—I think it was the first proper eye contact we'd made since I'd come back to the skinny side. 'Thanks,' he said. 'Funnily enough, I don't mind your strict rules at home, because I eat pretty badly at work. Lots of fast food and chocolate. So it's good to come home and detox each night. But I agree—no more hiding of stuff.' He shook the chips into the bowl. 'Are you going to have some?'

I hesitated for a second but didn't want to break this small moment of connection. 'Yeah, why not?'

The TV show was a gripping three-parter, and we ended up bingeing all episodes, demolishing not just the chips but a bowl of ice cream each and a bottle of wine too. When it was over and we were clearing away our dishes, Stu asked me if I was taking a break from my diet.

'No, I just felt like celebrating today.' He raised his eyebrows as if asking for more information, so I told him about my meeting with Lou.

'Evie, that's so great,' he said. 'I'm genuinely happy for you.'

He moved toward me for a hug. And suddenly it felt like I was back in my normal life. Good old annoying Stu, smelling like home. Messy, chaotic but comfortable. I looked up at him, smiling. And then we kissed. Lightly and sweetly. He pulled away quickly.

'Sorry Evie, sorry.'

'No, that's OK.'

'We shouldn't—it will confuse Vivi.'

'Yeah, you're right.' We looked at each other a moment longer. 'Well, good night,' I said, and went to my room. I lay awake for a while, wondering if there was a chance I could reconcile with Stu in this world. For a few hours things had been so pleasant. But was 'pleasant' enough?

I decided I didn't need to decide that night. Instead, I surrendered to the wine and went to sleep.

CHAPTER 36

Saturday morning was cloudy and cool. Perfect weather to spend in a mall. Vivi and I left Stu watching football on the TV and drove to the atrium-spined fashion mall near our house.

'What do you need?' I asked.

'I don't know,' said Vivi. 'Everything.'

'Well, let's start at the top, and work our way down,' I suggested, looking up at the glass-framed sky above. 'You point out things you like, and we'll see how we go.'

We walked together up an escalator to the third floor, where a conspiracy of boutiques and fast fashion chains lay waiting for us.

It had been a while since I'd taken Vivi to buy clothes. Sometimes I'd pick up a new pair of jeans or some cute t-shirts for her in the next size up when I was out getting things for myself, and Vivi had worn them unquestioningly, seemingly unaware she could influence what clothes her mother bought her. As a result, her clothes tended to the little girlish—larger versions of the sweet toddler outfits she'd worn since she could walk. But now she was 10 and starting to realize, through school friends, through YouTube and through advertising, that there was a thing called fashion and a thing called personal style.

I was curious to see what would catch her eye. Would she tend to goth or punk or sporty or tomboy or painted-on-eyebrow Instagram influencer? I feared it may be the latter. I steered us into Zara Kids to start. Vivi walked around with a happy look on her face, feeling the fabrics, gazing at the mannequins, tapping her fingers to the beat of the booming soundtrack enveloping us. Eventually she pointed at a girl-sized mannequin wearing a short sequined skirt, with a t-shirt knotted at the waist, a denim jacket and cowboy boots. I felt a secret swell of pride. It was cool, but age appropriate. What good taste my girl had.

'Do you want to try this on? The skirt?'

'Can we try the whole outfit?'

'OK, I guess so.' I walked to the rack where the skirts were hanging. '8, 12, 14—oh, it looks like they don't have any 10s in stock. How about you try the 12?'

'No, try the 8.'

'What? That'll be too small. Or if it fits you now, you'll grow out of it too fast. Here.' I handed Vivi the kids' size 12 in a non-negotiable motherly way. 'We can put a belt on if it's a bit loose.'

'No,' said Vivi, starting to sound impatient. 'That's not my size.'

I sighed. I could tell when she was working up to a mood. 'It doesn't matter what the label says. It's just a number.' I held the skirt against her belly. 'I actually think it might be close to fitting you anyway. Come on, let's find the t-shirt and try them together.'

Vivi followed behind me through the store, but her demeanor had darkened. Before, she had been almost bouncing with excitement as she flitted from rack to rack. Now her feet dragged, and she scowled. I was determined not to pander to this tantrum. I walked ahead of her with the relaxed confidence of a thin person in a shop where everything would fit.

***

Vivi made me stand outside the changing room as she pulled on the skirt. 'Have you got it on yet?' I asked through the curtain.

'Just a minute,' came her muffled voice. She sounded like she was putting on the t-shirt.

'Well? Let me see.'

Vivi pulled back the curtain, looking dejected. I thought she looked adorable. The size 12 skirt fitted her beautifully. I also noticed, with shock, tiny breast buds emerging under the thin fabric of the t-shirt. Already? Surely not. I felt a complicated mix of sadness and excitement.

'Oh Vivi, you look great!' I smiled.

'I hate it!'

'What? Why?' I was genuinely surprised.

She yanked at the side of the skirt. 'It's a size 12, mom. And I don't even need a belt. I'm only 10. I am so fat!' She folded her arm contemptuously.

'Rubbish!' I said. 'You are *not* fat. You're lovely.'

Oh God, Evie, can you hear yourself, I thought. Are you saying fat people aren't lovely? But I pressed on, eager to bolster Vivi's confidence. 'Sizes on clothes are never standard. My clothes are all kinds of sizes. What counts is how they look on you. And how they feel.'

It sounded good but I wasn't sure I truly believed it either.

'I'm only 10. I need the size 10.'

'Sweetie, the sizes are approximate. This is made for kids your age.'

'I'm 10 years old, mom. The size 12 shouldn't fit me. But whatever. I know I'm gross.'

Vivi turned and looked in the mirror, turning from side to side, twisting to see her bottom. I felt a sudden, overwhelming weariness. A deep sadness. Vivi looked up at me through the mirror.

'I bet this would fit you,' she said.

'What? Don't be ridiculous. I'm a grown woman.'

'Go on then, prove it.' She jutted out her jaw. 'Prove I'm not a disgusting whale.'

'Oh Vivi, let's not do this. You don't have to buy the skirt if you don't want it.'

'I want you to put it on, mom. I want you to see how fat I am. How hideous.'

I shook my head, conscious the people around us were starting to listen. 'You're heading into puberty honey. Your body's growing. You'll settle into yourself eventually.'

'What? So you *do* think I'm fat. C'mon, try it on.' Vivi stepped out of the skirt angrily and thrust it at me.

'Vivienne Michelle, I'm starting to get cross with you.'

'You're *scared* to try it on,' said Vivi, who had started to cry. 'You're scared you'll see that you're skinnier than me, and it'll make you happy. I remember all those times when you said you wished they made my clothes in your size.'

'Honey, I was joking—I just thought they were cute. I didn't really mean that I wanted to wear them. I don't want to be as small as a child.'

'Really?' Vivi sounded skeptical.

'Vivi,' I rubbed my temple. She stared back at me, angry, elevated.

'If you don't try this on I'm…I'm…I'm going to tell dad about your boyfriend.' My heart stopped.

'What did you say?'

Vivi shut the change room curtain in my face.

***

We sat silently in the car, each staring out opposite windows. After Vivi's dramatic outburst, I'd stepped into the cubicle while she violently wrenched her old jeans and well-worn t-shirt back on. I'd wordlessly rehung the sequined skirt and t-shirt on the rack, then grabbed Vivi by the wrist, pulling her firmly out of the shop and back to the carpark.

Now in the car, Vivi couldn't run away, and I couldn't be embarrassed by strangers overhearing any more shocking declarations.

I sat in silence, a turmoil of guilt and anger, wondering how to have this out. I still thought of Vivi as a baby. How was it that we were having such a grown-up conversation? I couldn't imagine how she knew about Ryan. I'd always been so careful. Hadn't I? The gaps in my knowledge about this thin world broke over me like thunder.

I was shocked Vivi was even aware of extramarital sex as a concept, let alone capable of joining barely visible dots to reach a conclusion about her mother's guilt.

I decided to prod further before I confessed to anything, to find out what and how Vivi knew.

'Honey, I'm so sad our day has turned out like this. I thought we were going to have fun together. Do you think we can talk about how you're feeling?'

Vivi shrugged but didn't say anything.

'You seemed to get upset about the skirt fitting you, but then you I said have a boyfriend. I just… I'm just confused about that. Where that comes from. What did you mean?'

She looked at me.

'I saw you,' she said. My mind whirled, trying to imagine where Vivi could possibly have seen me with Ryan. Maybe it was a time, pre-mirror-swap, when Fat Evie was safely (and chastely) in her fat world. Maybe Skinny Evie had been careless.

'It was at my school awards night. I saw you kiss him. And he was rubbing your back.'

'Who was?' I was still mystified.

'Mr Scullin. I saw how you looked at each other. And he whispered in your ear, and you laughed, then he went out of the room and a few minutes later you went out the same way.'

I tried to keep a straight face, relief and absurdity mixing together.

'Andrew Scullin? Your school teacher? Oh Vivi, he was just being friendly because I'd helped get a donation from my work for one of the prizes. Honey, look at me.'

Vivi was blushing but looked at me with a hopeful expression.

'Vivi, I promise you. Mr Scullin is not my boyfriend. What made you think that?'

'You did that thing. I've seen you do it before. You don't do it when you talk to girls. You talk sort of funny with boys, and you stand sort of funny.'

She was describing flirting.

'I guess when I talk to people, I'm trying to put them at ease, so I act friendlier toward them than maybe I really feel. Does that make sense?'

'So it's not true then? You don't have a boyfriend? You and daddy aren't getting divorced?'

I looked directly at Vivi and chose my words carefully. 'Vivi, I want to tell you three things that are true. Number one: Mr Scullin is not and has never been my boyfriend. Number two: daddy and I might get divorced. But whether we do or we don't doesn't change the fact that we both love you so much and always will. Our fights are never your fault and are never about you. Do you understand that? Never. Sometimes moms and dads decide they don't want to live together anymore. But they never stop being a family. OK?'

Vivi looked at me, still guarded. 'OK.'

I smiled and pulled a lock of hair off her face.

'What was the third thing?'

'What? Oh, number three.' I looked at her very seriously. 'You looked *really* good in that skirt, and I want to go back and buy it for you.'

Vivi smiled, as if she'd been carrying the secret of my infidelity for a while and that weight had now been lifted from her.

I felt relieved Ryan and I had broken up before this conversation. Technically I wasn't having an affair and I hadn't lied to Vivi. But I knew that was a flimsy basis for feeling off the hook. It was just lucky timing.

'What d'you say?' I said, hoping the distraction of the skirt would get me out of this hot water.

'OK,' she said. 'But can we cut the tag out? So no-one knows how big it is?'

'Of course, darling,' I said. 'It'll be our secret.'

Out of the car, I put my arm across Vivi's shoulders and pulled her in for a side hug as we walked. I really needed a coffee.

CHAPTER 37

My words to Vivi came back to me as I packed for my vacation a few days later. Did I really believe what I'd told her, that it's not what size you are but how you feel that matters? If I really believed that, why was I worrying, in this moment, that the tiny pinch of fat on my belly was now a moderate pinch of fat.

I realized I'd gained some weight as I was sorting through the summer shorts and bikinis I wanted to take with me. The microscopic scale of the bikinis was an overt challenge to my new-found body confidence. Did I dare wear them?

I thought about my weekly lunches with Renae, which had started to become a bit of a free-for-all. Those lunches were meals I looked forward to days in advance. But I was otherwise doing OK. There'd only been that one lapse with Stu, that night we shared potato chips and ice cream in front of the TV. Apart from that I'd been sticking to Skinny Evie's carefully prepped and portioned frozen meals. I'd been supplementing them with fruit, to appease Norman.

But fruit was healthy, I figured. No one ever got fat eating fruit, did they?

Now, as I held up an impossibly small two-piece, I wondered if I'd been a bit too relaxed. Angelica had warned me I'd wear the consequences of my choices here.

I decided to weigh myself. I'd been avoiding the scale since the night I'd come back and seen myself shrunk to just 114 pounds. Since then I'd avoided the scale on principle, reveling in the fact I was finally free from its tyrannical bad-day-making powers. I'd been using my clothes as my gauge, and they mostly still fit.

A familiar anxiety returned as I stepped on the scale. There should be a word for that feeling; that moment in those few seconds between stepping on a scale and its verdict being revealed. It was a kind of suspense that deserved its own terminology. Something ominous and German-sounding.

These thoughts were a momentary distraction. I was now focused on the number on the scale. One hundred twenty-four pounds. I'd gained ten pounds since I came back to the skinny side just over a month ago. That seemed quick. Maybe all that fruit hadn't been a good idea.

Despite this gain, I still looked thin and healthy. Maybe I was closer to a size six now, than a four. I could live with that. Like the well-worn reflex it was, I resolved that after the Gold Coast I'd get back on the wagon. Order the salad when I met Renae for lunch, and only have one or two pieces of fruit a day instead of three or four. That wouldn't be so hard. I wasn't beyond a point of no return.

I tried on the impossibly small bikini. It fit me—just—but the spaghetti-thin straps cut uncomfortably into my skin and I felt indecently exposed. Weight gain or not, I couldn't wear this. It was something I might have considered in my twenties, but not now. I went back to the swimwear drawer and found some more substantial bikinis, with fuller briefs, which I packed in my bag.

I sat back, satisfied. Despite those extra ten pounds, for the first time I could remember as an adult, I was actually looking forward to going to the beach.

***

I stood near the self-serve check-in kiosks at the airport, scanning the cavernous space for my travel buddy. Excitement echoed off the tiled floors and glass walls. Eventually Renae arrived, dragging a pair of vintage suitcases behind her.

I couldn't wait for this change of scene—away from Stu and away from Ryan. I wanted to stop thinking about both of them.

The only dent in my mood was a slight apprehension about leaving Vivi. It was only a few nights, and I knew she'd be fine, but it was still unsettling to be so far from her. I couldn't imagine how I'd cope if I had to share care with Stu and have her away from me for a week at a stretch. I figured I'd get used to that if I had to, but I started to appreciate better why he and I had agreed on the whole living-together-but-apart thing.

After squealing excited hellos and checking our bags in, we progressed through security to the departure lounge. It was only a short flight to the Gold Coast, but it had been so long since I'd had a proper vacation that I felt like we were going to the moon. We treated ourselves to glasses of champagne in the airline lounge (courtesy of BTL's corporate membership) before boarding our flight.

As we walked through the first-class cabin, I noted the generous reclining chairs available to those lucky travelers. A fantasy image flashed into my head—Ryan and I settling back on those wide seats, *en route* to Rome. I blinked it away, reminding myself of his rejection. Renae and I continued walking to the rear of the aircraft.

Despite my slender frame, I couldn't remember the coach seats ever being quite this narrow. It occurred to me that if I'd done this trip while on the other side of the mirror, the journey would have been much less comfortable.

Before long we were circling over sparkling blue and green water, with white arcs of beach stretching below the portholes.

The fairground feeling as the plane descended amped up our excitement, and we tumbled from the plane to the terminal to a taxi to our resort in quick order.

Before we could say 'cocktail please,' we were sitting at an outdoor bar opposite the beach, and only a short walk from our cabin.

When our drinks arrived, a fizzy tropical serum sprouting fresh fruit bobbing against icy shards, Renae and I looked at each other, tired and happy, and toasted 'to adventure.'

'Woo-hoo!' I called.

'Par-tay!' yelled Renae. Music was throbbing from speakers above the bar. The barman danced over and placed a bowl of fries between our drinks. 'On the house,' he said, jiving away.

Renae had booked four nights at the resort. On that first night we sorted through the enormous list of activities on offer, and both agreed we'd rather keep things unstructured. More than anything, we just wanted to relax, sit by the pool, read trashy novels, drink cocktails and gossip about the other guests.

The first day largely followed this blueprint. But Renae's eye was soon caught by a group of men on a buck's weekend. She started gravitating to their lounges, and following them to the bar, leaving me alone by the pool.

I didn't mind. I swam and sunbathed and dozed, sun-drunk in my bikini. It was the holiday of my dreams. Loose and lazy and untroubled by self-criticism.

I had vast empty hours to reflect on my options with the mirror.

My first trip through had been a shock, filled with surprises and mistakes and, ultimately, fear. The second trip had been wasted by a stupid craving for a stupid burger. But I no longer beat myself up about it. I couldn't undo it, and there was no point dwelling on it.

This third trip, I was starting to feel like I was getting the hang of life on this side. I'd managed to crack Vivi's tween veneer of indifference. I'd finally had a breakthrough with Lou. I'd had mind-blowing sex with Ryan, which, if nothing else, had emphasized my incompatibility with Stu, confirming the wisdom of our separation.

And I hadn't given up on winning Ryan back. Vicky might be young and clever, and probably beautiful, but she didn't know Ryan like I did. She didn't have the 15-year history that I did. I intended to exploit this advantage on my return.

Yes, things were looking up. I couldn't quite believe my luck in meeting Angelica and having this experience. I felt like I'd learnt more about myself in the past four months than in the previous thirty-nine years.

***

There was a Polynesian-themed outdoor banquet on the last night of our trip, with a pig on a spit and men in grass skirts walking across hot rocks for our entertainment. We turned a blind eye to the cultural appropriation and enjoyed the show.

After the meal there was dancing. The performers scissored their hips up and down to a fast drumbeat beside a fire pit, as the crowd of tourists, happy, drunk and sunburnt, cheered from our tables.

Earlier that evening a kind of sadness had descended on me, like that feeling on Sunday afternoon when you realize the weekend is almost over. But after a few glasses I'd been restored to a playful mood. Renae and I made eye contact, with smiles of uncomplicated joy.

I held out my glass to a passing waiter for a top-up of champagne and continued drinking.

Before long the line of grass skirts and leis and flowing dark hair and bikini tops was moving forward and back in waves before the crowd, beckoning the audience to participate.

Renae and I eagerly stood and began dancing an unco-ordinated hula. Laughing and posing for cameras and not caring anymore, I moved among the now-heaving crowd of performers and tourists.

Soon the drumbeats were replaced with a disco soundtrack, and in nearby palm trees some discretely mounted disco lights had started to strobe. The dancing became sweatier and more energetic. I was singing lyrics to the pop classics blaring from the speakers at the top of my lungs. At some point I realized I was drunk.

After some more jumping around, I became aware of grass rubbing against my knees. I'd fallen. I laughed at my clumsiness and kept trying to dance. Someone sat on my back and mimed a lasso with their arms, like I was a bucking bronco. I groaned and a voice far away wormed into my consciousness: no, you should stop now. Go and sit down. Drink some water.

I could feel something throbbing. Was it the loud bass from the speakers? No, the bass was echoing up from the ground through my hands and knees. This was a different throbbing, smaller, and on one side of my body. I crawled through the dancing legs to the edge of the dancefloor and saw the dinner tables.

Now someone was lifting me by the armpits. It was Renae. She was laughing and shouting something. We staggered to two chairs and flopped into them. Renae said something else I couldn't hear and poured me some water. It spilled down my front as I drank.

I could feel the throbbing still. No, throbbing was the wrong word, I thought. It was buzzing. I put my hand on my leg. There it was again. I wondered what it could be. I drank more water and put my hands to my face. I felt heat and sweat. The surface of the table was tilting up and down, side to side, like I was on a boat in a swell.

I looked up to tell Renae, but she was gone. I could see her walk-running to the hut on the other side of the bonfire, where the toilets were. There was that buzzing again. Why wouldn't it stop? I slapped it, thinking maybe a fly was trapped in my shorts. My hand hurt a bit. I'd hit something hard. I felt it again. It felt just like a phone.

The fog cleared in my brain. It *is* a phone. It's my phone. I reached into my pocket and pulled it out. I stared at it in wonder, feeling dizzy. It sat in my hand, silent, then buzzed again. I jumped and stared at the screen. Seven missed calls. Six messages from Stu. 'Call me—urgent.'

I unlocked the phone and tried to retrieve his messages. I listened and could hear a distant muffle but couldn't understand anything.

I stood up and swayed away from the party, stabilizing myself with the backs of chairs. I was halfway to our cabin before the noise of the party started to die down and the sound of crashing waves became dominant.

I didn't feel good. I stepped onto the porch of our cabin and fumbled the keycard from my back pocket. I waved it in the general direction of the card reader and missed. I focused really, really hard and managed to slap the card against the reader, as if I were swatting a fly. Success. The lock on the door flashed green and clicked open.

I propelled myself forward and almost crash-tackled the pillow on my bed. I rolled over and stared up at the vaulted ceiling. The room was spinning. As I lay splayed on the bed, I felt myself leaning to one side as if in a banking aircraft.

I became distracted by a stencil frieze that had been painted under the ceiling cornice. Even though it was faded and peeling in spots, the geometric pattern was ornate and beautiful. I became entranced, following the line of paint around the perimeter of the room. I kept losing my way and starting over. I decided I wouldn't stop until I'd succeeded in tracing the design with my eyes all around the ceiling. It was helping to steady me.

The phone rang again. Oh, that's right; I'd forgotten. I looked at the screen. It was Stu again. I scowled. Leave me alone. We broke up, OK. It's over.

But the ringing wouldn't stop.

Finally, I pressed the green button.

'Hello,' I shouted, my ears still ringing. 'I just got home from a party.'

'Evie?' He sounded muffled. It must be a bad line. 'Evie, can you hear me? Something terrible has happened.'

'What? Can you talk louder?'

'It's Vivi,' Stu said. 'I had to call an ambulance. You need to come home.'

CHAPTER 38

The taxi took me from the airport straight to the hospital. It was 10am. I'd taken the first flight from the Gold Coast at dawn. I'd left a note for Renae, who hadn't returned to our room following the party, and wasn't answering her phone.

Stu met me at the entrance to the hospital and led me up to the Intensive Care Unit. 'They might bring her out of sedation today,' he told me.

I had the tunnel vision of a scared mother, grabbing onto every piece of information, turning it over and around, looking for any angle that permitted a positive interpretation.

'That's good news, isn't it?' I asked.

Stu looked ashen. 'Yes, but we won't know the extent of the damage until she wakes up. If...' He didn't finish his sentence. I pushed away the thought of what he might have said.

We washed our hands and put on masks and gowns before entering a large room with several beds. White, bright light. Noisy with the pings, pops and clicks of machines measuring life, sustaining life.

And there was Vivi, my beautiful child, looking so tiny in that bed. Swollen and bruised and bandaged and unconscious.

I took her hand, gently avoiding the canula that violently pierced her skin. I knew how scared she was of needles.

Finally with her, and seeing for myself that she was breathing, I let go. I released the tears I'd been too scared to shed until this moment, when I'd needed every ounce of mental clarity to get myself home.

'Oh baby. Baby. Mommy's here. I'm here now darling. I'm so sorry. I should have been here. Oh sweetie, you're going to be fine. We're going to make you all better, honey.'

Stu stood behind me, his hands on my shoulders.

A person I assumed was a doctor spoke to us. He explained that when Vivi had bounced off the bonnet of the car that hit her bike, her head had landed heavily on the pavement. But she'd been wearing a helmet, and this had saved her life. They'd operated to remove a piece of skull, to remove pressure on her brain. She was responding well. She was no longer critical. She would survive. But we wouldn't know if there was any lasting damage until they brought her out of this medically induced coma.

I clung to the words 'she will survive' as to a life raft.

'What kind of damage do you mean?' I asked.

'To the brain. Her scans look good, but they don't always show us everything.'

'How long will she be here?'

'It's hard to say. Children are really great at healing, but everyone's different. She'll have a long road ahead in terms of physical therapy. But as I said, it could have been much worse. We think she'll pull through.'

The doctor left us, and Stu took my hand. He was crying from relief. 'She's going to be OK. She's going to be OK.' He hugged me. We stood, clinging to each other for a few minutes.

Finally I spoke. 'How did it happen?' Part of me wanted to say, 'Where were you? Why didn't you protect her?' But even in my anguished state I knew Stu would never have let this happen if he could help it.

'She'd been riding in the park across the road and was just crossing back to our driveway. It was a hit and run. Annika was in the park and saw it happen. She called the ambulance.'

'Where were you?' I whispered.

Stu frowned. 'I was in the backyard, hanging washing on the line. I heard it. That noise.' He put his fists to his ears and banged them against his head. 'It won't go away. I keep hearing it over and over. I keep replaying what I was doing. I'd thought about calling her in to help me hang the sheets out. But she was having fun so I let her keep playing. It was my fault.'

'No it wasn't,' I said flatly. 'It was mine.'

I'd realized that Vivi was only out riding her bike at that time because I was on vacation. Her accident happened on Thursday evening, when she and I usually went swimming together. If I'd been home, she would have been with me. She would have been safe.

***

Stu and I were exhausted. My parents came to the hospital to sit with Vivi so we could go home and sleep. Lou telephoned and also offered help.

We walked around the house in a daze. I spent a long time standing in the doorway of Vivi's bedroom, just staring at her things. I imagined her last moments in here, casually dropping her pajamas on the floor, papers and pens scattered carelessly across her desk, ready to resume homework later. Just an ordinary kid on an ordinary day. And now…

I felt a surge of hatred and anger for the driver of the car. The police had visited us in the hospital, and said they were following up leads based on Annika's description.

Stu was already sleeping, but I'd refused the pill he'd offered me.

The initial shock of Vivi's accident was fading. Now that I'd been assured she would survive, my adrenaline was subsiding. But I felt deep sadness about what lay ahead for her, even in the best-case scenario. Months of pain and incapacity as she recovered from her head injury, her broken leg, her significant abrasions. It wasn't fair. She was just a kid.

What I wouldn't give to protect her from this.

Suddenly the thought was floodlit in my brain: the most obvious solution, that I actually laughed for not having thought of it already.

Vivi was only hit by a car because I wasn't there. But in the fat world I didn't go to the Gold Coast. Renae had changed our plans so she could take her new boyfriend Curtis instead.

Maybe Vivi in my fat life, in my *real* life, maybe the real Vivi was safe. Maybe we'd done our usual Thursday swim. Maybe she'd been spared this awful trauma. This side of the mirror was all an illusion after all, wasn't it? Maybe if I went back, I would save her from all of this pain. I thought of Ryan and Rebekah. The fact Rebekah was dead on this side of the mirror, but alive and well—saved by circumstance—on the other.

I went to my bedroom and looked at myself in the mirror, barely registering my reflection. I was going back. If there was a chance I could save her, I had to try.

I leant my forehead against the glass. 'Mirror, mirror, let me out. I don't care if I am stout,' I said. 'And please, please, please, let Vivi be safe.'

The mirror softened as I pushed my weight into it.

CHAPTER 39

I tumbled onto the soft carpet on the other side of the mirror. I turned and saw my large shape huddled on the floor in the dark. I crawled to the glass. Yes, it was me. The mirror had worked one final time.

Stu was still asleep, but here in the marital bed, not the spare room.

I ran down the hall to Vivi's room.

She was there! Sitting up, well and whole, and looking guilty—she was reading her book with a torch.

'Sorry,' she whispered, assuming she was about to get in trouble for not being asleep.

I crossed to her bed and lay down next to her.

'Oh honey, I had such a bad dream. I dreamt something terrible happened to you. I had to come and check on you. Oh darling.' I buried my head into her hair, overwhelmed with relief and exhaustion.

'You're so weird, mom,' she said, laughing at me. She put her small arm over me. Her laugh was the best sound I'd ever heard in my life.

***

So that was it. I was back to the real me. My mirror adventures were over. Life was back to normal.

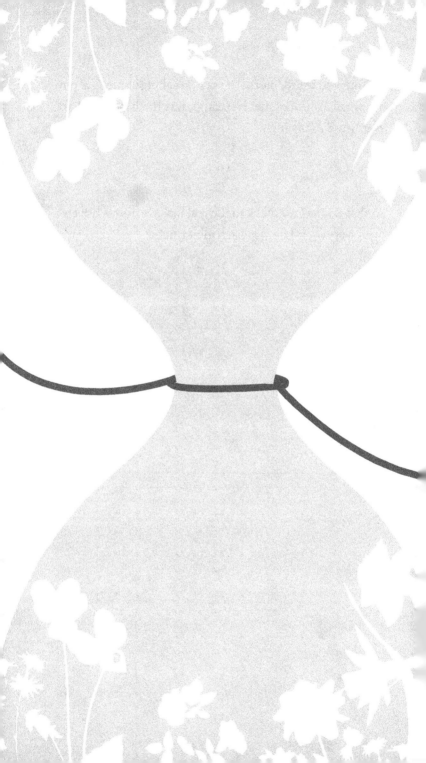

PART 3
AFTER

CHAPTER 40

For a few weeks I was walking on a cloud. The relief of having a healthy, untroubled child put any other worries in perspective. I was more present than I'd ever been in my life; mindful and so very grateful for ordinary days that didn't end in disaster.

Vivi was beautifully well, secure and thriving. I spent as much time with her as I could, resuming our Thursday night swimming and our Saturday mall-ratting. She was my joy. She was what I wanted more than anything. More than Ryan. More than being skinny.

My frolics in that skinny body had been fun at first, but also scary and complicated. And I realized it had all been play-acting. It had felt real, but it wasn't. This was real, here and now. This was the real Vivi, in living color, and this was my real body, and this was my real marriage. Stu, Vivi and I were a family. That was worth more than all the skinny clothes I'd left behind.

I never doubted my decision about coming back through the mirror to save her. I would do it again a million times if I needed to.

But as my relief faded over the coming weeks, the daily drudgery of life resumed. The novelty of normality lost its sheen.

I began to fixate on the stupidity of wasting that second trip through the mirror, just to come back for a hamburger. How could I have thrown away that opportunity so lightly?

Over time, I became ragingly unforgiving of myself.

I tried to accept it couldn't be changed. But as the weeks passed, I began spending more and more time imagining what could have been. If I'd made more careful decisions, things might have played out differently. It started to torture me.

Also still torturing me was the reality of my obese, middle-aged body.

No amount of 'loving myself' and 'showing myself grace' and nurturing 'self-care' would stop the fatigue that crushed me each morning when my alarm shrieked its herald.

I was chronically sleep-deprived, woken each night by throat-strangling sleep apnea or by anxiety, which would set my heart racing as I worried about just about everything. I was puffy and inflamed; my legs and back ached constantly. Afternoons in the office became a struggle as my energy slumped. Headaches and stomach irregularities returned with a vengeance.

I realized, sadly, that despite the gift I'd been given by Angelica, I was back to square one. Resolutely stuck in this body forever.

I remembered Lou's infuriating statistics. An obese woman has a less than one per cent chance of ever being a 'normal' weight. More than ninety-five per cent of dieters fail, usually ending up heavier than they began.

My options seemed limited and impossible. Either beat the odds and be that one per cent who succeeds or, even more impossibly, accept defeat. Accept I would always be fat. Hope that over time, with a lot of hard emotional work, I would learn to love my body anyway.

I started reading books about self-acceptance. I resumed intuitive eating, focusing on healthy, whole foods, eating less junk and continuing with at least 30 minutes of moderate exercise a day. I was the poster child for public health guidelines on how to achieve optimal health.

Except I was still obese.

The lifestyle changes I adopted—not for weight loss, but for health—resulted in no change to my blood pressure and no change to my many unpleasant maladies.

I went back to my doctor—the nice one, Dr Adichie, who didn't fixate on my weight—to ask for help.

I explained what I was doing, eating lots of fruit and veggies and exercising every day. She congratulated me. She told me that 'successful weight loss' in medical terms was a loss of ten per cent of body weight, and that this would significantly reduce my risk of 'poor health outcomes.'

I could tell she was trying to encourage me when she told me I only needed to lose twenty-four pounds to improve my health, but I knew that would make barely a dent in either my self-esteem or the physical discomfort caused by my size. After living in a body literally half as big, I couldn't see how a mere twenty-four pounds would make any difference at all.

But what else could I do?

I had no choice but to accept myself. I had to keep trying to love myself.

The only consolation was that I didn't feel alone. A good proportion of the adults I saw going about their business each day were also fat like me.

They too must be deficient in the mysterious willpower gene that led us to eat more calories than our bodies needed. What else could explain our collective heft?

CHAPTER 41

Over time, things at work felt like they were back to normal. The memory of sleeping with Ryan, and our epic fight when I was skinny, began to feel like the memory of a TV show I'd once watched, rather than the strange reality it had been.

I eventually stopped blushing in Ryan's presence and stopped getting tongue-tied. Finally, I was starting to feel like my old self. In control. Successful. Respected.

Then one afternoon Ryan knocked on my office door.

'Oh hey!' I smiled. We hadn't spoken that day, and I expected he was going to ask me something about work. Despite the way we'd left things on the other side—angry and hurt and bitter—I still cared for him deeply. Warm waves of happiness still filled me when he turned his dark eyes in my direction.

'Listen,' he said, 'are you free on Saturday? You and I haven't had a weekend outing in ages, and I thought it'd be nice to get back to doing that. I can't even remember why we stopped.'

I thought about how I'd abandoned our burgeoning flirtation on this side of the mirror in order to take things to the next level in Skinny Land. But I pretended innocence. 'I guess we both got busy. So easy to do these days.'

'Well, let's make a point of not forgetting, OK? I thought drinks at my new place might be nice. Saturday at 5pm? I'll text you my address.'

'Oh, um, sure,' I replied, a sudden flicker of hope or excitement flaring inside. This sounded a bit like a date. 'I'll have to confirm childcare arrangements, but yes!'

Ryan smiled and tapped the doorframe, as if he was pleased with my response.

***

On Saturday afternoon I stood in my closet, staring mournfully at my clothing options. Nothing that fit me looked right, and nothing that looked right fit me. For the millionth time I regretted the revenge burger that had robbed me of more time to make things right in Skinny Land.

In a fit of wishful thinking I placed my hands on the mirror and said the spell. Of course nothing happened. The mirror remained glassy and solid. An unambiguous thwack met my hopeful knock.

'Shit,' I muttered.

I turned to the blouses and tops hanging neatly in front of me. 'Well, ladies, it's gonna have to be one of you tonight. Who's up for some fun?'

In the end I chose a sage pleated chiffon blouse that skimmed lightly over the waist of my dark blue jeans. With some white trainers and the right makeup and jewelry I'd look good. Appropriate for casual drinks, leading to who-knew-what.

You know exactly what it's leading to, Evie, I warned myself. Good, wholesome friendship and nothing more, because you're still married to Stu. You have recommitted to him, remember?

Of course, I lied to myself. There is nothing going on. It's perfectly fine to spend time with my single, handsome boss on the weekend. So what if I told Stu I was going shopping? That doesn't mean I feel guilty.

At quarter past five I rang Ryan's doorbell. This was the first time I'd been to his apartment since his separation from the very much alive-and-well Rebekah. I was curious why he'd wanted me to come here, rather than meet at a gallery or café like we usually did. I tried not to read too much into it, but my mind couldn't help recalling our night in the hotel.

He opened the door, his pale blue linen shirt unbuttoned at just the right point, looking tantalizing but not sleazy. He had his relaxed weekend face on, unlined and smiling, and not a trace of the intense look of concentration he often wore at work.

'Evie, you came. Welcome.' He looked very happy to see me, and leaned in to kiss me on the cheek. He smelled like expensive soap.

'Yes,' I laughed. 'Stu and Vivi are busy building a Lego drone so I have the afternoon free. Thanks for having me.' I kissed him back and pressed my hand to his back. 'I can't wait to see your new...' I stopped mid-sentence as Ryan stepped aside and his living room came into view.

Sitting on two couches in front of me were Jeremy and Chelsea from work, and a very attractive woman I didn't know, who looked to be in her late 20s. Very attractive.

So, this get-together wasn't just Ryan and me after all. Why had I allowed myself to assume that? Why didn't I check with him? Now I felt like a dope. I flicked my hair self-consciously out of my collar.

'Hi Evie,' chorused Jeremy and Chelsea, looking happy to see me.

'Hello,' I smiled, conveying through my voice that I'd been expecting to see them and wasn't this just lovely.

'Of course, you know Jeremy and Chelsea,' said Ryan, 'but I'd like to introduce you to my new neighbor.' Ryan walked over to the young woman and put his hand on her shoulder. 'Evie, this is Vicky.'

My stomach flipped. Vicky? The Vicky from our fight? The other woman Ryan wanted to keep seeing after Skinny Me suggested we try living together? Could this afternoon get any worse?

Ryan continued with his introductions. 'Vicky, I've been working with Evie for more years than I care to remember. She really is the glue that keeps everything together at the firm. She's like our very own Mother Hen.'

Yes, the afternoon could get worse. Mother Hen. It was not exactly what I wanted to hear from my crush. Not in front of Vicky the Voluptuous. She smiled warmly and took my hand. 'Nice to meet you, Evie.'

'Likewise,' I muttered. Ryan had turned to talk to Jeremy and Chelsea, so I felt obliged to make small talk. 'So, you're neighbors then?'

'Yes,' she said, 'I live right across the hall. Our front doors face each other.'

'Oh, how nice.'

'I know. I was so relieved when I met Ryan,' she continued. 'It's luck of the draw in apartment buildings like this. You never want to get stuck with a dodgy neighbor. But I seem to have hit the jackpot with Ryan. He's wonderful.'

'Isn't he.' I said it as a statement, not a question, trying to keep my voice polite but perhaps registering slightly sardonic.

Ryan invited us to sit at a table he'd set up on his balcony, with a view over the lake. The late afternoon sun was glinting across the water and throwing a warm glow across Vicky's face and hair. The same sun bounced meanly off the glass table to shine harshly in my eyes, making me squint.

'So what's the occasion, Ryan?' I asked once we were all seated. 'I hadn't realized this was going to be a party.'

'Nothing special,' he said. 'It's not really a housewarming, but I thought it would be nice to have some friends over to toast the new digs. And Vicky is fairly new in town and doesn't know many people, so I thought it'd be nice to introduce her to these two youngsters,' he nodded at our junior staff. He turned to Vicky. 'You'll probably have more in common with them that with us more, ah, mature folk.'

'Speak for yourself,' I half-pretended offence.

'Ryan is so thoughtful,' Vicky purred.

'Why did you move here?' Chelsea asked in her usual friendly manner. 'Sorry! Tell me if I'm being nosy!'

'No, not at all. I came for work,' said Vicky. 'I was offered a residency at the hospital.'

'You're a doctor?' asked Jeremy.

'Training to be a pediatrician.'

'Impressive,' said Chelsea, good naturedly.

'Yes,' Ryan said, 'Vicky's a very impressive young woman. And if I ever get sick there's someone just across the hall who can do a house call.' They both laughed as if this was an established private joke.

I couldn't bear it anymore. I realized with horror I was on the cusp of crying.

I leant down to get my phone from my bag. I pretended to check my messages and exclaimed, 'Oh my goodness, I'm so sorry everyone, but my babysitter just texted to say she's hurt herself and I have to go home. Right now.'

I stood up. 'No, don't get up,' I said as Ryan started to stand too. 'I can show myself out. Enjoy your drinks. It was lovely to meet you, Vicky.'

I made it into the elevator just as the tears spilled over my cheeks.

CHAPTER 42

Back at work on Monday, at the end of our weekly all-staff meeting in the boardroom, Ryan asked me to stay behind as everyone was dispersing.

I'd spent the weekend, after meeting Vicky, chastising myself for being overly sensitive. And perhaps a wee bit possessive of Ryan.

He was entitled to his own life. He didn't owe me anything. We were work colleagues and nothing more. I was married. He was single. I had no right to feel sad that he'd met a sexy new woman. Why should I expect him to think of me in a romantic way? There were a million reasons for him not to.

By Sunday night I'd resolved to put it all behind me. The mirror was forever closed, forever in the past (stupid hamburger). I would do the grown-up thing and put Ryan behind me too. I would say goodbye to this fantasy. That's all he was. A fantasy.

I dressed for work in my most upbeat, flamboyant clothes. Why imprison myself in that drab uniform, that horrifyingly tedious comfort dressing? I was going to move on. I would only attract positivity if I projected positivity. I would choose my mood. I would choose my life.

Psychologically armed with this newfound resolve, I entered the premises of BTL on Monday morning with my head high.

But now Ryan had asked me to stay behind after the meeting, and I had a feeling from the look he gave me that it wasn't to talk about budget projections.

The bubble of my bravado pricked. I shrank within my clothes, my confidence eviscerated.

Yes, I had no right to feel sad about him meeting Vicky. But I *did* feel sad. There it was. Irrational or not, my heart was twisting with jealousy.

Jeremy was the last one out, and he shut the door behind him as he left the room. Ryan and I were alone, sitting on opposite sides of the conference table, staring at each other. Silence discharged between us, as palpable as the hum of the air conditioning.

Finally we both spoke at the same time.

'So you wanted to talk?' / 'Evie, I wanted to…'

We both laughed. I looked in my lap and gestured to him. 'Please. You go first.'

'Look, it's no big deal,' he said. 'I just wanted to check you're OK. You left so abruptly on Saturday, and I was worried.'

'I told you—the babysitter.'

'Yes, I know. And for the rest of the weekend I couldn't stop wondering why you lied about that. I've never known you to lie about anything. That's why I'm worried.'

I looked at him carefully. His face was gentle. Solicitous.

'What makes you think I was lying?'

'You told me when you arrived that you'd left Vivi with Stu, building Lego. Don't you remember?'

I looked down and scratched my eyebrow. 'Oh.'

I looked up at him again with tears in my eyes. I couldn't do this. It was too hard. My feelings were like a big beach-ball I was trying to keep submerged in a pool. It was coming up no matter how hard I pushed down. It was futile.

'Are you OK?'

'I was jealous,' I said, my voice very small.

His brow furrowed, confused. 'Jealous? Of what?'

I tilted my head. Did he really not know?

'Of Vicky. I think I'm in love with you, Ryan.' There, I'd said it.

Ryan just stared at me. His look of surprise was painful confirmation I was swinging way out of my league.

'Evie.'

'Look, it's stupid, and I'll get over it, and I don't expect you to do anything about it. You are you, and I'm…' I gestured at myself and thought 'fat and gross,' but instead said 'married.'

Suddenly it was easier to breath. I felt released. I hadn't realized how heavy this secret crush had been burdening me. Crushing me. I kept talking.

'I mean, these things happen sometimes. You know someone a long time and you suddenly start seeing them in a different light. I thought my feelings were trivial, transient. For a long time I dismissed them. But then meeting Vicky, well, it seems my feelings run deeper than I thought.'

Still he was silent.

'Anyway, it's not going to be a problem because I've made a decision. I'm leaving.'

'What do you mean?' he said quickly.

'Machiko Tanaka has been pestering me to join her firm. You know she's been asking me for a while, and I keep saying no. But I think maybe now is the time.'

'No Evie. I can't let you go.'

'Why? Anyone can do the job I do here. BTL will be fine without me.'

'But I won't be.'

My heart started hammering. He looked at me seriously.

'Of course you will,' I said.

He stood and walked to the chair next to mine. He sat and took my hand.

'Evie, what you just said, it's come as a bit of a shock. I don't know what to say. I just separated. I don't want to rush… I mean, I don't know what I think. But I know one thing for sure. You're as much a part of this firm as I am. You can't leave.'

I looked up at him. Our heads were close together, our hands entwined. It would be so easy to kiss him, but

I didn't dare. The humiliation would be too much if he rebuffed me.

For a moment I wondered if he was thinking of kissing me too. But then he looked away and patted my hand.

I stood up.

'I'll give you as much notice as possible. I'm happy to train my replacement before I go.'

I left him alone at the conference table.

CHAPTER 43

I rang Machiko when I got back to my desk. 'Is your job offer still on the table?'

I could hear the smile in her voice. 'Absolutely Evie. Can I take you to lunch to discuss what I was thinking?'

'Sure,' I said, feeling unhappy but grateful.

We agreed to meet at a place a few streets from her office. It was a café she assured me had interesting and tasty options. I didn't care. I would have eaten at a petrol station if she'd proposed it. I just wanted to get things sorted as soon as possible.

I left the office far earlier than I needed for the short walk, glad for any excuse to not be near Ryan. I arrived at the café with 20 minutes to spare, so ordered a coffee at the counter then took a seat near one of the windows. Most of the tables were full of office workers like me.

To pass the time I examined the menu. The Ryan-sized hole in me would never be filled with salad. Thankfully, the café had options that sounded filling and comforting.

Then I pulled out my phone. While I was scrolling, I became aware that a woman at the table next to mine was crying. I tried to ignore it and give her some privacy, but then I noticed she had a scrunched up, soggy tissue in her hand, and no napkin dispenser on her table.

I reached across and touched her gently on the arm. 'Excuse me,' I said, 'would you like this?' I placed my napkins in front of her.

The crying lady looked up at me. I sat back, surprised. It was Sally from the Wednesday morning running club. Sally, the mean woman, who fat-shamed and ridiculed the larger and slower people who crossed her path.

She didn't recognize me, because on this side of the mirror, in my fat life, she didn't know me. I'd never been to the running club in this world. Part of me felt a flare of satisfaction to see her upset. Good, I thought, remembering her rudely judgmental behavior. If anyone deserves bad things, it's her.

Then I remembered myself. That's not who I wanted to be. Maybe Sally needed someone to talk to. Maybe by being kind to her, I could make a dent in her fatphobic attitudes and help her see that fat people are human too.

But I couldn't lie to myself. My motives weren't entirely noble. I was also curious what would make a disciplined control freak like Sally get so emotional.

'Thanks,' she said, taking a paper napkin and blowing her nose. Clear mucus messily spurted from one side of her nose, and she needed another napkin to wipe her face clean. She reddened a bit. 'Sorry,' she laughed. 'What a mess!'

'That's OK. I'm Evie. Are you OK?'

'Thanks Evie.' She sniffed a few times. 'I'm OK.'

I kept looking at her, without saying anything.

Sally took another napkin and wiped her eyes, then scrunched the wet balls of tissue into her pocket and fanned her face.

'Phew! I don't know where that came from. I can't remember the last time I cried.'

'Really? I cry every second day.' I laughed, trying to lighten the mood.

Sally looked at me curiously. 'You seem familiar. Did you go to Westside Grammar School?'

I shook my head. 'Nope, I don't think we've met before.'

'Well, you look like I should know you.'

'Do you want to talk about what's bothering you?'

'To be honest, I'm hoping that if I never talk about it or think about it, it'll just go away. But I don't think that will work.'

My coffee was delivered to my table. I picked up the mug and blew off the steam, saying nothing. I figured Sally would talk if she wanted to. Sure enough, after a few sips of her own drink, she cleared her throat.

'I've just been diagnosed with cancer,' she said.

'Oh God!'

'No, no, it's fine, really. It's breast cancer, and they caught it early. They tell me that if you have to get cancer, this is the one you want to get. The survival rates are really good. But, still…'

298

'That's freaking scary,' I said. 'No wonder you're upset. It's a perfectly normal reaction.' I paused. 'Is there someone you can call? Someone to come and get you?'

Sally shook her head. 'I just feel like such a failure. My whole life I've focused on eating right and doing my sport. I'm a runner, you know. Like, a really good runner. I exercise every day. Even on holidays. I never get sick. Never even a cold. I always thought people who got sick were weak. Like they deserved it somehow. Like they weren't trying hard enough.' She snorted.

I kept drinking my coffee.

'The thing is, I didn't do anything special to be healthy. I just don't like eating very much. I get full so quickly I have to *force* myself to eat. I hate desserts and things. They make me gag. And I'm so restless—always have been since childhood—so exercising is just what I do to channel that energy. I get anxious if I don't keep moving. So it's not that I'm virtuous at all. It's just the way I was made. It was dumb luck. And now my luck has run out and my body has decided to betray me. It's sobering to realize it has all the control, and not the other way around.'

'Of course you have control,' I said. 'You control your attitude. You control your response to challenges. You control how you frame this setback. You either choose to give up, or you choose to see it as a different kind of marathon. You've got this. You cry a bit, but then you pick yourself up and keep going.'

Sally looked at me softly. 'Thanks.' I could tell she'd forgotten my name, but I smiled at her kindly. 'You know,' she said, 'I'd always been so proud of my fitness. But today I saw a frail old lady hobbling along with her walking frame and I was jealous of her. I envy all the years she's been gifted. What I wouldn't give to swap bodies with her.'

'I know what you mean. Age is a privilege denied many. The older I get the more I realize how important it is to just enjoy the present.'

'Seize the day, you mean?'

'I suppose. We only get a short time, so we should make it a good time.'

'Well, cheers to that,' said Sally, holding up a glass of water to chink with my cup of coffee.

'Cheers.'

Machiko arrived then, and in very short order offered me a job, which I accepted. I was leaving BTL in four weeks.

***

For a few days after seeing Sally, I felt less compelled to eat well. I should take my own advice and seize the day. Enjoy sensory pleasures while I can. Want that bowl of ice cream? Have it! Why not?

But then I'd wake in the morning, and every muscle and joint would creak as I lurched into the shower to warm myself up. I'd have to steady myself, gripping the bathroom counter as I put my pants on because my lack of core strength made it hard to balance. I imagined how helpless I'd be at 90 if this was how I was tracking at not-quite-40.

You have to keep trying, Evie, I told myself. The mirror's gone, but you have to keep trying. Remember what you told Sally. You can choose your attitude. You don't have to be militant, but you have to do something. Be more active, at least. Give your body half a chance.

And so I persisted with the daily evening walks, gradually building up speed. I persisted with the small home-made lunches to take to work. I persisted with the whole not-eating-my-feelings business, even though it left me cranky and crotchety and no one at home seemed to like me sometimes.

I dutifully interviewed, hired and trained my replacement at BTL—a very experienced legal secretary called Rory.

I went to my BTL farewell and said the right things, and avoided eye contact with Ryan and kept a tight lid on my feelings.

Ryan kept his distance from me. Sometimes I sensed him watching me, but I put it out of my mind. I counted down to my departure date, hoping the fresh start would help me mentally, emotionally and physically.

***

When I joined the team at Match Point, everyone was kind but it felt strange, unfamiliar and lonely. Give it time, Evie,

I counselled myself on the drive home each night. Give yourself a chance to find your feet.

At home, I continued with my 'good habits' and my 'trying again.'

Slowly, over many weeks, I managed to lose about fifteen pounds. But I didn't feel any different. No one seemed to notice, and my favorite clothes were as out of reach as ever.

The 'trying' continued to be hard. Many days I'd feel overwhelmed with my hunger, become food obsessed, over-eat then feel defeated.

Then at other times I'd do really well, sticking to healthy food and exercise for weeks at a time.

After one of these 'good' streaks, I was feeling so positive that I decided to weigh myself. I felt like I'd made some progress mentally and was sure the scale wouldn't bother me so much anymore.

I was wrong.

Despite my consistent healthy choices, I'd gained five pounds. And the weight gain *did* bother me. It bothered me a lot.

Standing on the scale, I remembered myself on the other side of the mirror, lean and lithe. In that moment, knowing I couldn't go back was torture.

It was frustrating and ridiculous that I wanted to go back, after everything that had happened. I didn't like myself on that side of the mirror. I didn't like the choices I'd made and the relationships I'd ruined. The pretty clothes hadn't been enough to make up for Lou's absence and the sting of

Ryan's anger. I couldn't believe I was considering returning to a life where Vivi might live with chronic pain.

But now, stuck in this body, I felt suffocated yet again by my size, and the burden of constantly thinking about it. I imagined unzipping my skin, and stepping back into the world, small and lovely.

I wondered if there were any loopholes I'd missed in Angelica's instructions; any way to bargain for another ticket to Skinny Land.

I decided to find her. Maybe she could bend the rules and get me back there. And if I could go back, things would be different.

I lied to myself about my motives for wanting to return. I told myself it was for Vivi's sake—I shouldn't have left her to face her rehabilitation without me. And maybe I could fix things with Ryan.

But deep down I knew the real reason. In that moment in my bathroom, feeling fat and frustrated, I just really wanted to be skinny.

CHAPTER 44

Later that day, sitting in my new corner office—still strange and uncomfortable—I pulled out my phone and scrolled through my long list of contacts. There he was. Dan the Builder. The phone seemed to ring forever, but finally he answered.

'Dan, it's Evie Swan.'

'Evie, good to hear from you. Look, sorry I haven't got back to you about the rectifications. Calendar's been jam-packed with jobs. But we'll get out to you as soon as we can.'

'No worries, Dan. It's only minor stuff—we can wait.'

'Oh, thanks. I'll try to send Will around there in the next fortnight.'

'Wonderful,' I said. 'Listen Dan, I was hoping to speak to your sister Angelica. I could have sworn I'd saved her number in my phone, but it keeps disappearing. Could you let me have it?'

Dan chuckled. 'Sure thing. She is a bit of an enigma, that one. Hard to pin down. You got a pen? I'll read it out to you.'

I scrawled Angelica's number on a sticky note. As soon as I said goodbye to Dan I tried calling, but Angelica wasn't picking up. I tapped out a text message. 'I need to see you urgently. It's about that mirror you put in my house. Please call ASAP.'

The next morning, after a fitful sleep, I parked across the street from Grimm's Clocks and Repairs, a shop I'd never noticed before, several blocks from my new office. Angelica was repairing some display cases for the business and had texted me to suggest we meet there at 9am.

I arrived a few minutes early and entered the dark, cool premises. I'd never seen anything like it. Clocks of all sizes and styles, from ornate grandfather clocks to artful wall projections, were crammed into a relatively small space. I weaved between the haphazard aisles then heard a laugh behind me, 'Don't get lost!' It was Angelica's familiar wheeze.

I spun around to see her holding a plane and shaving an edge off the corner of a timber counter. 'Thanks…' I began to speak but my voice was suddenly drowned out by the sound of five hundred clocks all chiming or beeping the hour. Angelica laughed again.

I waited for the last chime to strike, then started again. 'Thanks for seeing me Angelica.'

'It's a pleasure, love,' she smiled. 'How are you finding things?'

'Well, um, confusing. Mostly good, I think.'

'You came and went more than I thought you would. I figured you'd go across once and stay there forever. Wear all them pretty dresses and be happy.'

'You think I'm that shallow?' My feelings were hurt. I thought, with all her wisdom, that Angelica would sense my internal complexity.

'Well, the feeling I got—and I might be wrong, so by all means correct me if I am—the feeling I got from you was that you thought being fat was the cause of all your problems.'

I tilted my head to one side. 'I never talked to you about my weight before you gave me the mirror.'

'Didn't have to,' she said, resuming her work. Long, slow, methodical strips peeled off as she spoke. 'It was the way you stood, hand over belly. It was the way you talked, like every sentence was a question, as if you didn't have the right to state your opinions. It was the way you walked, like you were trying to hide behind your husband or your kid.'

I blushed. 'Could you read my mind?'

Angelica laughed. 'Nah, I'm not magic. The mirror maybe, but not me. You're just like most other women I meet is all.'

'What do you mean?'

'Well, it's not rocket science, honey. It's drilled into you, into *us*, from birth. Tell me something: did you ever play with a fat Barbie doll? Did you ever dance to the music videos of a fat pop star? Did you ever see your favorite movie star kiss a fat leading lady? Did you ever see a fat person on a commercial who wasn't selling weight loss products? Even skinny women are made to feel fat. And excuse me for saying so, but you ain't skinny.

So I knew for pretty much certain you were blaming yourself for being fat and blaming fat for causing all your problems.'

I didn't like being diagnosed like this, by a virtual stranger. I jutted out my chin stubbornly. 'How did you know I wasn't one of those body positive types. You know, healthy at every size?'

Angelica laughed. 'Oh my dear, the way you folded those arms across yourself when we spoke. You weren't proud of yourself. You were ashamed. Looking at you now, I think you still are.'

I realized I was hunching forward and leaning sideways into a cabinet, as if I wanted to hide in it. I straightened up. 'Well, I've certainly learned a lot from the experience you gave me. I understand now that being thin won't erase all my problems. But I can now say from personal experience that it's more pleasant existing in a thin body than a fat body.'

'Why'd you come back then?'

'For Vivi. I wanted to protect her.'

'And for that juicy burger too, I think.'

'OK, OK, I made some poor choices.'

'No you didn't, honey. You were just being human.'

'I've come to ask you if I can go back. I know you said only three times. But the burger was a lapse, and the Vivi thing—that was an emergency. If I could go back again I *know* I'd use my time better. I'd be more mindful of the opportunity you've given me. I just, I just can't do it here. I've tried. I've tried so hard. Every day it's the first thing

I think about in the morning and the last thing at night. It's exhausting. I want it to be fixed.'

'Then fix it. You'll work it out.'

'How? I've tried literally every diet ever invented. None of them work. Losing weight is impossible.'

'No it's not.'

'Then what do I do?'

'Like I said, you'll work it out. You have everything you need to find the answer.'

'It's not fair!' I winced, hearing myself talk like a toddler.

But Angelica just laughed. 'Listen honey, the rules were clear. If you wasted your chances, that's not my problem. You're stuck here. I couldn't get you back there even if I wanted to.'

That's it, then, I thought to myself. I'm stuck here forever. Fat forever. I was overwhelmed by a feeling of injustice.

'You lied to me,' I said bitterly. 'You said things were the same there. But they weren't the same. Lou hated me, my marriage was broken, Vivi was diet-obsessed, Ryan's wife was fucking dead! Those aren't small things.'

'No,' Angelica said. 'I told you things were mostly the same, but some different *choices* had been made. I was very clear that you'd have to wear the consequences of your choices.'

'Rebekah died of cancer—that's not a choice.'

Angelica shrugged. 'Maybe she chose not to wear sunscreen. You can't pin that on me.'

CHAPTER 45

So here I was, back where I started, fat, unhappily married and minus the consolation of a job I loved. There was nothing to do but get on with life. Put the mirror and my dreams of a future with Ryan behind me.

Although I'd felt closer to Stu after Vivi's accident, protective of our family, committed to our little trio, it didn't take long for our old problems to reassert themselves.

I found myself spending more and more time imagining a life on my own. I fantasized almost daily about the kind of apartment I'd rent, the neighborhood I'd live in, the furniture I'd buy without needing to compromise, and the solo vacations I'd take.

Guilt gnawed at me each night as I lay awake listening to Stu's seemingly contented snore. He never communicated. What was he thinking? Did he have these thoughts too? How could I ask him, without making everything implode?

Just like my diet, I felt fresh resolve each morning to stick with my marriage; to try to make things right.

But despite these intentions, the million little slights, omissions and annoyances that accumulated each day always led me back down that well-worn path to imagined separation.

For Vivi's sake I persisted. For my own sake I gave it every chance. I wanted to suggest counselling but was scared to. Knowing Stu's reticence to discuss anything even remotely intimate with me, I was certain he'd never agree to do so with a stranger. His fear of articulating feelings in front of anyone would be greater than his fear of me actually leaving him. I sensed that my marriage would be over if I suggested counselling. But it also might be over if we *didn't* get counselling. In this no-man's-land of confusion, I decided to keep hanging on.

At least by leaving BTL I'd been freed from the ordeal of seeing Ryan every day. It would have been unendurable to be around him now. A daily reminder of what I'd lost; of what might have been. Being near Ryan would have made the effort of my marriage unbearable.

I'd hoped that, by moving to Match Point and severing ties with Ryan, I'd have a fresh start—both at work and with Stu. But it wasn't working.

Then one night, the scales fell from my eyes.

It was a couple of months after joining the new firm. I was home late, rushing to prepare dinner. The caseload at MP was interesting but difficult. It was humbling to be the newbie after more than 15 years as the go-to person, able to answer every question.

I refused to admit I wasn't loving the new job, but I spent many hours complaining to Stu about the longer work hours, Machiko's rigid expectations and the egos of my competitive colleagues.

Machiko had been bred in the hot house of top-tier law firms, where one's value was inextricably tied to the percentage of time one spent in the office. When I started at MP I'd hoped to influence a change in that workaholic culture, which I thought was not only unreasonable and unhealthy, but also counter-productive. But I was beginning to suspect the task was beyond me.

As I chopped veggies for dinner, I unloaded to Stu about the run-in I'd had with Machiko about her habit of scheduling work meetings at 8:00am.

Stu was listening to my rant from the opposite side of the kitchen, one ear on me, and one ear (I suspected) on the football score being broadcast on the television in the next room.

I was warming to my theme and the knife, with which I was slicing potatoes, was shearing ever closer to my fast-moving fingers.

When the puddle of watery potato starch on the chopping board turned pink I realized I must have cut myself. It was one of those angled cuts that are hard to see until blood rushes to delineate its contours. The pain was delayed, not arriving until several seconds after the blood. But it was bad. Deep.

'Ah, fuck!' I exclaimed, recoiling. 'I cut myself.'

I grabbed a dishcloth and wrapped it around my finger, gripping tightly.

Stu turned back to see why I was yelping. He wandered over to where I stood near the sink, looking at me curiously.

He extended an arm in my direction, and I gratefully leaned forward to accept his embrace.

But he didn't embrace me. The reason he'd leaned forward was to grab his tumbler, which was behind me on the counter. He filled it with water and started drinking, looking down at the dishcloth in my hand.

'I cut myself,' I said again.

'Do you need anything?'

What a question. Perhaps some sympathy. Some affection. Or a god-damned Band-Aid.

That was the moment I knew my marriage was over.

'Listen Stu,' I said, 'I'm going to ask mom if Vivi can have a sleepover tomorrow night. I need to talk to you about something.'

He shrugged. 'OK.'

Two days later, I was single. Stu moved into the spare room.

CHAPTER 46

All through that winter I continued Sunday Pilates with Annika. The friendship I'd tentatively initiated that day in front of my house had continued. She accepted me as I was, and I loved being in her company. It was easy.

We would sometimes end up in each other's kitchens after Pilates, drinking tea and chatting non-stop.

But never about weight loss.

I was intrigued she never talked about it. Most other women I knew, if you talked to them long enough, would eventually say something about their weight or their appearance or their diet. But never Annika. I found this particularly interesting, because I now knew she was maintaining a significant weight loss.

Whenever I was in her kitchen my eye would stray to that photo on her fridge. Fat Annika. It seemed impossible she was the same person.

But I'd never asked her about it. I didn't want what happened to me and Renae to happen to me and Annika.

I didn't want that weird dynamic where we silently compared ourselves and our dieting strategies.

And I wanted Annika to think I was cool, that I was progressive and body neutral like her, that I was above the boring old dieting mindset that seemed to preoccupy so many people, to the detriment of good conversation.

However, after weeks of a persistent ache in my lower back, I was no longer able to stop myself. I wanted to know how she did it. I decided to initiate The Talk.

Annika had just handed me a steaming cup of green tea, and I was perched on a stool at her kitchen island, facing her refrigerator, the glow of Pilates still lighting me up inside.

'Every time I come here I look at that photo,' I began nervously, pointing at the photograph. 'That woman looks so much like you.'

'Well that's unsurprising,' said Annika. 'She *is* me!'

'No!' I pretended shock, hoping this would be last lie I'd ever tell as a result of that stupid mirror.

'That photo was taken about nine years ago. Since then I've lost about 130 pounds.'

'But, isn't that impossible? I've tried my whole life to be thinner, and it's *never* worked. I'm just about ready to give up and accept it's never going to happen. But something tells me to keep trying because I feel so unwell all the time. How did you *do* it?'

Annika looked at me seriously. I could see she was weighing her words carefully.

'Well, I've never raised this with you, because it's none of my business and, honestly, when I think of you, I don't think of your weight, so it's never at the forefront of my mind. But if you want to hear how I did it, I'm more than happy to share.'

'Please,' I said. 'What magic did you use?'

Annika laughed. 'It wasn't magic, although it did feel like that at first. I actually managed to cure my diabetes, which felt incredible. That was the real reason I started in the first place, after someone at work suggested it. The weight loss was a side effect.'

'A side effect of what?'

'Well, Evie, you need to start with fundamentals. If you don't understand the *why*, you'll never understand the *how*.'

She shifted in her chair and looked at me straight. I could tell she was taking this seriously. The levity of our previous conversation was gone. 'Why do you think we gain weight?'

'Because we eat more calories than we need,' I said quickly, with conviction. That was common knowledge.

'And why do we lose weight?'

'Because we've eaten *less* calories than we need.' These had to be trick questions because they were so basic.

'Not entirely correct,' said Annika.

'Which bit?'

'Both bits.'

I tilted my head to one side. Then I had a flash of understanding. 'Oh, I get it, you had weight loss surgery. Stomach stapling or something?'

'No. I did it without surgery.'

'Then what? I don't understand.'

'Exactly. Neither did I, and neither do most people. And that's because we're given the wrong information about obesity. We trust that information, because it comes from doctors and health organizations. Then we follow their advice, which is bad advice, because we want to be healthy. We're told we just need to eat less and move more, and it's not true. At least, it's only part of the story. It's not the full story. And then, when we predictably fail, because that strategy almost always fails, we blame ourselves. We think the problem must be us. We didn't do it right, or we cheated. We lacked willpower.'

Annika's voice had risen, and she spoke with passion. 'Sorry,' she said, checking herself. 'The fact it's still happening makes me really mad. Scientists have known what the problem is for decades.'

'And what is the problem?'

'Well, it's not as simple as too many calories. You could eat 1200 calories a day and still not lose any weight if you ate those calories throughout the whole day.'

'I don't get it,' I said in a tell-me-more tone. I was feeling excited, like Annika was about to share a spell as powerful as Angelica's incantation.

'Fat storage is controlled by the hormone insulin. Fat *release* is also controlled by insulin. If you can control your insulin, you can control how much fat you have on your body. If you understand how insulin works, you will understand how to lose weight and never gain it back.'

'Please,' I laughed, 'keep talking.'

'OK. So insulin is a complicated hormone that does lots of things, but for the purposes of weight loss it has two key functions. When insulin is *high*, your body is physically unable to use your stored body fat for energy. It's like insulin has locked the door on those fat cells. You can't get to them. So your body has to get the energy it needs from the food you just ate, or from short-term stores of sugar in your liver, called glycogen. But when insulin is *low*, that signals to your body there's no food coming, so after it uses up the glycogen in your liver, the body can dip into its fat stores for energy. Those fat cells are unlocked, and the fat is used for fuel. Your body stops being a sugar burner and starts being a fat burner.'

'So you want insulin to be low?'

'Exactly.'

'Is it carbs that make insulin high? Is that why low-carb diets are popular?'

'Yes. Carbs generally spike insulin pretty high. But it's not *just* carbs. Every time you eat your insulin goes up. Even zero-calorie foods and drinks will raise insulin. Did you know that just *tasting* something sweet, like chewing gum, or having a zero-calorie drink, will trick the body into thinking food's on its way, and make your insulin go up? It's called the cephalic phase response.'

'So what do you do then?'

Annika took a sip of her green tea and smiled at me. 'You fast.'

CHAPTER 47

'You mean you don't eat anything? Isn't that starvation?'

'No. Starvation is when you *can't* eat. Fasting is when you *wait* to eat. Listen, you sleep every night, don't you?'

'Usually,' I said, thinking of the 3am anxiety that shook me awake many nights.

'And do you eat when you're asleep?'

'Of course not.'

'So you're already fasting,' said Annika. 'You're probably fasting seven or eight hours in every 24. All you need to do to lose weight is gradually increase the length of that non-eating period.'

'I've heard of 16:8 before. I read an article once and tried it, but I hated it. I was so hungry I couldn't do it. There's no way I can *not* eat for 16 hours.'

'Yes, you can. Once you understand about insulin, it'll help you understand how to do 16:8 effectively. I bet you were drinking things with calories during your fasting period. That's what would have made it hard.'

'Just my coffee.'

Annika nodded knowingly. 'With creamer?'

'Yeah, it'd be way too bitter otherwise. I could never drink black coffee.'

'Yes, you could.' I pulled a face. Everyone was different. What made Annika so certain I could drink black coffee. But she ignored my slight pout and continued with her lesson.

'The creamer in your coffee makes your insulin go up. Creamy coffee and any kind of sweetened drink, even artificially sweetened, is going to trigger your hunger hormones. It's much, much harder to fast if you drink anything apart from water or unsweetened tea or coffee.'

I looked at Annika's cup, half full of green tea. 'Are you fasting right now?'

'I sure am,' she said. 'I fast every day for about 22 hours.'

'What?!' I exclaimed. 'How can you do that? Aren't you starving all the time?'

'Not at all. I sometimes fast for three days straight, so 22 hours is nothing.'

'Three days! I don't know about this, Annika. It sounds dangerous.'

'No, it's exactly how our bodies evolved to survive. We fast and we feast. Just think about it. There were no supermarkets in caveman times. You only ate if you caught or foraged food. Natural selection favored those who could thrive in environments where food was scarce.'

'Yeah, but cavemen had a life expectancy of 20 years or something. I'm not sure they're a great example to emulate.'

'Well, they didn't know about bacteria and germs. They had no antibiotics or vaccines, and no dentists. They would have been dying of infections all the time, or eaten by angry bears. But they weren't dying from metabolic diseases. How long do you think humans can survive without food?'

I hesitated. It felt like a trick question. I imagined the longest stretch of time that seemed feasible, and I doubled it. 'One month?'

'Well, the amount of time you can safely fast depends on the amount of fat you have on your body, because fat is a fuel source, remember? But the longest fast ever recorded was done by a Scottish man in the 1970s. He fasted for 382 days.'

I sat in shocked silence, my eyes bulging. Finally, I found my tongue. 'And what about you?'

Annika smiled. 'Fortunately, I didn't need to lose as much weight as him, and I didn't want to do a continuous fast either. I can't imagine any doctor supporting such an extreme approach these days. But once you know how insulin works, you don't need such an extreme approach.'

'So what did you do?'

'Well, I started really slowly. First, I cut out all snacking between meals. No snacking at all, and no flavoured drinks. Especially no soda. That was probably the hardest part, because it'd been a lifelong habit to constantly graze and nurse a drink. Then I tried to limit the added sugar and junk food. Tried to include veggies in every meal, that sort of thing. You could probably lose weight even while eating junk food if you fasted consistently, but it would take you longer. Besides, junk food is never going to be healthy for you, and I was trying to get healthy. But I didn't 'forbid' any food, I just tried to reduce the less-good choices, you know? Then I tried 16:8. So no more breakfast, and only black tea or coffee in the morning. Once I got used to that, I increased my fasting time and reduced my eating window, so I was only having one meal a day. We call that OMAD in the fasting community. And that's what I still do today, to maintain.'

'You still do it? Even though you lost all the weight? When will you stop?'

'Never. I don't *want* to stop, Evie. The feeling when you fast is so good that I'm going to do it for the rest of my life. I can't express to you how freeing it is to live this way. How peaceful. I can eat literally anything I want. I never weigh my food or count calories or track macros or feel guilty about anything. I eat what I feel like, then I stop. It's so simple, and it costs nothing. I haven't paid a single cent to lose this weight. In fact, I've saved money, because I'm buying less food. Not to mention the time saved by not need to cook.'

'What about socializing, though? What if someone invites you out to brunch?'

'Then I go, I eat and I have a great time. I just resume my normal fasting routine the next day. Every day is a chance to re-set.'

'This sounds too good to be true,' I said. 'So back to your story. You lost 130 pounds just by eating one meal a day?'

'Well not entirely. That's how I started, but after a couple of months I hit a plateau, because my body got used to one meal a day. So I stepped it up a bit.'

'To the three-day fast?'

'No, no. I only do extended fasts a few times a year, for health reasons. There's evidence that longer fasts might protect you against all kinds of nasty diseases. But that was a fair way down the track for me. When I was trying to lose weight and OMAD became less effective, I started doing alternate daily fasting, which—as I'm sure you'll be madly Googling when you get home—you'll see referred to as ADF. That's where you eat lunch and dinner on one day, then zero food the next day, then back to lunch and dinner, then zero food. It means you get two overnight fasts in your fasting window, which is really powerful for weight loss. So it's about 42 hours of fasting, followed by an eight-hour window where you eat two meals and no snacks, then back to 42 hours fasting. And *that's* how I lost the bulk of my weight. Once I was at a point where I felt good in my body, I returned to OMAD.'

'One meal a day.'

'Exactly. You're a quick study, Evie.'

'Believe me, I'm hanging on your every word here.'

'I know. It's life-changing information. I don't know why doctors don't tell anyone about it.'

'Maybe they're not allowed to. Maybe it's not safe. It sounds a lot like an eating disorder.'

'Yeah, I hear that sometimes. Look, anorexia nervosa is a psychiatric disorder that involves self-starvation.

It's awful and it's deadly. Intermittent fasting is just a tool. Like any tool, it can be misused. But that doesn't mean people struggling with metabolic issues shouldn't benefit from it. Thousands and thousands of people every year are dying from obesity-related conditions. I think doctors should be promoting fasting much more than they do. It would save lives.'

'So I won't starve myself?'

'You're not going to starve. You have hundreds of thousands of calories stored in your body, just waiting to be used. You just need to know how to release them for energy.'

Annika took a sip and I kept listening.

'Actually, I heard about a study that asked doctors what they do to lose weight themselves. Can you guess what their preferred approach was?'

'Fasting?'

'Bingo. So if it's good enough for doctors, why not for us? And as for disordered eating, I *did* have an eating disorder when I was fat. It was a disorder of habitual, frequent feeding, which led to constantly high insulin in my body. It wasn't my lack of willpower that made me fat, it was my hormones. If I hadn't discovered fasting, I don't know where I'd be now.'

I kept thinking there must be a catch. It couldn't be this simple, after all these years of struggling. To hear that I didn't need to count calories or weigh my food or pay for help was astounding. All I had to do was look at the clock.

I tried to remember all the other reasons I'd been told why diets didn't work. Wouldn't the same apply to fasting?

'OK, for arguments' sake,' I said, 'let's say I actually managed to lose some weight this way, wouldn't I wreck my metabolism in the process?'

Annika smiled. 'Oh Evie, this is my favorite bit, apart from the no-hunger thing. Are you ready for this? Fasting makes your metabolism get *faster*.'

'I don't believe you,' I laughed.

'It's true. Just imagine you're a caveman again. You haven't eaten for a week, and you need to kill an animal or you and your cave babies will die. Do you think it'd do you any good to be fatigued and shaky and foggy brained? No. You'd need to be super alert, ready to spring at the nearest bison, or whatever. Fasting increases your adrenaline and your growth hormones, to make your muscles stronger and your reflexes quicker and your brain more alert. Some people even say it makes your eyesight better, so you can get that next kill.'

'But won't your body eat your muscles for fuel because it went so long without food?'

'Only if there's no fat on your body. Why would the body eat muscle when it's storing fat specifically for that purpose? That wouldn't make any sense.'

'What about the math though—calories in, calories out. You can't argue with physics. Surely fasting only works because you're eating less often, so you're eating fewer calories.'

'Like I said before, you might not lose any weight eating 1200 calories a day if your insulin was elevated. So low-calorie isn't necessarily the answer. And lots of exercise to increase "calories out" isn't necessarily the answer either. People think they can burn fat just by ensuring they run their dinner off on the treadmill. But that assumes we can control how our body uses energy. We can't.'

'So you don't need to exercise to lose weight?'

'No. I run in the park because I love how it feels, but I only started doing that after I lost weight. Exercise will help with your mood and your sleep and your strength and your stamina. You *should* exercise, because it's vitally important for good health. But it's definitely not as critical to weight loss as everyone makes out.'

I exhaled. I was itching to go home and read up on all this stuff. But Annika's explanation was so detailed, and her voice was so animated and sincere, I was certain what she was telling me was true.

'OK, I need to go home in a second because it's time for me to cook dinner,' I laughed at the irony. 'But one last question: what did you mean by the no-hunger thing?'

Annika drained her cup and put it on the bench in front of her. 'You know that feeling of constant hunger when you diet, when you eat small meals and snacks throughout the day? How you finish a meal but feel like you could eat it again three times over, and immediately start thinking about your next meal? How you even *dream* of food.'

'Uh-huh.'

'That won't happen with fasting. You fast, then you feast. And when you feast, I really mean that—you feast. You eat as much as you like, preferably high-fat and fewer carbs, until you are completely full, completely satisfied. And it changes your mindset. You stop feeling deprived. I can cook a whole meal for Charlie and our friends while I'm fasting, and not be the slightest bit tempted to have a taste. Now, I'm not going to lie; you're sometimes going to feel a bit hungry. But it's never unbearable. It peaks like a wave, then goes away entirely. And over time those peaks get smaller and smaller. In our society we're trained to fear hunger. But you learn pretty quickly when you're fasting that hunger is not an emergency. It's just a feeling. In fact, a little bit of hunger is good for you. It signals that your body is switching from burning sugar to burning fat. And if you do an extended fast—three days or longer—after the second day, your hunger hormones drop to nothing and you actually feel no hunger at all. Zero. Once your body realizes it has all the fuel it needs—your fat—it doesn't need to remind you to eat. It's just like magic.'

'Abra-fucking-cadabra,' I said.

CHAPTER 48

I went home to cook dinner and ate it with enthusiasm, then I went to my room with my laptop and watched YouTube videos about fasting for six hours straight.

Everything Annika had told me seemed to be corroborated. But to be safe, I decided to see my doctor to discuss it. Vivi had just avoided a major health crisis and I had no intention of jeopardizing my own health, especially now I was a single mom.

The next day I ate three meals, with no snacks. When Norman growled at me in the morning, I drank black coffee with a pinch of salt. A YouTube video had suggested I do that to take away the bitterness, and it was actually drinkable. When Norman growled at me in the afternoon I drank mineral water. The fizz helped me feel full.

I had planned to do the no-snack thing for at least a week, to ease myself in, but I was too excited and impatient. I decided to dive right in. That second day, after my black coffee, I skipped breakfast entirely and had a couple more coffees to get me through to lunch.

By the third day, I was able to get to lunchtime with only one black coffee and I realized, with amazement, that fasting for 16 hours was actually kind of easy.

That was the day I went to see Dr Adichie. When I told her what I wanted to try, she was very relaxed about it. She told me her own sister had lost thirty pounds with intermittent fasting. She arranged for me to have a blood test, so we'd have a baseline to monitor any changes.

Out of curiosity (and, I have to admit, slight annoyance), I asked whether she ever suggested fasting to her overweight patients.

'Well, that's a difficult conversation to initiate, Evie,' she said, looking serious, 'especially if they've come to see me for something else. And most people would find the idea of fasting far too daunting. I think it's better to tell people to introduce small healthy changes and gradually build on them, rather than tell them not to eat for long periods.'

I was surprised my otherwise progressive doctor seemed to have such an orthodox mindset, even after seeing her own sister succeed with fasting. Daunting? Surely being told to skip a few meals wouldn't be as daunting as being told you had diabetes, or that you needed medication for hypertension. I wanted Dr Adichie to understand how unhelpful that approach had been for me.

'But if they keep eating lots of small meals, they're destined to fail. Their insulin will stay elevated. They'll just be hungry, and lose barely any weight, and give up. Instead of being taught about nutrition, and then being blamed for not complying with a complicated diet, patients should be taught about biochemistry. If I'd known 20 years ago what insulin does to the body, I would never have gotten fat in the first place.'

Dr Adichie sat back in her chair. 'It's certainly a complex problem. There's lots of social and environmental factors too. I'm really glad you feel like you've found something you think will suit your lifestyle.' For the first time in all the years I'd been her patient, there was a crispness to her tone.

***

That first week, I lost over five pounds. I tried not to get too excited. I always lost weight quickly at the beginning of a diet and told myself it was probably mostly water weight. But I didn't care if it was 'just water.' Not having to lug around an extra five pounds of water was surely a good thing.

After the first month of 16:8 I'd lost fifteen pounds, and was getting impatient. The idea of one day fitting into the smaller dresses in my closet now felt like a more realistic prospect. The sixteen-hour fast felt easy now. I decided to try OMAD.

I bought some urinalysis sticks from the pharmacy to measure my ketone levels. I'd learned that ketones are produced by the body when it uses fat for energy, and that ketones can fuel the brain instead of carbohydrates. From what I'd read—which, by the end of that first month, was every book about fasting I could get my hands on—the brain thrived on this fuel source, to the point that it might even protect against degenerative diseases like Alzheimer's.

I felt this mental clarity profoundly. My previous, persistent headaches were gone. I was alert throughout the day, with no mid-afternoon slump, and I was able to read late into the night. I no longer fell asleep after two pages. I called it my ketosis buzz.

The weight continued to drop off me steadily after I switched to OMAD. Over a couple of months, as this eating lifestyle became routine, other amazing things happened to my body. My back stopped hurting. Skin tags fell off my neck. My feet no longer ached in the morning. My energy levels shot up. My asthma went into remission. It truly felt like a miracle.

But despite my excitement and relief at finally, FINALLY, feeling calm and in control of my food choices, and finally, FINALLY starting to lose weight in a sustainable way, I was not completely happy.

I hated my new job. I missed my BTL work family. Most especially, I missed Ryan.

CHAPTER 49

The Switching Yard was a popular weekend market held at an abandoned train depot in town. People went there each Saturday or Sunday to buy their fruit and vegetables, gifts and trinkets, vintage clothes and furniture or to just have a coffee and wander the stalls. Months ago, Ryan and I had come here a few times, chatting and browsing (and, in my own head, pretending to be a couple).

I was here with Renae now, formulating a plan.

I was single. Ryan may or may not be with Vicky. But I had decided I needed him back in my life. At least, I had to try.

'Mmm, those donuts smell amazing,' Renae inhaled deeply as we walked past a baker's van.

'They do. I might get one to share with Vivi at home.'

She looked at me. 'Are you sure?'

'Yeah, I'll save it for when my window opens. We can come back for it just before we leave.'

Renae shook her head. 'I still don't know how you can go so long without eating.'

'Me either!' I laughed. 'If you'd told me a year ago, I wouldn't have believed you. But you get used to it. Anyway, what do you think about me emailing Ryan. Will I sound pathetic?'

'Maybe. But don't let that stop you.'

'Gee, thanks.'

'No, Evie, I mean it. You can't control what he thinks. He might think you're pathetic, but he might not. The worst he can do is say no. And then you'll have your answer, instead of wondering about it.' She slurped her cappuccino.

'You're right. I just feel so embarrassed. I told him I love him. To then ask him if I can come back to my old job seems a bit…desperate?'

'Rubbish. You have a years' long track record there. He knows you better than that. Besides,' her eyes twinkled, 'he might love you too!'

I grimaced. 'I doubt it. Not with *Vicky* living across the hall.'

'Vicky Schmicky. She's a child. You, my friend, are a woman.'

'A Real Woman,' I laughed, remembering the plus-sized clothing labels that had frustrated me for so long. Renae didn't get my joke, and kept talking.

'So all you need to do is email him and ask to meet for lunch. Like old friends. Which you are. Then you just say straight out that you hate your new job and you want to come back. I'm sure he'll take you in a nanosecond.'

I turned and looked at Renae. She was such a wonderful person. 'You're right.'

'I know.'

'OK, I'll do it.'

'How about you do it now.'

'What, here?' People were jostling past us in the crisp midday sunshine. A busker 30 feet away was grinding some klezmer tunes on an accordion to an appreciative horseshoe of onlookers.

'Sure. You have email on your phone, don't you?'

'Yeah.'

'Well do it. Email him right now, then you can focus on the important bit.'

'Which is?'

'Planning what to wear!'

***

Renae was right. Ryan messaged me back straight away to say how happy he was to hear from me and that yes of course we could meet for lunch. In fact, he suggested we catch up the very next day. He proposed the nice café at the art museum, where we used to go to together. I swelled with hope and fear.

Deciding what to wear turned out to be fairly easy— there were many more options available to me now. I wore one of the old dresses that, until recently, hadn't fit. One of my ghost dresses. It was a size 12. It now fit perfectly, accentuated my curves and emphasized my more slender waist.

I arrived at the café for our rendezvous a few minutes late. I hadn't meant to, but I'd had difficulty finding a park. I'd rushed down the street to make up time and now stood in the doorway, breathless, looking for which table he was at.

And there he was.

He looked up and saw me. His eyes widened a bit—he was noticing my weight loss, I guessed—then smiled his lovely, familiar smile. He stood as I walked toward him.

'Evie.'

'Hello.' I moved to give him a friendly kiss on the cheek, but before I could, he enveloped me in a tight hug. I closed my eyes against his chest and inhaled.

Finally he relaxed his grip and looked down at me. We stared at each other for what felt like forever.

Then he kissed me.

***

Ryan fit into my life like an old pair of jeans. Comfortable and comforting.

After I returned to BTL, we agreed to take things slowly. I didn't want to jump out of one relationship into another one without carving space out for myself.

Although I was desperate to spend every moment with him, I only stayed over at his place on nights when I wasn't responsible for Vivi. I wanted to be sure my feelings for Ryan were not based on some unconscious comparison with Stu, stemming from previous marital dissatisfaction, but could stand independently. And I wanted to give Vivi space to get used to the idea of this new relationship before being thrust into the midst of it.

But taking it slow didn't mean keeping it secret. Everyone knew. It would have been hard for them not to. We couldn't take our eyes off each other.

CHAPTER 50

As predicted by Annika, my weight loss plateaued again after a few months of OMAD. I took a deep breath and decided to try alternate day fasting. I'd hesitated about this, because it would mean not eating dinner every second night, when I usually sat with Vivi to talk about her day. I worried about setting a bad example, about modelling dysfunctional eating habits, even though I was convinced by then that what I was doing was very healthy.

On that first night of ADF, when Vivi tucked into her chicken schnitzel, potatoes and broccoli, I sat in my usual spot at the table, drinking mineral water. Amazingly, I didn't feel deprived at the sight or smell of her food. Norman had long since given up pestering me. He only emerged for short, half-hearted rumbles from time to time, never with the intensity of before.

'Why aren't you eating, mom?' asked Vivi. 'Are you sick?'

'No, I'm fine. I'm fasting.'

I expected her to ask what that was, but instead she said, 'Oh. Zaina's family does that.'

'Zaina from school?'

'Yeah, she told me they do it for their religion.'

'Yeah, lots of people do,' I said, amazed and relieved that this thing which had been so novel and a bit scary to me had already been normalized for Vivi at her culturally diverse school. 'People have been fasting for thousands of years.'

'Are you religious now?'

'No,' I laughed, although I felt like Annika was my guru. 'I'm fasting because I want to give my body a break from digestion, so it can have a chance to rest and repair. I've learned it's really healthy to have long breaks between your meals. But only if your body has stopped growing. It's not good for kids. It might stunt your growth or something. But I'm plenty big enough, so for the next little while I'm only going to eat dinner every second night.'

'Aren't you hungry?'

'Not really.'

'Why is it healthy? Cause it makes you skinny?'

'No. Skinny people aren't necessarily healthy, and fat people aren't necessarily sick. The fat in your body is just stored energy. But often if you have a lot of fat it's because you have a lot of insulin. That's a hormone in your body that's really important. But if you have too much of it, it can make your body stop working properly. Adults can keep their insulin levels healthy if they don't eat for a day or two.'

'OK,' she shrugged, popping a bite of chicken in her mouth. I could tell she was losing interest.

I stopped talking about it then, but I couldn't wait to teach her more about fasting as she approached adulthood.

I felt profound gratitude that, armed with this information, she need never experience the struggle I'd endured, the self-blame and embarrassment and low self-esteem that came from trying to control my weight using incorrect information.

Settling into a comfortable ADF routine took some trial and error. Occasionally I overdid it in my feeding window, eating far more than my appetite was telling me to. I'd given myself permission to not restrict food and I sometimes ate to the point of discomfort. Rather than panicking, I analyzed this response with forensic interest. Am I sufficiently hydrated? Do I need electrolytes? Am I snacking in my eating window? Gradually I found a pattern that worked well for me. What helped the most for me was eating as little sugar as possible. I filled my two ADF meals with high-fat, lowish-carb meals, and gradually the impulse to overeat on my feeding days lessened.

Amazingly, over time, the focus of my fasting practice became less about weight loss and more about health and longevity.

At first, I'd been frustrated I hadn't learned about the role of insulin much earlier in my life. But now I had a different perspective about the journey I'd taken to reach this point.

Weirdly, I now felt a certain gratitude for having been obese. That was because my quest to lose weight had led me to accidentally learn a lot about biology, which was important information for anyone, regardless of their size.

It had led me to understand that inflammation could cause chronic illness, and that fasting was a really effective anti-inflammatory.

It had led me to learn about sugar, the damaging effects it can have on our bodies, and that we can happily thrive without any sugar or carbohydrates in our diet at all. The few parts of our body that need glucose don't have to get it from carbohydrates. They can get it from fat and protein, in a process called gluconeogenesis. Notwithstanding this knowledge, I didn't give up carbs entirely. They were far too delicious. And with daily fasting, the occasional pasta meal or slice of buttered bread didn't make me gain any weight (although I was hungrier during my fast the next day).

My search for answers had also led me to hear about autophagy. This is a process, stimulated by fasting and exercise, where your body searches for old or damaged cells, takes them apart, gets rids of their waste products, and uses them to make new, healthy cells.

Everything I learned reinforced that fasting had enormous potential to keep the body young. Long after I was at a healthy weight, I'd continue fasting to improve my chances of having an active and healthy old age. I'd started fasting from a desire to get skinny, but the amazing array of 'non-scale victories'—the surprising collateral health benefits—made me never want to stop.

Once I began ADF, Annika and I started synchronizing our fasts so we could enjoy our feasts together.

Ryan started skipping breakfast when he noticed how much energy I had from doing so. He loved how it made him feel, as well as the beautiful simplicity of it. And he found that his workouts at the gym were more effective when he lifted weights in a fasted state.

It was so nice to have my loved ones sharing this lifestyle with me. Even my parents got on board and were soon raving to all their friends about the fountain of youth they'd discovered.

As my weight loss became more noticeable, people started asking me what I was doing. Without intending to, I'd become a walking endorsement for the power of time-restricted eating.

And even though I never initiated those conversations, I had no hesitation about telling people, as Annika had done, about my skinny spell.

CHAPTER 51

The morning of my fortieth birthday dawned still and calm, with a soft orange glow creeping across the park. I laced on my sneakers and scrawled a quick message on a Post-It note on the kitchen counter: 'Gone for a walk.'

Lou had slept over the night before. Her birthday present to me was a day of complete freedom to do as I pleased. She would be at my beck and call for the full 24 hours, to watch Vivi if I wanted to go out, to cook, to clean, to talk or not talk. Whatever I felt liked. I silently thanked the universe, for the millionth time, that she was my sister.

I drove ten minutes to the base of Seaview Mountain and parked amongst a small group of other early risers. I put headphones on, and pressed play on my favorite podcast.

As I crunched up the gently sloping gravel to the start of the track, I paused on a small wooden bridge to do a couple of hamstring stretches. I looked ahead of me with a mix of pleasure and dread. I knew this was going to be uncomfortable, but the view at the top was amazing, and the feeling powerwalking back down the hill was exhilarating. I took a deep breath and started up the hill.

It was a gentle incline at first. Then all of sudden, after turning a corner, the path rose vertically before me. There was a tree at the end of this short steep stretch, with beautiful globby nobs and knots. I kept my eye on that tree and walked slowly, one foot in front of the other, focusing on my breathing. Trying to keep it steady. Trying to stay at a pace where I could still talk if someone was with me. Before long, I arrived at that tree, and gave its trunk a grateful pat. I took a sip of water and looked at the view. It was starting to emerge between the tree trunks, but I still had several more legs up the zig-zaggy track before it would open unobstructed before me. I faced the path again and looked for the next tree to focus on.

In this way I was able to move my body up the steep slope.

While I wasn't sure exactly what I weighed now, I knew I was significantly lighter than this time last year, when Lou had told me I'd always be fat. I'd lost most of that weight without any vigorous exercise at all—just gentle walks and Sunday Pilates. And while I doubted I'd ever run the way my skinny alter ego had run, I did miss that post-vigorous-exercise glow that Skinny Evie had been addicted to. So recently I'd begun to trade up my gentle walks for more challenging, hilly hikes. But not every day. Most mornings, I still preferred to stay in bed for as long as possible and wake myself slowly with black coffee. On those days, I would take my sneakers to work and, instead of eating at lunchtime, would loop around the park near my office.

My closet was roomier now. After Stu moved out, I did a big cull of my clothes. Due to my fasting success, instead of clearing out dresses that were too small, I needed to get rid of dresses that were too big.

I also thew away items from my previous dull work uniform that still fit me. I swore I'd never wear black pants again.

I bought new clothes in my new size. I decided to invest in good quality brands, rather than cheap fast fashion, and the cut and quality of the fabric made me feel fabulous. I marveled that I could wear small sizes and still enjoy carbonara for dinner. I felt like the world had been lying to me my whole life, and I'd suddenly woken up to it.

Without the preoccupation of weight and weight loss and food taking up so much space in my head, I was able to focus more of my attention on my friendships, and spent a lot more quality time with Vivi, Ryan, my parents, Lou and her family, Renae and Curtis, and Annika and Charlie. Sometimes we bonded over food, and those occasions were never fraught with anxiety for me. I just ate and enjoyed myself.

Filled with fresh gratitude for my newfound focus on things more interesting than how fat or thin I was, and feeling a post-hike glow, I returned from my walk realizing I hadn't weighed myself in weeks. My clothes and my energy levels were a sufficient barometer.

I stared at the scales in the corner of my bathroom as I dried off from my shower. I wondered about stepping on. But then I thought about what I'd do with that information. I couldn't identify a single reason why it was relevant to me anymore. Why should I let a stupid arbitrary number dictate the happiness of my day, when I'd just been on an amazing hike that made by blood pump and my lungs burst and my sweat run and my mind expand.

I pulled on my new jeans and brushed my newly shortened hair. I didn't look like I'd imagined forty would look. I just looked like myself. What was all the fuss about this number anyway?

I picked up the scales and took them outside to the trash. I opened the lid and tipped them in. Good riddance, I thought. Away with you.

***

'So, what's the plan for today?' Lou sipped her coffee in my kitchen with me. 'Massage? Facial? Pedicure? Shopping?'

'None of the above,' I said. I had a cunning plan for my birthday, that I hoped Lou would love. 'I'm taking you to see something.'

'Me? But today's all about you. I'm here to watch Vivi.'

'She can come.'

'Where are we going?'

'You'll see.'

A hour or so later, I maneuvered my car through back-streets and past warehouses on the edge of the city. I pulled up in front of an empty shopfront with a large 'For lease' sign in the window.

'What's this?' asked Lou.

'I'll tell you inside.'

I led her and Vivi to the door of the empty store and unlocked it with a key the letting agent had given me. We walked inside the high-ceilinged space.

It was the gallery Lou had used in the skinny world.

'Wow,' Lou said, looking up and around.

Vivi skipped off, making echoing noises in the cavernous space. She twirled and sprinted, unable to resist the urge to run that always seemed to overtake children when let loose in large rooms.

'This is a great space,' Lou said. 'Why are we here?'

'Oh Lou, can't you just picture it? It would be a perfect gallery for your business. There's room for hangings and a dark room and an office. It would be amazing for you.'

Lou looked at me with wide eyes. 'Are you crazy? I can't afford this.'

'So get a loan. Take a risk. Look, here's the information.' I handed her a sheet from the realtor. 'Just imagine, Lou. With space to move and create, out of that little corner of your living room, and away from the boys and Mario, there's no limit to what you could do with your art.'

Lou walked around quietly, not saying anything. Not contradicting me. I could tell her mind was racing.

Eventually she turned to look at me. 'I love it,' she said. 'I'll have to think about it. But maybe I could make it work.'

CHAPTER 52

As I dressed for my party, I looked beyond the imperfections on my body that a photo editor might airbrush away, and focused instead on my glowing skin, my happy face.

Standing in front of that mirror, I wondered about the people I'd left behind on the skinny side. Were they real or imagined? If they were real, were they OK? Had Vivi recovered? Had Ryan come back to Evie—to me—after his dalliance with Vicky?

I used to think I didn't like myself very much on that side of the mirror but I realized now that version of me had been doing the best she could with the information she had. She'd made some crazy choices. But chronic hunger can drive a person mad. All I felt for her now was sympathy and affection.

I suddenly had an idea.

I went to my desk and pulled out a notepad. I wrote her a letter. I didn't know how I'd get it to her, but I wanted to try.

Dear Skinny Evie

Thank you for sharing your life with me. I don't know where you went when I was in your body, but I hope you had some reprieve from Norman when I took your place. I'm happy that I chose my real life in the end, but I'm so glad I was able to try yours too.

I've learned so much in the past year and I want to share some of this knowledge with you. I remember how miserable you felt in that always-hungry body. One of the things I've learned is that you don't need to feel that way. You don't need the meal-prepped frozen lunches and the dawn running club and the constant vigilance and deprivation to stay thin. You don't need to be scared of food.

I've found freedom, and you can too. Please try intermittent fasting. Read about it. Learn about what insulin does. It changed my life and I want it to change your life too.

With much love, (less) Fat Evie xxx

At the bottom of the letter I wrote the name of the books and podcasts that had helped me the most, then I sealed the letter in an envelope and went back to the closet.

I knelt down on the floor and inspected the small gap where the bottom of the mirror met the top of the skirting board. I felt around doubtfully with my fingers. It didn't seem likely anything would happen, but what did I have to lose? I shrugged and pushed the edge of the envelope into the narrow space.

As I did, I closed my eyes and thought of Angelica. I said 'mirror, mirror, let it through, show her what she has to do.'

Suddenly the paper in my hand jerked, as if being fed into a shredder. I let go and watched it travel under the mirror. But it didn't shred. I saw it land, intact, on the floor of the closet on the other side. I said a silent prayer for the other Evie.

***

The party was at Lou's house. She and Mario were gregarious hosts, and everyone was happy. Vivi and her cousins charged through the house, screaming with excitement and the adults ate and drank with abandon.

Chelsea arrived at the party with Jeremy about 20 minutes late. 'You look amazing,' I cried out, spinning her around. 'Thanks for coming.'

'I wouldn't miss it for anything,' she said. 'Sorry we're late.'

'Uh-uh,' I chastised her. 'What did I tell you about apologizing?'

She smiled self-consciously. 'Damn, I keep forgetting. It's such a hard habit to break. How's this?' She cleared her throat and said regally, 'Thank you for waiting.'

'Perfect,' I said.

Ryan arrived alone, ten minutes later. He'd warned me he'd be a bit late because he was organizing a surprise. He pulled me aside, near the door. 'Happy birthday, gorgeous.' His kisses still left me breathless. My heart raced.

'So, what's my surprise?'

'Hmm, should I *tell* you now, or *show* you later?' he kissed me again. I swooned with happiness.

'Why not both?'

'OK. I've hired a yacht. You and I are sleeping on the harbor tonight.'

'What?'

'Well, the sleeping part is optional.' He winked, squeezed my hand, then headed into the kitchen to get himself a drink.

Several hours later, after the cake had been cut, and a bottle of expensive champagne uncorked, I surveyed the sea of faces there to celebrate my milestone. I turned my head to wipe away a tear. I'd never imagined I could feel this happy.

I finished my champagne. 'OK,' I yelled, knocking a knife against my glass for attention. 'I feel like dancing. Turn up the music!'

The dancing was very animated, and after a particularly ambitious gyration I heard a loud tear. The seam under my sleeve had ripped. 'Oh no,' I shouted to Lou, pointing to the gap in my shirt, 'I liked this top.'

'I can fix that,' she said. 'Come and change into one of mine for now.'

I followed Lou down the hall to her bedroom. Her closet was sparsely filled with tops and pants in shades of black, white and grey. She rifled through a shelf and pulled out a simple black sweater.

'Try this,' she said, holding it out.

I put on her top and Lou tossed my torn one on a bench in the corner of the room. 'I'll fix that tomorrow, if I'm not too hung over.'

'Thanks Lou-Lou,' I said. 'What would I do without you?'

'Barf, don't get sentimental just cause it's your birthday.'

I hugged her anyway. 'I can't help it. I'm 40 now. I'm feeling emotional. What would I do if you ever stopped loving me again?'

Lou laughed, patting me on the back and sighing with mock patience. 'Oh Evie, don't be silly. You'll always be loved.'

EPILOGUE

It was a few weeks before my forty-first birthday, and I was getting dressed in my closet.

'Mom!' Vivi called.

'In here!' I answered.

She came to the doorway, her reflection appearing behind me in the mirror. 'What time are the movers coming?'

'They said any time between 11 and 2. Why?'

'Mel asked me to go over for a swim. Can I?'

'When?'

'I dunno,' she shrugged. 'Most of the day. You won't need me when they're here, will you?'

'I guess not. Do you remember where you packed your swimsuit?'

'Yeah, I think so. But I can borrow Mel's if I can't find it. Is it OK if I go?'

'OK, that's fine. You'll have to walk yourself there because I'll be busy supervising things here. And be careful crossing the road. Look both ways, OK?'

'Mom, why do you always say that? I'm not a baby.' She walked off to find her bathing suit.

As I watched her retreating reflection in the mirror, I thought I noticed a slight limp. But it was just a split second and then it was gone. A thought flickered into my mind, but I dismissed it. That was impossible.

I finished getting dressed, pulling on my red chiffon tea dress, the long-time favorite that had taunted me, unworn, for more than a decade. But now, after a year and half of fasting, it fit me again. I wore it regularly now, and not just on special occasions. It made me happy, so it was on high rotation in my wardrobe.

Although I had no idea what I weighed, I was nearly as thin as the Evie on the other side of the mirror. I'd never get to her level of skinniness, but now I didn't want to. The still soft flesh on my arms and hips mirrored the softening of my attitude to myself. I felt so much better in my fasted body than I'd ever felt in her calorie-restricted body. I felt a million times happier.

Ten months previously Stu and I had finalized our divorce, and six weeks ago I sold the house that I'd kept in our settlement. Today was my last day with this mirror. Tomorrow, it would be someone else's home, someone else's closet, someone else's mirror. I wondered if it would work for them the way it had worked for me.

Ryan and I had chosen our new house together. He told me, when we started looking, that he had no interest in interior decoration. I wondered if Rebekah's decision to pivot to that profession had left him with some sour grapes.

But I didn't complain. His declaration of no interest meant I had carte blanche to design the home of my dreams. But I wouldn't be calling on Angelica if we needed to do any renovations. I didn't need her now. I wouldn't leave this life for anything.

I stared at my reflection in the red dress. I still couldn't believe the transformation that less than two years could make. I looked like a curvier, rosier version of Skinny Evie, without the crippling hunger and anger and worry lines.

Looking at myself, for the faintest moment I saw the flicker of an eyelid. But I hadn't moved my eye.

Was she there again? Had the portal reopened?

I touched the glass. My reflection did too. Hand on hand. I breathed hard. For some reason I knew. I could feel it. That was her.

The woman on the other side of the mirror turned her head slightly and looked down at our pressed-together hands. My heart filled with love.

Had she read my letter? Had she found peace with the beautiful body that, for so long we'd both fought and punished and hated? If that *was* her, she'd gained some weight. But she was glowing. The mirror Evie looked back up at me and nodded. Her eyes glistened and I felt my own tears welling.

For another second we gazed at each other, somehow communicating. I knew she'd read my letter. I knew she was OK.

And then she was gone. Instantly I knew the reflection was just my own again. The portal was closed and my doppelganger was lost forever to that parallel universe where things were the same but different in small and giant ways.

But somehow, through this crazy shared experience I could never explain or understand, we would be connected forever.

I would always hold that other version of myself close in my heart. I supposed that was like loving myself. A thing I used to never think possible. The thought made me feel full and expanded and light and grounded all at the same time.

I straightened the skirt of my dress and smiled.

ACKNOWLEDGMENTS

My journey to intermittent fasting (IF) started in about 2017 when, at a family BBQ, my brother Pete casually mentioned this weird new dieting thing he'd heard about. At the time I dismissed it as extreme and unhealthy. But, with a BMI in the 40s, I paid attention to any snippet of information that might hold a clue to helping me lose weight once and for all.

In the years following that conversation I made half-hearted attempts at IF, but I never researched why it worked. I never understood the role of insulin. I also didn't give up my milky morning coffee. I'd white-knuckle through to 11am, then calorie restrict the rest of the day, and eventually give up because it was too hard. But Pete had planted the seed about IF, for which I am so grateful.

In September 2021, I accidentally stumbled across an interview with Cynthia Thurlow, discussing her viral Ted Talk about IF and fasting's particular benefits for middle-aged women. The talk is called 'Intermittent Fasting: Transformational Technique', which you can find on YouTube (at the time of writing it has over 13 million views). I watched it straight away and started fasting the next day (with no milk in my coffee). Thank you, Cynthia, for being the catalyst for me to give IF another go.

I soon fell down a YouTube rabbit hole, in which I found Dr Jason Fung. His videos were so informative, with brilliant analogies to make this complex science understandable. Dr Fung's book, *The Obesity Code*, changed my life. It is my number one recommendation for understanding why IF works. It explained to me why I'd always struggled to lose weight and why getting my insulin under control was the answer. I've also found helpful information from Dr Fung's colleagues, Megan Ramos and Nadia Pateguana, in 'The Fasting Method Podcast'.

One of the most useful resources I found in those early days of fasting was Gin Stephens' podcast, 'Intermittent Fasting Stories'. Gin's warm and wise approach with her guests, who each week share their own IF success stories, was reassuring and inspirational. Gin's books, *Delay, Don't Deny*, and *Fast, Feast, Repeat*, are easy to read and focus on practical steps for incorporating IF into your life.

There are more IF resources than I have room to list here, but two publications I've found particularly interesting are: Dr Mark Mattson and Dr Rafael de Cabo's article in the *New England Journal of Medicine* in December

2019 called 'Effects of Intermittent Fasting on Health, Aging, and Disease,' and Dr Mattson's follow-up book, *The Intermittent Fasting Revolution.*

On a personal note, I'd like to thank my mum and dad, who've been amazingly supportive while I wrote this book. Through my whole life they've been a loving and constant presence, and I'm so lucky to have them. Big thanks also to my sister Emma, the most fun person I know, who was an early reader and gave me some helpful feedback. To my dear friend Isolde, who was so encouraging after reading my manuscript—that meant so much. And special thanks, too, to Leife Shallcross, my bestie, who was able to provide insights about the publishing world based on her own experience as an author. The fairytale Evie reads to Vivi in my book is *The Beast's Heart*—Leife's retelling of Beauty and the Beast, told from the Beast's point of view.

I could never have launched this book into the world without the excellent assistance of the team at Green Hill Publishing, in Adelaide, Australia. They've helped me navigate the self-publishing process with professionalism and enthusiasm. This time-poor wannabe novelist couldn't have done it without your help—thank you!

Finally, my heart is too full of love for Dave, Ed and Millie to adequately express here how much you mean to me. Thank you for giving me space and time to bash away at the keyboard alone, when you wanted to be with me. I love you so much.

ABOUT THE
AUTHOR

Sarah Wilbow lives in Canberra, Australia, with her husband, two gorgeous children, and two beaglier dogs. Sarah is trained as a lawyer and works as a public servant. Her long-held ambition to write a novel floated to the surface during the COVID-19 pandemic, when she suddenly had a bit more time on her hands. During the writing of this book, Sarah lost 35kg (77lbs) by fasting every day. She has a big collection of fancy dresses she can now actually wear.